Monkey Me Monkey You

Gail Hulnick

Monkey Me Monkey You

Gail Hulnick

WINDWORD GROUP

The WindWord Group Publishing & Media
2950 Newmarket Street, Suite 101-297
Bellingham, WA 98226

www.windwordgroup.com

This is a work of fiction. Names, characters, businesses, places, events, and incidents are either the products of the author's imagination or are used in a fictitious manner. Any resemblance to actual persons, living or dead, is purely coincidental. The publisher does not have any control over and does not assume responsibility for author or third-party websites or their content.

ISBN:

978-1-947527-46-1 (Paperback)
978-1-947527-45-4 (eBook)

Books may also be purchased or the author contacted by emailing admin@windwordgroup.com

OTHER BOOKS BY GAIL HULNICK

MEDIA MYSTERIES

The Lion's Share of the Air Time

A Bird in the Sand

Sleeping Dogs Lie

Kangaroo Court

THE RESORTING COLLECTION

Resorting to Murder

Resorting to Larceny

Resorting to Fraud

Resorting to Short Stories

Resorting to Arson

RUMBLE STRIP BOOKS

Canada 150

USA Off the Interstate

Europe: Could we live here?

Benelux and a Boat

CONTENTS

CHAPTER 1

Nevada Leacock crouched behind the reception desk and tried to focus on possible escape routes. She could feel Taylor next to her, shaking and sobbing. A shooter was somewhere in the office, hunting for something or someone.

She reached for the receptionist's hand and gripped tightly, even letting her fingernails dig into the young woman's palm. Maybe a little pain would help her regain control.

Taylor inhaled deeply but silently, and then returned the squeeze.

Immediate problem solved, Nevada concentrated on making some sort of action plan to get out of this situation. Alive.

In the five minutes since they'd heard the first shot, the entire office had gone deathly quiet: no voices; no doors opening and closing; no phone ringtones. You might have expected a stampede toward the elevators, but Nevada guessed everyone had the same reaction as she had—dive for cover under the very convenient desks and tables. Not a good idea to run out into the open, trying to get to the lobby or the stairs. Not when you had no idea where the shot came from or who had the gun.

She felt fear rising in her gut and swallowed twice. She needed to stay in control.

Even though it was only 8:45, it had already been a busy morning, with steady traffic from the elevator. Eighty people worked here at Fraser Greene Publishing (New York), and every department had some sort of Monday morning meeting. One of Nevada's groups, the nonfiction/biography and autobiography section, had already started gathering for their meeting in boardroom C. She'd scheduled it early because she liked to get a solid jump on the week.

She'd been here since seven, because Jasper Inniskillen had requested a meeting. Once one of Fraser Greene's bestselling authors, he had recently jumped ship to go over to their nearest rival, Mondarix Press. They'd stayed in touch, even though they no longer had the publishing offices at Fraser Greene in common. He was a dear friend from way back and was one of the contacts who helped her find this job in publishing after her career in broadcast journalism reached its terminal stages. Jasper was not usually high-maintenance, but his request to see her had a tinge of urgency to it. Odd, because although she had moved several other items to the side to make time for him—and told him she was doing that—he didn't show up. After waiting till eight, Nevada had called him. His apologetic wife answered his phone, but said she didn't know where he was.

Nevada had just begun leafing through the morning's snail mail, left for her on the reception counter when the first shots rang out. Her dive for cover was instinctive and experienced.

She disconnected her hand from Taylor's, then wiped her other hand on her skirt, and tried to settle herself a little more comfortably. Her knees couldn't be relied on anymore; sometimes, she moved around and barely thought about them and sometimes they ached and screamed to be noticed. So far, they were holding up. The reception desk had two levels: the top counter, to hold the computer monitor and to make a barrier for the receptionist, and then a second counter about eight inches lower to hold phones and keyboards. There was clearance of about thirty inches between the second counter and the floor, and it was in that space that Nevada and Taylor hunkered down.

Five minutes ago, this had been a normal office lobby: bright lights, loud voices. Now it was silent and somehow darkened. It had only been five minutes, but it seemed like five hours.

It was a safe space, under the desk. For now. Nevada knew she should just wait there and hold her breath. Over her years covering hard news, she had learned many ways to survive. But when she heard a door open, very close by, and then shut with a careful click, she couldn't overcome her urge to find out what was happening.

She slowly and silently straightened up, just a few inches, trying to get a sightline through to the outer office without raising her forehead above the counter. Who knew where the shooter was? She couldn't tell from the sound of the shot. They might be right there, just three feet away, just waiting for her to straighten up and provide a target. But they might be in one of the back offices, maybe even off into one of the corner suites.

She couldn't see a thing.

Then, somebody opened a door—maybe help was on the way? She thought she could just try again to grab a quick look. It would be a good idea to hurry, though, so she straightened up, glanced over the edge of the counter, then ducked back down, as low as she could go. She'd seen nothing: just the usual array of couches, side tables with magazines, and video screens on the opposite wall showing a rotating series of the covers of Fraser Greene's current bestsellers. So strange how the ordinary and everyday could suddenly seem bizarre.

Taylor was breathing hard. ""Should we try to run?" she whispered.

Nevada shook her head.

"What should we do?"

"Just copy me," Nevada replied.

She could see from Taylor's expression the nausea that came with fear was spreading through her body. Nevada felt one brief wave, then it was gone. No time for that; they had to get out.

She slowly rose to pick her way around the corner of the desk. Taylor reached for her hand again, but Nevada ignored it. The lobby was still as quiet as a churchyard.

Then, the elevator doors opened.

Hannah, the new intern, stood there, hesitating before walking out. Obviously, she sensed that something was off.

"Go! Go!" Nevada hissed at Taylor, grabbing her by the elbow and propelling her toward the open door. They crossed the lobby at a run, then hurled themselves into the elevator. Taylor crumpled into a sobbing heap at Hannah's feet while Nevada reached up to pound the 'close door' button. As the open space shrank at what seemed like a sloth's speed, Nevada heard two more shots.

A man appeared in the hallway that led to the C-suite offices.

"Call 911!" Nevada hissed at Hannah.

"I don't know if my phone will work in an elevator," Hannah said.

"Just do it!"

As the teenager put her head down to look at the numbers while she tapped them, Nevada put her hand up and yanked her to the floor. In the final seconds before the door completely closed, Nevada stared at the man and tried to memorize as many details as possible: brown pants, brown shirt, no tie, running shoes, gray hair, medium height, clean-shaven.

He raised his right arm and she saw the gun he held. The door closed. Nevada heard a thump and then the sound of what she assumed was a bullet hitting metal.

***

When she, Hannah, and Taylor emerged from the elevator in the lobby, they found police officers crouched around the entrance, ready to guard their escape. It was chaos: a crowd was forming on the sidewalk, horns blasted as drivers tried to express their frustration over the gridlock on the street, and police officers rolled out tape and tried to get control of the situation. One officer in uniform and another in plain clothes, presumably a detective, stepped forward to lead the three women from the building to a safe spot outside. In the distance Nevada could hear sirens wailing, and moments later, a van pulled up into the space cleared in front of the building.

"Over here, ma'am." The police officer was tall and broad-shouldered, his hair cut short. It was Nevada's reporter training; she instantly took note of his appearance, for future reference. "What's your name?"

"Nevada Leacock."

"What's happening in there?"

Nevada looked at the circle of police officers that was growing around her. Three men, one female police officer. She was still holding the hands of Hannah and Taylor, all three of them clutching at one another in relief. The panic was gone, but the shock was taking over.

She took a deep breath. "I work at Fraser Greene. We publish fiction and nonfiction books. We're on the twenty-second floor. Someone is up there with a gun."

The police officer nodded. "We had a 911 call about shots in the building. We'll want to talk to you later about what you saw, but right now, let's get you checked out. Where's the medic? Here, put a blanket on her. She's shivering."

"I'm fine," Nevada said. *What did he mean, shivering? I've seen much worse than this.* "I saw one man walking the hallway. Everybody took cover in their offices, I think. I didn't see anyone else. I was out by the front reception desk. We were hiding there ... Taylor and me. Hannah was coming up in the elevator and when the doors opened, we ran." She looked around at the circle of faces. "I'm Nevada Leacock."

"What do you do at Fraser Greene?" The police officer had his notebook out.

"I'm an editor," Nevada answered.

A man in full SWAT gear approached from the van. "Okay, we're going in," he announced, nodded toward the other police officers, then led his team toward the entrance.

They crouched in a line, shoulder to shoulder. Suddenly, the doors swung open and people began streaming from the building. Nevada saw her boss, the managing director, followed by a dozen people from Contracts and Legal. She stopped counting at twenty, and as dozens more staffers poured out, it looked as though everyone who worked at Fraser Greene might be safe. The point now was to see who was *not* in the group that had escaped.

"Who's in charge?" The police officer took over.

Of course, Bernadette would be the one to step forward.

The SWAT team leader turned to her. "And you are?"

"Bernadette Shanley, Fraser Greene Publishing Managing Director," she said.

The officer looked at the man standing behind her. "And you?"

"Crawford Burr, Fraser Greene CEO." That was unusual. Crawford did most of his work outside the office.

The police officer in plain clothes flashed his badge. "What can you tell us about what's going on? Is everybody out of your office?"

"On the way out, I asked every department head to round up their staff members once we got outside," Bernadette said. "We'll need to do a head count."

"How many people?"

"Not sure. Most of the meetings hadn't started yet. But we know who was expected in."

"How did you get out?"

"Came down the stairs," Crawford said.

"How many shots?"

"There was one, and then three more, then nothing. We waited for about ten minutes, then people started to come out of their offices. We didn't see anybody. Nothing was going on, no talking, nothing. Somebody said, let's get out, and people headed for the stairs. If the shooter is still up there, he let us go."

"Maybe he's dead," the police detective said.

Nevada shook her head. "Four shots total. I heard the first three, then the fourth one when he fired at the elevator door when we were getting out. So, it doesn't sound like you're going to find a body up there."

The SWAT leader looked up from his walkie-talkie, which had been crackling nonstop. "No sign of any activity on any other floor," he said. "We're evacuating the entire building, though. We'll send our team in, find out what's what."

The police detective said. "Until we have a firm ID on everybody, we don't know whether there's a hostage-taking going on. Officer, could you get all these people to step back?

Get them some coffee and have the paramedics check them all out."

Nevada watched as the police filed into the building while she allowed herself to be guided toward the ambulances. Someone pointed her toward a camp chair and she sat down. More like sank, really. Her arms and legs felt as though they'd all gained about fifty pounds.

"Ma'am?"

She looked up. A pair of police officers, one male, one female, loomed over her.

"We have a few questions about what you saw in there."

"Of course."

Over the next few minutes, she tried to answer the man's questions, but her mind was like a cricket on steroids. Had she really been trapped in an office with an active shooter? How had she managed to get out?

"Collared or not?"

The man growling the question at her took another generous gulp of whatever it was he had in his cardboard cup.

"I beg your pardon?"

He crumpled the cup and looked at her with what felt like fake patience. "Was the gunman wearing a shirt with a collar or a T-shirt?"

"Oh. Sorry. Collared. Brown."

The police officer checked his notes. "Yeah, I got the brown."

Nevada lifted her feet one after the other, just to prove to herself that she hadn't turned into concrete after hours of standing here, answering these questions. She knew it hadn't really been hours, but time was moving slowly. She ached to know exactly how much time had passed, but she didn't look at her watch or her phone. The cop might take that as some sort of challenge, and react badly.

Like a light bulb going on, Nevada suddenly felt herself done with the murkiness of her reaction. She gave herself a shake, like a wet dog getting rid of the proof of his recent swim, and focused on the police officer. "Brown pants, brown shirt, no tie, running shoes, gray hair, medium height, clean-shaven."

The officer scribbled down the description, then nodded to her. "We'll get this out. Detective will want to talk to you more later on… maybe get you to give a description to a sketch artist. We'll need you to come in to the station."

Nevada nodded. "It's close. I'll walk over."

Half a block from her office building entrance and the yellow tape that now festooned the light posts, garbage cans and bike racks nearest the door, Nevada's burst of adrenaline ran its course. She stopped. The pedestrian traffic streamed past her and she realized she was blocking the flow. Stepping back into the shelter of a doorway and taking a few deep breaths, she tried to get her balance back. Ever since the attack this morning she'd been alternating between some sort of weird automatic pilot, holding herself steady through the arrival of the police and the questioning, then shivering with hysteria held down just below skin level.

Now, she felt like she had to fall apart, and for that, she needed her husband.

Owen's was the only name she had on speed dial. She almost never used it during the working day. This had to be one of those exceptions.

It went to voice mail. Not surprising—he was with patients almost constantly. He usually phoned her back within fifteen minutes.

"Owen, I've just been in a police incident. Don't worry, I'm fine, just shaken up. Well, not really shaken up. You know me. Call me as soon as you can."

The streets and alleyways were surging with people traffic, as usual, but she saw far more police uniforms than usual. If the shooter had slipped out of the building through a back door, he might still be in the area—maybe even watching the action by the front door. She'd seen that happen in enough movies and TV cop shows.

Nevada reminded herself of the description: brown pants, brown shirt with a collar, running shoes, medium height, gray hair, clean-shaven. No tie. But as she looked around, she knew it was no use. In this sea of people, no matter how many faces she saw, she'd never spot the man she'd seen behind that gun. The one whose face and form were seared into her short-term memory.

And how long would that last? She needed to capture as much as she could before it was gone.

The precinct nearest the publisher was housed in one of the few beaux arts buildings that hadn't been converted to condos in the '80s. Nevada was hustled into a small room furnished with a table and two chairs.

The door opened and a lean man in a gray suit and blue tie walked in. "Hello, Ms. Leacock. Thank you for coming in. I'm Detective Travers."

She nodded and took the chair that he indicated. "I saw you when we came out of the building. Is there any more news? Were you able to pick up the shooter?"

"Not yet, but we'll get him."

The comment came from a woman who was standing in one of the back corners of the room, leaning casually against the wall, her arms folded. It was directed to Detective Travers; she didn't make eye contact with Nevada.

"Can I ask you, Detective, is everybody okay?"

Travers looked up, then exchanged glances with his partner. "Yeah, there were no injuries. Everybody shaken up, of course. Especially the guy who got the note."

"What note?"

Again, he looked over at the other detective before answering. *Was he getting permission?* "The gunman was on the premises for seven minutes. He walked past your receptionist, then along the hall to the executive area. He fired three shots, then one more later, according to everybody we've talked to, and we've recovered the bullets."

"But nobody was hurt, you said."

"He didn't shoot at any people. Only the walls."

"He shot at the walls." Nevada wanted to be sure she'd heard correctly.

"Yep, and the elevator door. No bullets hitting any people."

"On purpose?"

"We think so."

The way he was checking with the other detective was creeping Nevada out. She turned in her seat and addressed the woman. "And you are?"

"Diaz," was the answer.

They all waited five seconds, then Travers took over. "It seemed that he walked in, sent everybody into hiding from the shots, then made his way into your CEO's office and left a note."

Nevada shook her head. "So weird. I'm happy no one was shot. What did the note say?"

```
"It's not my fault. It was the
full moon."
```

"That is strange."

"We were hoping you or one of the other staff would pick up a reference of some kind," Diaz said.

Nevada shook her head. "I'm sorry."

"It's not a title? Something being published soon? Maybe an important quote from one of your previous books?"

"Nothing comes to mind right away," Nevada said. "But I'll give it more thought. Maybe try running the words through some of our files. I'll ask the others, too."

"Thank you," Diaz said, then reached for the doorknob. "I think we're done here."

Travers took the cue and stood up, but Nevada didn't. "Was Mr. Burr in his office when the gunman left the note?"

"We can't answer that question right now," Travers said.

Again, the silence in the room. Nevada had plenty of experience interviewing police officers on sensitive matters, but she'd never encountered quite such a high brick wall.

"Where does that leave us then?" she asked.

"Where?" Diaz looked puzzled. "Detective Travers will call you if there's anything further we need. Let him know if you remember anything else significant or if anybody tells you anything they didn't already mention to the police."

"What do you think it's about, Detective Diaz?"

"I'm not going to speculate, Ms. Leacock."

"Well, then, what are the next steps?"

Diaz's smile was tense. "Also, not going to answer that question. If there's anything relevant for your company to know, we'll inform ... we'll go through the proper channels." She opened the door and headed out into the police station's lower hallway. "By the way," she tossed the words over her shoulder, "It's Captain Diaz."

Nevada was silently kicking herself as she stood on the sidewalk in front of the building an hour later, raising an arm to flag down a taxi. "I should have recognized her," she thought. "In the old days, in any city, I would have picked up on her in the first few minutes. I always knew the names and faces of everybody who makes the decisions. I must be slipping."

It had been three years since Nevada had left her job as a news director, but after so many decades as a journalist, she still expected herself to look at things the same way. So many things had changed recently in her life but until today, none of that had bothered her. She was fifty-five, but she felt thirty-two, and the move to New York with Owen when the hospital offered him his dream job was just one more adventure, as far as she was concerned.

"No, I'm not slipping," she thought. "This is a big city. There are probably thousands of captains and chiefs. You can't be expected to know them all."

It was only after the taxi pulled up in front of her and she settled herself in the back seat that she stopped to think about where she was going. Her day was supposed to include a visit to the Javits Center to check on Fraser Greene's set up for Book Fair, due to begin in twenty-four hours. While she probably should go home, relax, turn off the phone, and try to process everything that had happened, the idea of going to the Convention Center appealed to her more.

Some people might think of taking a break, going for a walk in a park or on a beach, or would desperately just want to be home. But for Nevada, Book Fair would be the place to go to get her balance back after the events of the morning. Hundreds of thousands of square feet covered in books—that was her idea of a perfect place to run after a trauma.

CHAPTER 2

When Nevada stepped through the front doors of the Convention Center, she felt as though she'd landed in Oz. The comparison was apt, given the experience she'd been through this morning. She'd been through a tornado, smashed through a world in black and white, then awakened in the wizard's realm, throbbing with emerald and yellow brick.

On this late day in May, the air outside was heavy with an early heat wave. Inside, Nevada felt she needed a jacket. The convention center floor stretched out in front of her like one of the broad boulevards through the heart of Paris. Books as far as the eye could see. The advertising banners proclaimed the titles of the upcoming bestsellers, while dozens of publishers' booths displayed stacks of advance reading copies. All there for the taking.

It was like seeing all the money and all the precious stones in the world laid out on tables for anyone to pick up, look at, and fondle.

Nevada felt overwhelmed. Ever since she'd arrived in New York and found her way into a job in book publishing, she'd been hearing about Book Fair and what a crossroads it was for the industry. Just like the Frankfurt or London Book Fairs, it was a time and place for thousands of authors, editors, and execs to come together. She'd been looking forward to it for months, and as shaken as she was by the morning's experience, she didn't want to miss a minute of this event.

She dropped her tote bag to the concrete floor and decided to stop for a while to get her bearings. Off in the distance, she could see one of the anchor booths of the trade show, shouting the name of its owner in massive lettering on a sign the size of a billboard. The big five publishers could afford to take up the most space and visual real estate, while the mid-sized and small presses, with their smaller wallets and smaller shoes, made for smaller footprints.

Her job today was to visit the Fraser Greene booth, double-check that all the promotional material was there, and watch for opportunities to network with anyone in the book business: editors, authors, booksellers, and librarians. Everything and anyone. It was going to take some determination to carry on as usual, but determination was her rocket fuel.

"Nevada! Hey there!"

The man calling her name rushed toward her with a smile on his face. Well, not really *rushed*. Hard to rush when you are over eighty years old. Charles Delaney was a legend in the publishing world. Nevada had known him since childhood, when her father's career as an actor put their family in touch with many people in the arts worlds. Charles was one of the people she had turned to when she wanted help in finding her way into a publishing job. He understood her feeling that since she was closer to the end of her working life than the beginning and that she wanted to try out a few of the unexplored roads that had always intrigued her.

He knew everybody who was anybody, and when she came to New York because of Owen's new job, Charles quickly set her up with a lunch with Crawford Burr. Apparently, she'd been presentable and acceptable, because a day later her email inbox pinged with an offer of employment and a week later, she set her briefcase down on a walnut desk on the twenty-second floor of the Ackerman Building on Sixth Avenue.

"Charles! How *are* you?" Nevada met his outstretched arms for the hug and double air-kiss that all business encounters seemed to require. She missed the old days when a handshake was all that was necessary.

With Charles Delaney, though, she didn't mind so much. Besides having details of the history of New York publishing and summaries of almost every important book ever printed, ready to roll out at a moment's notice, he was a normal, smart man—the kind you like to work with.

"How's it going?" Charles asked.

"We're busy with set up, like everybody else," Nevada said. She hesitated—should she tell him about the events at the office this morning?

"I saw the news." Charles stepped in to bridge the gap. "Must have been terrifying."

Of course. Why would she assume other people didn't know about the incident? There must have been half a dozen reporters in that crowd gathering in front of her building this morning.

"It was mostly confusing, in the moment," she said. "We heard what sounded like shots, hid under the desks, and then got out."

"Nobody hurt?"

Nevada shook her head. "Apparently, he deliberately fired into the wall." She chose to leave out the detail about the gunman sending one bullet in her direction, toward the elevator.

"Any idea who? Or why?" Charles asked.

"None."

"They didn't catch him?"

"Not yet."

"I don't want to make light of it, but I can imagine some miserable author finally losing his cool and going after a copy editor for adding too many commas."

"Or after the accounting department over the size of his royalty check," Nevada said. "Or maybe not an author at all. Maybe somebody whose manuscript has been lying in the slush pile for five years."

Charles grinned at her. "I'm glad to see you still have your sense of humor."

"You gave it back to me," she said. "Up to now, I think I've been in a state of shock. Not where I should be, with all the work that needs to get done before we open tomorrow."

Charles pulled a phone out of his pocket and stared at it. "I'll leave you to it. I've got a few things of my own going on today. Darn Rubios."

"I beg your pardon?"

"Sorry, Nevada. A problem at home, with my housekeeper and her husband. Take my advice, do as many of your own chores as you can."

He walked away, mumbling into his phone. Then Nevada's phone demanded her attention.

"Owen."

"Hey, what's up?"

"Have you seen the news?"

"No, I've been with patients all morning."

"Take a look at it and then get ready to pile on the pampering tonight," she said with a smile. "I'm having a rough day."

"Wish I could. But it's going to be a long day for me. I probably won't get home till ten. Maybe eleven."

The intensity of the wave of disappointment surprised Nevada. Disappointment and dread. "Why?"

"It's a long story. Let's plan to take some time off this weekend and I'll tell you all about it. Gotta go, honey. Talk later."

And he was gone.

Weird.

Nevada watched the crowds of staff and building employees dashing around setting up. Forklifts maneuvered between booths, delivering pallets stacked with books. Designers put up banners and signs, while editors, marketers, and every available pair of hands from the publishing houses laid out brochures, author one-sheets, and bookmarks.

She had seen a few major conventions and conferences in her time on the political beat, and this was certainly somewhat smaller, with less fanfare. No confetti, streamers, or marching bands. But they probably compared when it came to emotion. According to everything Nevada had read about Book Fair, in preparation for her first time working on one, it was a high point of the year, and even their careers, for some authors and editors. Anticipation ran high, as some publishers watched the cards being dealt on books that they'd bet the farm on. Individual acquiring editors mentally crossed their fingers (although they'd never admit it) as they watched the books they'd picked go out into the world. They had guided them through the maze of development, editing, design, and marketing to this launchpad toward the bookstore and library shelves, waiting to be seen and adopted by readers.

And readers there would be at this convention. Yes, it was a trade show and there would be much business done during the first few days, but it was also Book Fest, where 20,000 avid readers were expected to descend on the building, line up to meet their favorite authors and get an autograph, and ideally, go home to spread the word among all their friends about the terrific new author they'd discovered.

She knew it was a good thing, for her mental health, that she was here. After the shooting this morning, if she had been at home alone or sitting in the quiet of her office, she would be sliding into a funk, letting the aftershock anxiety and her overactive imagination get to her. What if he had better aim? What if she, or anybody else, had been unable to take cover and had been wounded? Or killed? What if the media reports were filled with headlines about dozens of casualties at a New York City publishing house targeted by a madman?

Nevada tried to snap herself out of it. What good was it to get upset about what might have happened? It didn't. And there was so much that was odd about the event. Her thoughts veered away from the 'what if' and toward the 'why'. Why was that man in their hallway? How did he get in with a gun? Nevada could speculate about a dozen scenarios that might explain things. He was a political nut with a beef about one of the bold-name biographies they published this year. He was an author who felt his book would have been a much bigger success if only his publisher had committed more marketing money to it. He was an editor who'd been let go in the latest round of downsizing.

Of course, it was entirely possible that it was just random. Any New York skyscraper, any floor, any company. Just a place to make some noise and get some attention.

Nevada shook her head. Didn't seem like that though. If that's what it was about, why didn't he cause more damage? Why didn't he stick around? It seemed he had just vanished, moments after shooting at a wall and an elevator door.

She gazed across the convention floor toward the Mondarix Press booth, which was probably two thousand square feet. Twice the size of her New York apartment. Banners proclaimed the publication of Jasper Inniskillen's latest thriller. Jasper had complained about what he saw as a lowering of his profile when he was still at Fraser Greene; it appeared he'd found the attention he was looking for when he crossed the street to go to Mondarix.

"Have you read it?"

The young woman asking the question stood to her right and was also staring toward the *Lockdown* poster.

"Yes, have you?"

"Not yet," the woman said, then turned to make eye contact. "But I'm trying to get my hands on a copy. I'm one of his biggest fans. He's the reason I started writing. He's just so inspiring. Did you know he's written forty-five novels? Forty-five! He must be on his computer three-quarters of the day!"

"He is a hard worker," Nevada said.

"Do you know him?" The woman stuck out her hand. "I'm Josselyn Madden. I write thrillers like he does."

"Are you published?" Nevada asked.

"No, not yet. I've sent out letters to agents and to a few small publishers who take unsolicited submissions, but nothing but rejection, so far."

"Are you thinking of self-publishing?"

"I don't have the money or the free time for that," Josselyn said. "I work full time in a hotel and I couldn't find enough time to write AND learn everything I'd have to, to publish it myself."

"If you work full time, what are you doing here?"

"I work nights. Front desk at the Hilton. Awesome place to get writing done. After midnight is the best."

"It might also be a great place to learn how to self-publish," Nevada said. "University of YouTube and all that."

Josselyn made a face. "I'd rather concentrate on being a writer. There's a lot of work in being a publisher."

"You're right. You have to take the manuscript, design an interior, design a cover, check the facts, edit, proofread, produce, print, market, and distribute—and then the booksellers start their job. Tough enough when thirty people are trying to get it done, let alone one."

Josselyn stopped glancing around at the banners and the booths, then looked Nevada over. "What do you do?"

Nevada dreaded telling her, for a moment. But it probably was a silly idea to be at Book Fair, trying to deny what it is you do. "I'm an acquisitions editor."

"You consider submissions and decide what books will be published?"

Nevada nodded, then braced herself.

"May I give you my card?" *There it was.*

"Sure, I'll take it, if you want," Nevada said. "But that's not the way it works. Maybe in a movie or a fantasy novel, but there's a process here in New York. You have to get an agent."

The woman didn't look daunted. "Do you know any agents looking for new clients?"

Nevada stared at her for a few moments and wondered how she'd got the credentials to get in. "Is this your first Book Fair?"

"Yes! I'm so excited. It's just amazing, isn't it? Books everywhere ... and they're giving them away!"

"Come back tomorrow on opening day," Nevada said. "It will be even better. Today is mostly setting up and mostly employees of the big publishing companies. But if you come tomorrow and take in some of the education sessions, you'll learn a lot."

Josselyn met her eyes and raised her chin. "I came today exactly because I thought there *would* be a lot of publishing people and not so many library people or bookstore people," she said. "If I want to take seminars, I can do that all day long at a college or university. Or online."

"You have a point," Nevada said. "Well, good luck with it."

"But wait!" The woman tried to fall into step with Nevada as she headed for the Fraser Greene booth. "What's your name? Do you have a card? Which company are you with? Simon and Schuster? Sourcebooks?"

Nevada pretended not to hear and picked up her pace. She moved so quickly, and so many people filled in the space between them, that she lost Josselyn in the crowd.

CHAPTER 3

Nevada had a moment of guilt for not exchanging cards with the woman. She knew Josselyn's dream was that this acquisitions editor would give her a direct cell phone number, promise to introduce her to an agent who would take her on immediately. Then the agent would ask to be sent a copy of her manuscript, read it over a weekend, offer her a six-figure advance and then shepherd her book through three edits onto the *New York Times* bestseller list. Nevada grinned to herself. *Sorry, Josselyn, but I already have a really full schedule today. I don't know if I can manage the items on my own to-do list as it is. You'll have to try to find someone else to find you a pot of gold.*

At the Fraser Greene booth, the interns and assistants were stacking galleys under the tables, ready for distribution over the coming days. Last year, it was Jasper Inniskillen's novel, *Hostage,* that had received FG's big promotional push at the convention. It was the last of his books that they had under contract, and he'd taken his latest work of fiction over to their biggest publishing rival, Mondarix Press. Nevada was curious about what her competitor would do to support Jasper's new thriller, *Lockdown,* and she intended to wander over to their booth to check it out as soon as she'd finished her setup tasks. She'd seen the huge banners hanging from the ceiling, but there was usually more, much more, done to support a high-profile author from whom the publisher expected to reap major revenue.

She was also very curious about Jasper's no-show this morning. He was the one who had contacted her, asking to talk. His wife, Fiona, a lovely woman with the tolerant tone you might expect of the spouse to a celebrity, had been quite apologetic when Nevada tried to reach him when he didn't show up for their appointment. Perhaps he got stuck in the crowd being controlled by the police on the street outside the building?

Her phone buzzed and she pulled it from her pocket, looking down to check the name. *Fiona Inniskillen.*

"Hello, Nevada? I'm sorry to bother you, but have you seen Jasper?"

"No, Fiona, I haven't. Why? Isn't he at the house with you?"

"He left about nine o'clock and said he was going into the city to meet you. He promised to call me when the meeting was done, but that was hours ago."

"I didn't meet with him, Fiona, but we had a police incident at the office, so…"

"Police?"

"We're all okay. It will be all over the news."

"Are you worried?" Nevada smiled her thanks to Hannah, who had dragged a chair over for her. Good for her, to be right back at work after the scare they'd all had that morning. Nevada would expect that behavior from a reporter, but it was quite gutsy for a bookish person.

"No, not worried, exactly. He goes lots of places, in a day, or a week. But it was unusual for him to miss his meeting with you this morning, and he didn't say where he was going when he left."

"Maybe he took the dog for a walk."

"No, the dog is here."

"I'll call you if I hear from him."

"Thanks, Nevada. I will, too."

Nevada considered calling one of her counterparts at Mondarix Press, Jasper's new publisher, then reconsidered. Why would that be her responsibility? When Jasper was in the Fraser Greene stable—was the star of the Fraser Greene list, in fact—she was happy to be on his speed dial around the clock. When he decided he could get better treatment and a better deal at another house, she'd been hurt, and then philosophical. It was just business, and why shouldn't he do what was best for his career and his family? No hard feelings, and she'd seen him several times in the past year without flinching, as they worked through the last book he owed them. But she didn't want to continue to let him depend on her, and she had other authors who needed her attention.

She was surprised that Fiona had called. Her experience of the famous author's wife, over the years of contact back in the day, was of a very bright, sophisticated woman. She must be quite concerned, to be calling Nevada to try to track him down.

Nevada first met Jasper in the 90s when a book tour brought him to Vancouver and the TV station where she was news director. She'd become long-distance friends with Jasper and with Fiona.

Nevada stared at Jasper's name, blazing across a piece of cloth that hung from a ceiling that looked to be about half a mile above her.

"What do we call that? Do we call it a poster?" The man standing next to her had his head tilted back. His voice put her in mind of Cary Grant, but his face was much less memorable.

He wore his gray hair short and a beard in the goatee style that so many men over sixty seemed to prefer.

"I think we call it a huge marketing budget," Nevada said.

He laughed. "Yes, Book Fair is quite a stage."

"Your first time here?"

"No, I attended quite a few times, when I worked for Penguin."

"Who do you work for now?""Myself," he said. "I'm self-publishing. I've done four thrillers, fifth one coming out next fall. Is this your first Book Fair?"

"Yes. I'm new to publishing," Nevada said. "My background is in TV journalism, but various events set me up for a new career. Act three."

He smiled. "Age is just a number, right? I hope to be doing new things when I'm eighty."

She had the feeling she could kid around with him. "When is that? Next year?"

"Ha! Very funny. What kind of books do you do?"

"Nonfiction. A few novels."

"Makes sense with the journalism background. Author? Art director? Copy editor?"

"Acquisitions."

"And what's your big book here this year?""I have a biography of the female head of a high-tech company publishing tomorrow," Nevada said. "But I don't think you'd call that 'big'. And I've just signed a couple to do a coffee table art book on the power players in the collecting world. That might make a splash, but it will be two years or more until it's ready for the world to see."

"What else are you looking for?"

"Biography or autobiography. Political or business."

He nodded. "That's where the big bucks seem to be. Although we do hear, from time to time, about a novel with a lot of buzz and an enormous advance."

"A lot of them have the buzz building up after the TV or movie version has been produced."

"That's true. That's the case with Jasper Inniskillen, isn't it?" He swept an arm up toward the banner flying over the center of the Convention hall. "He hit it big with *Hostage*, then it was made into a series, then this next one commands all the rafters' real estate at this little party."

"Yes, but that's quite a story, too," Nevada said. "In publishing circles, anyway. Fraser Greene published *Hostage*, then Jasper jumped ship to go to a different publisher."

The man crossed his arms and stared at the banner. "You seem to know quite a bit about things. Who do you work for?""Fraser Greene."

"Ah. Not quite one of the big five, but not one of the little guys, either," he said. "Do you like doing nonfiction, or do you want to add more novelists to your stable?"

Nevada felt herself ready to launch into a discussion of her career plans. Why was she preparing to tell this total stranger about herself this way? She recognized he had the listening skill that most successful journalists have. Somehow, they induce people to want to disclose. Almost as valuable as the talent for frequently turning up on the scene of action happening. Some people go through their whole lives without experiencing anything but their usual nine-to-five and their family events, while others seemed to find themselves on a street outside a bank robbery, in a mall where a public wedding proposal is being made, or on a freeway a half mile from a tornado.

Not great for the average person, but solid gold for a journalist.

"My name is Daniel Pyne," he said, handing her a business card.

She handed hers over. "Good luck with the self-publishing."

"And good luck with the biography launch."

Nevada turned away just in time to see a vigorous hand waving at her from across the aisle. Book Fair was certainly nothing if not a maze of paths crossing.

"Nevada! Hey!"

Bernadette Shanley was Fraser Greene's Managing Director and had held that position for more than twenty years. She was edging toward retirement age now, and whenever the subject came up, she had many plans for golf holidays and world travel to discuss, but Nevada had the feeling she would have to be pushed when the time came. Nevada could relate to that: at fiftyish, she barely recognized the woman she saw in her mirror. She reacted to many things in the same way she had thirty years ago and some days, she even felt like a teenager.

Bernadette was a petite woman who had let her hair go to its natural gray many years ago. She made up for the boycott on hair salon hours with time spent among the clothing racks in the best stores in New York. Every day, she was turned out in an outfit that was runway-ready. Many times, Nevada had rushed back to her own office after encountering Bernadette, to make notes about the suit, blouse, scarf, and shoes she had just seen on her boss.

"Nevada, how are you? We're all still frazzled from that ... that ... *episode* this morning at the office, but I guess no one has the time to just go home and let it sink in. How are you doing? Is the setup okay for you? Do we have all your author galleys ready to pass out?"

Nevada nodded. "All is well, Bernadette. How about you?"

"Oh, you don't have to worry about me. I feel confident that Crawford has everything under control now, and the police will sort this out soon." The executive had finished greeting Nevada and was scanning the spaces around her for others she might recognize. "Have they talked to you? Did you recognize the guy or have any idea who he might be or why he was in our office?"

"No, have you?"

Bernadette shook her head decisively. "Not a clue." She stared upward at the Jasper Inniskillen banner. "Quite a show, isn't it?"

"I guess they want to get as much mileage as they can out of the launch of his new book."

Bernadette hesitated, as if she were fighting with herself. Then, she chose a side. "If you hadn't messed it up, that book would be ours and Fraser Greene would be making the big splash at this year's Book Fair."

That was aggressive. Nevada wasn't going to let it go by. "I don't really think that's accurate, Bernadette. Jasper is a grown man, quite an independent one, and he has every right to choose his publisher. His contract was expiring and he was attracted to a better deal."

"You were the one who could have got him to sign a new contract. Especially since he introduced you to us and paved the way for your job and your corner office, you owed it to him to get him what he wanted at Fraser Greene."

"Charles Delaney introduced me. Jasper is an old friend who just showed me a few of the ropes."

"Whatever, Nevada, you had the best connection of any-one with Jasper."

"I tried, Bernadette. You know I tried. Crawford just wasn't interested in meeting Jasper's terms."

Bernadette looked at Nevada and seemed to look right through her. "It wasn't that black and white. And no, I don't know that you tried."

"What possible reason could I have for wanting Jasper to leave us and go over to Mondarix Press?"

"I don't know the answer to that, but something, somehow, will turn up," Bernadette said.

"Do you think I should make another attempt to get Jasper to come back?" Nevada asked.

"I do."

"Then I will."

"You do that," Bernadette said. "Listen, I have work to do. Let me know if you hear anything from the police about the shooter."

As she watched her walk away, Nevada couldn't suppress the feeling that Bernadette had left much unspoken. As it was, the words she had spoken seemed like an accusation. Did the managing director really feel that Jasper's change in publishers had something to do with Nevada? She had only been at Fraser Greene a year or so; how could she possibly have so much influence?

She wandered over to the Mondarix Press booth, where advance copies of *Lockdown* covered the tables. Beside them were full-color brochures with extravagant quotes of praise for the book, punctuated by details of bookstore readings and signing stops throughout the U.S. and Canada. How had the Mondarix Press people been able to convince him to do that? Last year, Nevada had tried to get Jasper to do a book tour and he'd refused. Said his mental health couldn't sustain the stress of a book tour.

Nevada shrugged. Maybe they'd offered him a lot of money. Whatever. She'd probably hear more of the story this week. Book Fair was a quagmire of gossip.

She strolled past several other booths. The erotica people were out in full force. For some reason, they were set up right beside the children's picture book people. Floor signage proclaimed the titles of the latest from various specialty publishers, and then Nevada started to see more announcing Book Fest, which was due to start on the weekend, the day after Book Fair finished. Tens of thousands of avid readers would crowd the space, hoping to meet their favorite author, get an autograph, and perhaps a free book.

Just as she always did, when the subject of Jasper Inniskillen's flight to Mondarix Press came up, after defending herself, Nevada reverted to second-guessing herself. Had she done everything she could to prevent his leaving? Was there something she could have said or done to convince him to stay with Fraser Greene, his publisher of twenty years? She wasn't his main contact at FG, Bernadette was, but she had a longstanding contact with him that went back another ten years. Maybe she should have leaned on their friendship to get him to agree to stay put?

"Excuse me, but where do I find the authors?"

The woman asking her the question was a few inches shy of five feet tall, with white hair worn long and hanging down past her shoulders. She was dressed in sneakers that looked sturdy enough for running a marathon, anonymous black pants and jacket, and a rope of turquoise around her neck.

"Well, I'm not really sure ... I mean, I don't think there are that many here today," Nevada said. "If any. Was there somebody in particular you're looking for?"

"Jasper Inniskillen. I'm hoping to get an autograph. Isn't this the day of the big convention? I read in the newspaper that there would be dozens of writers here, signing autographs."

"It starts tomorrow," Nevada said. "Actually, it's Book Fair tomorrow. That's for meeting publishers, but quite a few authors, too. But the really big event for readers to meet authors is Book Fest. That's on the weekend."

The elderly woman looked around the convention floor, and Nevada had the feeling she was overwhelmed. She could understand that; she was finding the whole thing rather overpowering herself.

"You have to have tickets for both of the events," Nevada said. "The Book Fair ones went on sale about six months ago, and you have to be approved to get one. It's basically a trade fair, not a for-the-public event. Are you in publishing?""No, I'm a retired teacher."

Nevada looked down at the woman. No sign of a lanyard. She looked around, then voiced her thought. "How did you get in here?"

"I used an old trick we used to use to get into the state fair, when we didn't have the money to go." The woman was twinkling like a fairy godmother in a children's bedtime story. "You hang around the entrance until there's a pack of people going in, then you slide in with them, match their pace and bingo! You're in. Helps if you pick a busy time, too."

Nevada matched her smile. "Very clever of you. But I'm afraid it won't do you much good today. There's nobody here but publishing company employees, trying to get ready for the big displays starting tomorrow. Then the Book Fest on Saturday is where you want to be to meet authors ... although there will be some here in the earlier part of the week. But for Book Fest they hand out tickets and show you where to go to get free books. It's a lot more organized for readers."

"But I've heard it's double or triple the size of crowds," the woman said. "I'm not much good in crowds." She looked as if she could be trampled in no time.

"It's going to get crowded in here, too," Nevada said. "But good luck. You must be quite a fan of Jasper Inniskillen's, to go to so much trouble."

"When you're a fan, it doesn't feel like trouble," the woman said, then stuck out a tiny hand. She was wearing dainty, lace trimmed gloves. "I'm Olivia Theale."

"Nevada Leacock. I'm an editor."

She watched a look of disinterest cross Olivia's face. "Oh, an editor. Well, thank you for your time and for the advice."

Just then, over the older woman's shoulder, Nevada saw a figure pass through the crowd that seized her attention. It looked like the gunman from this morning! Brown shirt, brown pants, gray hair. Clean-shaven, no tie. It wasn't much to go on and it was more than the dry list of facts, anyway. It was almost as if there were a motion of some sort, drawing her attention toward him.

She nodded to Olivia, then set off to follow the man.

CHAPTER 4

Nevada watched the gunman walking quickly toward the west wall and decided to shadow him. "Please excuse me, Ms. Theale, but I see someone I have to catch. Have a nice day!"

As she hustled toward the last spot where she'd seen him, her eyes raked the scattered rows of people passing among the booths without success. Just that one brief glimpse. Was it the same man? Did he still carry the gun?

Since she'd moved to the States from Vancouver, Canada, four years earlier, she'd become used to the notion that many people on the streets and sidewalks around her might be carrying guns. Probably were, Owen would say. Both she and her husband paid no attention to that aspect of American life, figuring that if it became a factor in their life, they'd deal with it then. She supposed her career of covering the news, traveling to so-called hot spots around the world, and learning to work with the sound of bombs or explosions going off in the distance had toughened her to the point of ignoring the fear. Some foreign correspondents faced a life of post-traumatic stress disorder after they changed jobs, but she wasn't one of them. She'd made up her mind long ago to refuse to dwell on the danger there might be in a situation. Cross bridges only when you come to them. Perhaps she was suppressing a tsunami of fear that would rise up one day to drown her, but it hadn't happened so far.

Many people would have gone home and pulled the covers over their head after what happened this morning, but that just wasn't Nevada's style. She had work to do this afternoon and she would get it done.

But she couldn't ignore something so obvious as the man showing up again, here, in this place where a lot of Fraser Greene employees were working on the company's biggest promotional and networking push of the year. Did this mean he was somebody in the publishing business? If he'd been able to get approved and received credentials, he would be. On the other hand, she'd already met three people who'd fumbled their way in here on setup day. How exclusive and carefully managed could it be?

Thousands of others would be here for the three official days of Book Fair, starting tomorrow. She assumed security was tight—they'd certainly searched her bag thoroughly when she came in—but shouldn't they get a heads up about what she'd seen?

Nevada began to look around for a security guard to alert to her concerns. Or should she call one of the police detectives from this morning? She thought she still had his card. As she was searching through her bag for it, her phone rang.

TOBY ENCELL

Oh no. She had promised to call him this morning. Well, she was quite sure she had a good enough reason for dropping the ball on that. Maybe he'd heard about the shooting and wanted to talk about it? More likely, it had to do with his own writing.

Her phone buzzed only twice, then the call was gone. He hadn't waited for it to go to voicemail. Fair enough; he knew she'd see his name and return the call.

Toby Encell, as a first-time author, needed a lot of hand-holding on his autobiography. Even though he had conquered the worlds of telecommunications, then sports, business, and had even done a not-too-embarrassing foray into movies, he was behaving like a little kid at his first day of school on this book project. Nevada had urged him to hire a ghostwriter, but he wouldn't hear of it. He believed that his communication skills were a significant part of the reason for his business success and he saw no reason to hand the writing task over to someone else. Someone else who wouldn't have the grasp on the subject that he would, as he'd explained to Nevada repeatedly during their early meetings.

"Nobody will have the balls to tell it like it is!" he said.

Could I get him to see that no one said 'tell it like it is' anymore?

"I was there. It all happened to me. I made the decisions, and I'm the one to write it. It's an autobiography! Not a biography. There will be lots of those, once I'm done making my mark. And they can all use this autobiography for reference! I'm the one with the experience and the knowledge to pass down."At that first, do-the-deal lunch, Nevada had tried to get him to slow down and focus. "The ghostwriter will handle it whatever way we want," she said. "But let's talk about our goal in doing this book. Is it to make money and to tap into your fame? Is it to be part of the publicity engine?""No, I don't care about the publicity," he had roared. He really did roar. She'd read that word many times before, as a description for a way of speaking, but when she met Toby, she knew what it really meant.

"Then why are we doing it?"

"I have a story to tell," Toby said. "Things I need to get off my chest. Back in the day, when I was starting out, a bunch of us worked together and over a lot of late nights, a lot of ideas got shared."

Nevada wasn't sure what that meant. *Is he telling me there's a confession he wants to make? In this book?*

Toby had sipped on his lunch martini and chosen his next words carefully. "Anyway, it happened a long time ago, but it's a story that no one's heard before. I've been pondering the title for a long time—"

"Yes, Crawford has a few ideas about that," Nevada said. *Would Toby buy into that?*

"It's my book and I'll choose the title."

Apparently not.

"I like *Monkey Me Monkey You* for a working title."

"Meaning?"

"Meaning 'copy me'. But recognize that I'm the original." Toby had signaled the server for another drink. Nevada had declined, deciding that she needed to keep a clear head.

"I am the original, and I'm not the original," Toby had gone on. "Over the years, I've studied many great men and adopted the best of what they said and did. Copied. I saw what they did and then I did it. And now, in my book, I'm going to show people, so they can copy me."

"I see," Nevada said. "Is it about more than just your inventor beginnings?"

"Yes, it will be my family story, too. It's not been told before and it's going to upset a lot of people, but I don't care. It needs to be heard, and it has things in it that are important. That have implications for other people, and other people's families. And secrets. And money."

Well, that certainly had sounded promising. Besides being a success on his own, Toby Encell came from the Encell family, which owned the fine art business in New York. They were notoriously secretive and averse to any personal publicity.

So, despite her hesitation over some of his phrasing and her hope that he'd be able to do better than "things in it", she pushed for the house to sign Toby Encell to a book deal for his autobiography and started the process of guiding it through to publication.

Nevada sighed as she looked at the poster of Toby's face, anchoring one corner of the Fraser Greene Booth. So far, it was a publicity bonanza and a creative sinkhole. Toby didn't lose any opportunity to promote the upcoming book, and the company had wagered a quarter-million dollars on publicity, in addition to the quarter-million it had given Toby as his advance against royalties.

The money was chump change for him and Nevada often wondered why he hadn't chosen to plough it back into marketing the book, the way some eager newbie authors often agreed to do with their advances from tiny presses. She had asked Toby about this once, and he'd replied that he thought there was a principle that mattered here. Living the life and writing the story was his job: producing the book and marketing it was Fraser Greene's. Even though he said he would help with the marketing, he expected Fraser Greene to do the heavy lifting.

Despite her irritability over this, she knew the book would be a marketing and publishing success. Toby Encell was the one of the ten most famous entrepreneurs in the world and the only one who had not yet peppered the world with mid-life memoirs and observations-about-business books. The appetite for sneak peeks into his current life was matched by curiosity about his past and his family.

And that was matched by his reticence and his reluctance to get rolling on this project. The whole thing was bewildering: why had he signed a book deal if he was going to play shy guy about getting the pages out there? Crawford had predicted Toby wouldn't go for the Nevada's suggestion of a ghostwriter, and he was right. In all their meetings, the billionaire insisted, with every bit of charm and confidence she had expected, that he could manage the writing himself and that was one line item on a budget that he could save them all. But months had passed now with no sign of a workable first draft and after dancing around the issue of a firm deadline, Nevada had finally set one at the start of the year.

Pages were due next week.

Would that be why Toby was calling her today?

Nevada looked his name up in her phone's contact list and tapped it.

"Nevada Leacock! Thanks for the quick response. Listen, I'm making some progress on my book outline—it's done, actually—and I want to run it by you."

Cuts right to the chase. "That's fantastic, Toby. Do you want to email it over? Or courier actual pages?"

"No, in person is better," he said.

Should have expected, she thought. More handholding.

"I'm at the Javits Center, setting up for Book Fair tomorrow," Nevada said. "Would you like to come over here? See the scene?"

"No, let's save that for another day," Toby said. "How about you meet me at The Press at 1:30?"

Nevada managed to say the first of the two letters to signal her agreement, then he cut off the call. But really, it was a rhetorical question. She stared at his name under the E section of her contact list, shaking her head, then looked up just in time to see the brown-clothes man walk through her field of vision, about fifty feet away.

It was him! Was it him? She hadn't seen his face earlier this morning—at least she didn't think she had, but her memory was clouded by her state of shock over realizing that shots had been fired and they were under siege. She would deny it was fear, but it definitely was shock. She hadn't been able to recall for the police detective whether he'd been wearing a mask and defended her lack of specificity by recalling that she'd only seen him twice, and very briefly: when she peeked over the reception desk for a split second and then, when he'd run toward them in the elevator, as the door was closing. Face mask? She just wasn't sure.

The man she saw across the corridor wore no mask and wasn't in any hurry. He seemed to be the same height and build as the man she'd seen, same gray hair, same brown clothes, and running shoes. He carried several rolls of posters under his arm.

Nevada stuffed her phone in her purse and set out to follow him. What did she have to lose? He walked past the row of academic publishers, past the indie group, and was heading toward the opposite corner of the hall, where Sparrow, one of the other giants, sprawled over two thousand square feet of space.

A thought struck like Florida sunshine hitting a northerner's eyes. *Take his picture!* She wasn't one for snapping photos of strangers in public, as the street photographers liked to do, and she certainly hadn't joined selfie culture, using her phone to document her daily life. And of course, this wouldn't be a selfie, since Brown Clothes Man wouldn't be taking his own photo. But she remembered occasionally that she had this amazing tool in her pocket, and that she could take photos, tell the time, make notes, record a memo, and phone a friend all with this same device.

You're distracted, and he's getting away! Nevada groped in her bag for her phone, then hurried along an angle that she thought would allow her to intercept him in a good spot to get a picture. Close, but not too close. As casually as she could, she turned her back to the crowd, then just as he passed by, turned back, and snapped the photo.

He didn't notice, just strolled on past her toward the Sparrow booth. Definitely looked like the guy. But would you expect somebody who'd just invaded a business office and fired four shots to be walking around Book Fair delivering posters that same morning?

CHAPTER 5

Nevada almost walked over to confront him, but she remembered her recent promises to Owen to take better care of herself and to live a little more cautiously now that she was in her fifties.

"Try to let things go," he'd said, most recently, when they were discussing whether their landlord really needed the telling-off she thought he had in store.

She fumbled for her phone and tapped in Detective Travers's number. After getting his assurance that he'd have officers over there as quickly as possible and would be in touch with the Convention security people, she made a promise that she'd keep an eye on Brown Clothes Man and wouldn't approach him or do anything to spook him. She ended the call and maneuvered herself over toward the Sparrow display. It wasn't hard to fit in among the dozens of people standing around the stacks of books. Even though it would be another twenty hours before Book Fair opened to the rest of the industry, today there were thousands there working, setting up their own displays and eager to get around to case out the competition.

Nevada watched her quarry move around behind the Sparrow Publishing tables, putting up posters, setting up books, doing his job. He didn't seem furtive at all. In her years of reporting, she'd followed many people, sometimes just to watch what they were doing and sometimes to find the right moment to approach them to request an interview or a photo. She knew how it looked when someone was aware they were being followed. Brown Clothes Man seemed to be completely oblivious to her interest in him.

She didn't plan to do anything more than just watch, and ten minutes later, when Detective Travers and two other men in plain clothes showed up, all she had to do was make eye contact with the detective, then nod her head in Brown Clothes Man's direction. They started a quiet conversation with him— good plan, to keep everything under the radar here. It would be nuts to cause any unnecessary panic at an event like this.

The man looked puzzled, but not particularly upset. Nevada watched as he put down his roll of tape, pointed out his stack of posters to another Sparrow employee, and walked off down the hall with the three detectives.

***

Nevada had never been invited to a meal at The Press. Even though the lunch service had been in full swing for an hour and a half, every table was taken and there was a lineup at the door. The odds were low, because The Press was almost entirely built on reservations, standing ones that various captains of industry maintained day after day and week after week, with no flinching at the tabs that tickled the ambitious end of three figures.

She stood at the entrance, looking past the marble pillars, crystal chandeliers, and mahogany panels, over the various balding and silver heads, to try to spot Toby Encell. Unnecessary effort, it turned out.

"Ms. Leacock." The maître d' smiled. "Mr. Encell is waiting for you. Do you have a coat or anything you'd like to check? No? Please, follow me."

They threaded their way through a tapestry of expensive suits, white linen tablecloths, and priceless carpets laid against the polished wood floor. Nevada saw Toby seated against the mirrored wall in a dark green leather booth, a perch from which he could watch the comings and goings throughout the entire room.

He had started in on his lunch, with knife and fork in hand, and he raised the fork in a sort of simulation of the upward motion he might have shown if he'd stood up to acknowledge her arrival at the table. Still, she thought, it might not be much, but it was more than you'd get from a lot of men these days. Courtesy and chivalry were the passenger pigeon and the dodo of human communication, Nevada believed. Almost extinct. Gone but not forgotten.

She smiled warmly at him. "Toby, so nice to see you! Thanks again for the invitation to lunch." As she slid into the booth, she realized he would not move to one side to balance out their positions behind the table. He was in the center. That's all there was to it.

She stopped moving as soon as she felt she had enough real estate for her backside. He smiled, nodded, and took in another mouthful of steak.

The server was at her side instantly. "May I offer you a cocktail? A glass of wine? Perhaps you'd like to see the list?"

"No, thank you. I'd just like water, and a ... " Nevada quickly glanced over the menu, "a slice of the quiche."

Toby's attention was laser-focused on his meal. That was about what she would have expected, Nevada thought, as she watched him eat: his ability to concentrate was probably one of the keys to his stupendous success.

And stupendous it was. Toby Encell had started out in cell phones in the 1980s, with the help of some seed money from his family's fine art gallery fortune. He had invested in telecommunications, software, and then internet startups, and had steered his company into waters navigated by only a handful of business geniuses. Since then, he'd acquired dozens of companies in sports, financial management, and movies.

When Nevada had first discussed this autobiography project with him, he told her that up to now he'd been too busy to document his activities in a book. Not in any form, actually; apparently, he had been asked to authorize several film projects, too. But he wanted control over the way his story was told, he said, and so far, he hadn't met anyone he trusted enough to loosen his grip on the details. At the beginning, Nevada had pushed for an authorized biography, but after that rock kept rolling down the slope, she tried the ghost-writer approach. Nothing doing, Toby said. Many people have done their own autobiographies. How hard can it be?

She supposed that to a man who had amassed a fifteen-billion-dollar net worth, four hundred-or-so pages of a book might seem simple, but they'd already hit a few potholes in this road. Toby just couldn't seem to get his head around the fact that they had deadlines to meet. He seemed to think, as so many authors did, that his part, the writing part, was all there was to it. He thought that everything else that went into a book—the polishing of the words, the design of the pages, the cover, the printing and binding of the pages, the distribution to the bookstores, (not to mention, convincing those bookstores to stock and sell the books!)—that all of that happened magically and in the space of a few weeks.

If Nevada could have handed all of this off to Crawford Burr, she wouldn't have given it another moment's thought. Let Crawford get Toby to see that he should write faster: let one alpha male talk to another one. Toby would listen to Crawford and would get it done. But Crawford seemed disinclined to get involved; meanwhile, the managing director and the vice-presidents, particularly the Marketing VP, were breathing down Nevada's neck, sending her daily emails to remind her how much the company had invested in Toby Encell's autobiography and how much of her job description included the care and feeding of important authors.

"Nevada, how are things?" Toby summoned a server and his plate was whisked away just as her quiche arrived.

"Just fine, Toby. I hope all is well with you."

"I wanted to see you to touch on a couple of points that have come up." He watched her for a moment, and she felt his unspoken command to get on with her lunch. She felt as though she was still catching up from having been five minutes late.

The quiche was heavenly and she regretted she didn't have the luxury of savoring it. Finishing it off quickly, she blotted her lips with her napkin and turned in the booth to face him. "What's up?"

"My son, Royce, wants to be involved in the publishing process for my book."

His son, Royce? I didn't know he had a son, Royce.

"So does my father, Rolf, apparently," Toby said as he sipped his coffee and played with the spoon.

I didn't know he had a father, Rolf.

"I thought this was an autobiography, but my family … some members of it … seem to think it is a project that involves them, too. Royce sees it as a springboard into publishing, I think. He has been trying to find a way in and evidently, now believes it's all about who you know. My father doesn't have enough to do, and is looking for a new project. Just the way he has ever since I was a young man, he wants to get his fingers into my business. I've blocked him many times, but this go-round, I'm just tired of it."

Nevada was beginning to get the picture. "You want me to handle this."

"Keep him away from it," Toby said. "Or find some small way for him to be involved that doesn't involve talking to me and telling me what the pages should be."

Nevada grinned at him. "I have some experience with family members needing some help to stick with what they know and are supposed to be doing."

"And are good at, am I right?" Toby made eye contact for the first time during this lunch. "He's a gifted fine art appraiser, and he's run a successful gallery for sixty years. Why would he want to get involved in publishing at this point? Royce, I can understand. He is still flailing around, trying to define his career and his place in the world. But my father? It makes no sense!"

Nevada didn't know what to say to all this, so she simply nodded and tried to look sympathetic. Eventually, he would run out of words to say on this topic.

He did, but not before he got to the point of the lunch. As he called for the bill, he said, "I want you to set up meetings with both of them and find out what's going on. Give them something minor to do. Something that won't derail the project or get in our way but will make them feel heard. Can you do that? Good." He scribbled his initial and slid out of the booth. "I'll be out of town for a few days, but we'll reconnect when I get back."

"But Toby, what about the first chapters deadline next week?" She was speaking to his back.

Nevada sighed and went back to sipping her water. She didn't stay long, though. It was an oasis, a restaurant like this, but she was eager to get back out onto the busy Manhattan sidewalk, hail a cab, and get herself back to Book Fair.

When she walked through the double doors of the convention center, she immediately saw how much progress had been made in just a few short hours. Booths the size of penthouse floor apartments lined the aisles, with side walls made of bookshelves, panels, and one in case, billowing, Arabian-style silk curtains. If the place had seemed busy at eleven a.m., the mid-afternoon scene was twice as busy.

She found a chair in a quiet corner of the Fraser Greene booth and pulled out her phone. A text from Detective Travers –

> ```
> Talked to him. Wrong guy. Had an
> alibi.
> ```

Nevada was floored. She had been absolutely certain it was the same man. Otherwise, she wouldn't have called the cops.

She also had texts from Bernadette and from Jasper Inniskillen, both saying the same thing:

> ```
> call me.
> ```

Jasper first. She'd been worrying about him since she'd seen him for lunch last week, and his no-show this morning added to her anxiety. Despite his defection to Mondarix Press, they'd stayed in touch. She could tell he felt somewhat guilty about making the move, and she wanted to reassure him that there were no hard feelings. So, she had accepted his invitation to lunch at the Tavern on the Green in Central Park last Monday. The spring flowers were just coming out and everyone was in a kindly, vibrant mood after the long winter.

"Nevada!" Jasper had been on his feet to meet her, calling out her name in a way that had the diners at most of the nearby tables looking up to take note of them. His hair, as usual, needed a cut and his beard was showing the results of the cocktail or glass of wine he'd started without her, but the friendliness of his smile canceled out all that.

"Jasper! Nice to see you." Nevada settled herself into the chair and treated herself to a moment of enjoyment of the surroundings. This was one of New York's most famous restaurants, quite a remarkable perch in a crowded landscape, and was one of Nevada's first destinations when she came to live in New York. It was every bit as appealing as it looked in the movies.

"You know, I think you're the first person who's ever asked to meet me here," he said as he waved the menu in her direction. "it's not a place locals think of, unless somebody's getting engaged or graduating from something. Even then . . ."

"Oh, I think I'll be a forever tourist," Nevada said. "Almost anywhere in the States, I think. It's because of all the movies and TV shows we see, growing up in a different country."

"What are you drinking?"

"Too early in the day for me," she said. "I'll just get sleepy. What are you drinking?"

"Cosmopolitan. Girly drink. That's how I deal with the daytime issues. Save the Scotch and the rum for after five."

Nevada shook her head. "None of my business, of course, Jasper, but do you ever think about your health? What you eat, what you drink, when you exercise?"

"Uh, no. Except in the moment. You know. Look, let's change the subject. How are things at Fraser Greene?"

"They're fine. I have half a dozen new nonfiction projects, most of them with the word 'secrets' somewhere in the title."

Jasper laughed. "Hah. How are things with the Tobias Encell autobiography?"

A shrug was all she could manage. A project that had started off with so much promise was now about to jump the tracks over Toby's inability to respect other people's deadlines. She had a feeling she was seeing only the beginning of the train wreck on that one.

But that was overly pessimistic. It was early days, far too soon to label Toby a problem. Jasper, now he was a problem.

Wait a minute, that was overstating things, too. Jasper was a train that had already sailed.

Hah. She loved a mixed metaphor.

Nevada recalled that their conversation at lunch last week touched on a half dozen different subjects before she got to ask him about his new publisher.

"How about you, Jasper? Are they treating you well at Mondarix?"

"Yeah, it's alright." Jasper was absorbed in the menu. Next to his concentration on wines and spirits, cuisine and the contents of a plate were second on his list of personal interests.

Nevada would not let go of this, though. "That's not saying much, Jasper. When you told me you were switching publishers, you raved about how much better the deal would be over there. Comforted me a bit, in the face of the outrageous betrayal you were inflicting on me." She grinned to make it very clear that she was joking.

"Nah, all I did was take some work off your list so that you could concentrate on the authors you really wanted to take care of. Like Toby Encell," he said, then turned to the server who'd just arrived. "I'll have the burger."

"The grilled chicken salad for me, dressing on the side, Perrier," Nevada told the server, then turned her attention to keeping up with the banter.

"The issue wasn't the workload. It was the fact that the Fraser Greene execs thought that since they caved to your pressure to take Charles's advice to hire me there that you'd be indebted to them for life. Or at least for as long as you keep turning out the books," she said.

"That's all they love me for, the turning out the books." Jasper was looking around the room to see whether he spotted anyone else he knew. "That's all any of you love me for."

"Only the good books," Nevada said, as she picked up her fork to attack the salad that had appeared in front of her. When all you're having is rabbit food, every mouthful mattered. "We don't love you for the bad books."

For a moment, she thought she might have offended Jasper and that he'd misunderstood her attempt to be funny. Then he grinned at her. "It's refreshing to see you, Nevada, you know that? At Mondarix Press, there's just so much sucking up and brown-nosing that I just wish, once in a while, that someone would insult me. Treat me like a regular human being."

"Just give it time. Your star will fade there. Everybody's does. Then you can come back home to Fraser Greene."

"Can I?" He put his fork down and stared into her eyes rather than at the plate of lemon penne that had engrossed him a moment before.

"You know you can at any time, Jasper. Everybody there would love to have you back."

"Because I can't get over this feeling that I made a terrible mistake. Sometimes, I'm awake for hours in the night. I should be writing, but I'm just going over the pros and cons of switching ... one more time. Fiona says I shouldn't remake a decision that's already made, but I can't help it."

"Listen to your wife," Nevada said. "She makes a good point. And listen to your instincts. One day, if the right thing to do is to come back to Fraser Greene, you'll just know that, in your gut. Or your heart. Or whatever. And then you'll do that."

That conversation last week had Nevada watching every day for a message from Jasper that he was ready to talk seriously about coming back. She had to be careful not to be seen to be encouraging him, and she certainly never wanted to be accused of poaching him, but at the same time, she wanted to make it clear that he would be welcome.

The meeting that they'd missed this morning might just have been one of their periodic 'checking in' get togethers, but it might have been the conversation at the crossroads. She had to speak with him.

Her call went to voice mail.

> Jasper? It's me, Nevada. Please call me back.

After she left her brief message, she stared at her phone and couldn't quite bring herself to put it away. She wanted to say more, and to tell him all about the events of the morning. She wanted to find out what he was working on today and what his thoughts were about the work in the weeks to come, whether he planned to hang in at Mondarix Press or not. Most of all, of course, she wanted to hear about his current state of mind.

Nevada looked around the vast convention hall and the crowd of people buzzing around in it, and knew that she had to find a little quiet space and time. She almost made it over to an alcove with a couch and table that no one had claimed when she heard Bernadette call her name.

"Nevada! Could I speak to you for a minute?"

What could she say? Bernadette was her boss. One of them. Nevada pasted on a smile and walked toward the managing director.

"Listen, bring me up to speed on the Encell autobiography. Is he going to make his deadline?"

"I hope so, but I don't know."

"Well, stay on him," Bernadette said as she looked around the room for other Fraser Greene staffers she could harass.

"I will, Bernadette. I'll stay on everyone I'm supposed to."

Bernadette shot Nevada a look, but she got nothing but wide-eyed cheeriness in return. If Nevada meant to deliver sarcasm to anyone, she'd wait until her position was more secure and her job title a few more rungs up the ladder. She watched Bernadette bustle away, then walked as quickly as she could over to the solitary chair. Dropping into it, she closed her eyes and breathed deeply a few times. It really did work; she felt herself push away the tension and slow down to a healthier pace.

She sat and willed herself to relax, and when her phone buzzed, she was tempted to ignore it. But there was just too much going on. She had to take a look at the call display.

Fiona Inniskillen.

CHAPTER 6

"Hello, Fiona?" she said. "What's up?"

"Nevada! Thanks for picking up. I've been hearing on the news about everything that happened at your office this morning. Why aren't you at home, taking a break?"

"Wish I could. But Book Fair opens tomorrow and I have a lot to do."

"I won't keep you long, then. I just wondered whether you'd seen or heard from Jasper yet."

Nevada frowned. "No. I tried calling him about fifteen minutes ago, but he didn't pick up."

"That's typical. He really is the most unreliable man." Nevada thought she heard a breath of affection in the midst of Fiona's irritation, but she couldn't be sure. "Okay, well, I have quite a few more people to check with, so I'll let you go."

"Is there a message you'd like me to give him, in case he does call me?" Nevada couldn't help herself; she was incapable of letting a call like this come in without becoming curious about the next development.

"Yes, tell him, it's the Mondarix Press insurance clause. They're on the phone bugging me," Fiona said. "No, never mind. It's too complicated. I have to explain it to him myself. You know how he is, Nevada. He has no ability to focus on the serious things. His brain is just full of silly, made-up stuff all the time."

Nevada wasn't sure she would describe the thoughts of one of the most successful writers of their time in that way. But then, she'd never lived with someone like Jasper Inniskillen, so she probably shouldn't judge Fiona too quickly.

"I'll just mention that you called me, if I hear from him," Nevada said.

"Great. I'm on my way out to an appointment, but he can reach me on my cell. He always can. I'm never hard to reach. He goes off for hours to his writing room, but I never cut myself off like that."

"Is that maybe where he is?" Nevada asked.

"I checked there first, of course. He's not there. And his car is gone."

"I'll let you know right away if he calls me back."

After Fiona was off the phone (with no 'thank you', but then Nevada hadn't done anything for her yet, so perhaps it was excusable), Nevada decided to try again to contact Jasper. This time, when the voice mail recording started, she was ready with a longer message.

```
Jasper, it's Nevada again. I'm
hoping to speak with you before
the day is over. I know you've
been off on your own today—may-
be the muse is visiting? Always a
good thing. I heard from Fiona,
by the way. She wants you to call
her. I also talked with some of
the senior people here at Fraser.
I didn't exactly say that you want
to return, but when I just dropped
the possibility—as a sort of 'what
```

if?'—they were very excited. I
think you should feel confident,
Jasper. You can do whatever you
want. Fraser wants you, Mondarix
wants you—but the question is,
what do you want? Let's get together and we'll talk about it.
I'll be your sounding board—if
you can forget that I work for one
of the sides, that is. Hey, we go
back a long way. Let's not let
this ... this phase be more important than our history, yeah?

She let the recording go on in silence for a few seconds
before realizing she had nothing else to say. Well, she'd been as
clear as she knew how to be.

The afternoon wore on and she worked her way through
to the end of her to-do list, but Nevada didn't want to leave
the building. She pitched in wherever the Fraser Greene staffers needed a hand with the setup, then spent about an hour
strolling around checking out the other booth displays. Once
the Convention started, she wouldn't have a lot of time to do
that. She had booked meetings in almost every available time
slot, and for the major ones, with the biggest bookstore buyers
and the foreign rights agents, she liked to set aside half an hour
before each, to get her game face on and have the priorities of
that potential client clearly at the forefront of her attention.

The industry became more competitive with each passing year. The margins were razor thin, as they liked to say in
the business magazines. Very little profit, with huge and ev-
er-rising costs for raw materials, processing, marketing, and
distribution. The shipping price on a book was often more
than the author, the publisher, or the bookseller got. But it was

an industry that gave employment to many people and each book gave jobs to hundreds, if not thousands, who could pay their rent, buy their groceries, and live their lives, thanks to a reader's desire to buy a book.

Maybe books should list credits at the back, the way movies listed the names of thousands who had worked on a production. Everyone from the cast to the producers to every crew member, driver, and assistant. Most readers had no idea.

Her feet were aching, even though she'd chosen a pair of ten-hour shoes for this day. Maybe it was time to do new categories for them. The three-inch heels that she'd been able to manage over a long day were perhaps just a bit too high now, although she wasn't ready for all-day flats or sneakers just yet. Maybe as soon as the clock ticked over to sixty.

Sometimes she looked at the spikes and stilettoes that the younger women wore daily and it seemed like such a stretch to remind herself that she'd once rocked those heels, too. She'd been proud, at age twenty-five, that she could run, no matter what heel she was wearing. Run from the station cruiser to a police line at a crime scene, run to catch a reluctant witness on the courthouse steps during a high-profile trial, run to catch the last train out of some hot spot.

Long ago.

Nevada spotted a folding chair that someone had propped up against one wall of the Fraser Greene display. It was such a large encampment that it seemed odd to call it a booth. It had four walls surrounding a meeting space that was divided in the middle by a fifth wall. Two editors could have simultaneous, private meetings with suppliers, sellers, library buyers, and other players or one editor could throw a small party while the other went head-to-head with a foreign-rights publisher on the other side of the wall. There was even a door, if they wanted to connect the two rooms.

Out in front, tables surrounded the walls, which were adorned with posters of dozens of their bestselling authors and books. The tables were covered in advanced reader copies, bookmarks, pens, notebooks, mugs, and T-shirts, all imprinted with the Fraser Greene logo.

Nevada set up the chair behind the table and sat down to flip through the season's catalog. She'd been on the final approval team for the design and contents, and she was pleased with the final result.

"Nevada, could I speak to you for a minute?" Hannah North, the new intern, looked as fresh as if she'd just come in to work and hadn't been on the job for nine hours, with several of those hiding from an active shooter.

"Absolutely, Hannah, what's up?" Before Hannah could launch into whatever it was, Dane Saunders appeared at her side. The Fraser Greene Marketing VP was so jumpy it seemed as though sparks were shooting from his head, and Nevada appreciated the table that stood between them. "Nevada, something's happened. You're not going to like this. I hate to be the one to tell you … "

His eyes seemed to glaze over, and Nevada wondered if he was ever going to say anything. She waited. "It's Jasper Inniskillen. He's been found dead."

CHAPTER 7

Nevada's head spun for a moment, and she was grateful for the chair. She looked around for Hannah, just to have a second pair of ears to verify what she thought she'd heard, but Hannah had disappeared.

"What did you say?"

"Jasper. Inniskillen." Dane's face was close to an ashen gray color. "Someone heard it on the radio news and just called me. All they know so far is that he's dead."

She wrapped her arms around herself. "Dead! Where was he found?"

"Don't know."

"Cause?"

When Dane shook his head again, Nevada jumped to her feet. "Do we know any details so far?" She was reaching for her phone as she asked. A quick connection to the internet and she had everything that had been made public so far.

> Jasper Inniskillen, 62, found dead in the driveway of his home.
>
> Shot through the head.

It had taken only four clicks before Nevada found the internet post that gave that detail. How did someone know that already? The poster didn't give attribution to the police.

True or not, it didn't take long for the news to spread through the Book Fair floor. Nevada saw many upset faces, and the energy had changed. It was quieter, darker somehow. Across the hall, she thought she could see one of the massive Jasper Inniskillen banners being lowered from its spot above the Mondarix Press booth. Someone was certainly being decisive over there. Nevada didn't know that she'd be able to move so quickly or know what needed to be done in that situation.

Most of the people seemed not to know what to do. It seemed disrespectful to carry on with getting ready to sell books and make money when the news of Jasper's death was so fresh. And not just a tragic death—the loss of someone dear to the community and to individuals in it.

And a violent death.

That fact was reinforced for Nevada when Detective Travers suddenly appeared in front of her at the Fraser Greene display. "Ms. Leacock, do you mind speaking with me for a few minutes?"

"What about?" she asked, then realized it was the wrong answer. "About anything, of course. What can I do for you, Detective? Is it about this morning?"

"It's about Mr. Inniskillen," Travers said.

"Are they connected?" Nevada didn't know what to make of that, but she knew she felt shocked.

"Don't know," Travers said. "But a shooting at a publishing office and a shooting of an author, on the same day ... we have to ask the question."

"Of course," Nevada said. She had an ache in the back of her throat, but she pushed it down and resolved to remain professional.

"Mr. Inniskillen was once one of the Fraser Greene authors, isn't that right?"

Nevada nodded. "We've just published a biography that he did of Agatha Christie, but after that, he's Mondarix Press's author."

"All quite recent?"

"Within the past year. He chose not to sign a new contract with us and he went over to them for his new thriller," Nevada said. "It happens."

The detective narrowed his eyes and stared at her for a few moments, then slapped his notebook shut. "I'll be in touch."

"Just a second, Detective. Could I ask … about the man I saw yesterday? You picked him up, then let him go. You texted me he was the wrong man, that he had an alibi?"

Travers nodded.

"What was his name?"

"Mark Diotte."

Nevada waited for some glimmer of a memory, but nothing surfaced. It was not a name she knew.

"Thank you, Detective."

As she watched him walk off toward the convention center doors, she thought she'd never seen such an unlikely visitor to a book fair. Somehow, she couldn't imagine him with a book under his arm, and given the speedy pace he set past the publisher booths, neither could he.

Nevada saw Bernadette beckoning to her from the other side of the booth. Not now.

She had a sudden feeling that she couldn't stand to be there any longer. She didn't know where she wanted to be. She just knew it wasn't here. She felt a need to go, to move … to take some action that might help her cope with the news about Jasper.

When she first emerged from the concrete cavern out to the plaza in the warm May sunshine, she wanted to walk.

Aimlessly and without direction. But after a few blocks, a new intention formed—she wanted to go to Jasper's house. She wasn't sure why—maybe she wanted to see Fiona and offer her condolences?

Nevada turned in her tracks and headed back toward the convention center parking garage where she'd left her Audi that morning.

Her car was her haven, even on the crowded, noisy streets of Manhattan, and as she settled back on the cream leather seat and let the music coming from the high-end sound system spin its magic, Nevada felt herself relax and come back into connection. The horrendous news about Jasper had sent up the inner walls she always used to surround herself when faced with trauma. For the past hour, she'd disassociated from everything she'd seen and heard since this morning and just concentrated on getting through each moment. Just as she'd done back in her war correspondent days, she focused on one single object—her bag, a camera, a notebook—and forced everything else around her, all the noise, the pain, the suffering, into the fuzzy spaces around the edges.

But now that she was alone, she could let herself breathe again. She started to feel some of the pain. Grief hits in a million different ways, from different directions, and often, when unexpected. It's also something that needs to be allowed, Nevada had learned, and she knew she couldn't cut herself off from her feelings about Jasper for long without risking all sorts of other problems.

When she pulled into Jasper's home, the lights that lined the driveway were piercing the evening darkness. The yard was filled with cars, some of them parked on the lawn. Jasper wouldn't have liked that.

Nevada could see Fiona sitting on the front steps of the palatial house, a uniformed police officer standing in front of her. Two other officers were walking around the garage and a fourth had just gone inside as she pulled in.

Fiona spotted her as soon as she parked and rose from the steps to greet her. "Nevada! Thank you for coming."

Nevada reached out for a hug. Not something Fiona usually would have tolerated. "Of course. I wanted to see whether there was anything I could do."

"There's nothing," Fiona said. "The police want me to stay here ... and I will. But I feel like getting away from here, from where he ... was."

Nevada nodded sympathetically. "Do you want to tell me what happened, Fiona?"

The tall, blonde woman shook her head rhythmically, as if she were in some sort of trance. "No. I can't talk about it anymore."

"Of course," Nevada said again, as if she had had this conversation dozens of times before and Fiona's statements and reactions were what to be expected. "Let's just walk, shall we?"

"I'll walk with you, if I may."

Daniel Pyne handed Fiona a sweater, and she put it on. If Nevada was surprised to see this indie author here, she decided she would not show that or almost any reaction or emotion to anybody this evening. Her previous state of frozen forbearance seemed like the safest place to be, right now.

Fiona's face brightened briefly with a smile. "Yes, Daniel, please do."

He put the sweater over her shoulders and the three of them strolled along the circular driveway toward the road in front of the house. Cherry trees that had just finished dropping the last of their annual festival of pink lined the driveway and then continued into a grove in the space nearest the street.

"I'm so sorry for your loss," Daniel murmured to Fiona.

"And I'm sorry for yours," she replied.

What was the connection here?

"Did you talk to Jasper today? Or yesterday?"

"I spoke to him yesterday," Daniel said. "I asked him to meet me for lunch downtown, and maybe go over to the Strand for some shopping."

"What did he say?"

"That he'd think about it. Surprised me, because he's never turned me down before."

Something in the tone of his voice made Nevada look at him sharply. Was he getting choked up? "I didn't realize you were friends with Jasper," she said.

"Close friends. They go way back," Fiona said. "To college days."

"I guess it's just never come up when you and Jasper were talking," Daniel said. "I knew your name, of course. And I heard all about Jasper's move from your shop over to Mondarix Press."

"And his plans to go back," Fiona said.

Nevada almost came to a full stop—which wasn't far to go because they were moving so slowly. She had been holding onto this hope that Jasper would decide to return and she'd been doing her best to convince him, but this was the first sign she'd had that he had made up his mind.

"Really?" Daniel said. "He didn't tell me he'd decided definitely."

Nevada looked back and forth between them. Which one had Jasper's confidence, and which one knew the truth?

"He said he felt it was like family there and at the new place there was nobody who cared much about him," Fiona said. "He thought if he went back, he'd be happier and he'd make more money. Would he, Nevada? Would he have made more money?"

Then, in 2014, Toby's business activities took him to Germany. He had never been particularly interested in his family history. His entire focus and mindset were on the events of the future. But when he found himself in Berlin one week, he decided to visit the address he had for his parents' home before they left Europe. A conversation with neighbors who had never left led him to follow a trail to his grandparents' former home, his father's and uncles' schools, and then to classmates from seven decades past.

All were delighted to meet the descendant of one of the friends of their youth, particularly because Toby was American. He heard many tales of Rolf's exploits in the neighborhood, but when he tried to steer the conversation to ask for memories of his uncle Tobias, suddenly the recollections dimmed and the details dried up. After this happened three times, Toby was sure there was something more behind the reticence and he continued to probe, gently and politely. Finally, in a tiny, deserted café, across a table from a man well into his nineties, Toby heard for the first time, "Tobias Encell became a Nazi."

Nevada recalled the disturbing words that ended Chapter One.

All my life I had watched my father and later, my uncle, watch out for being watched. We were warned not to give out any personal information to anyone ... not even our best friends at school. 'Don't take our business out into the street' was the way the order was phrased. And it did feel like an order.

Now I understood why they seemed so jumpy about being seen, about having anyone know their names or where they lived. They were in hiding. Rather, Uncle Tobias was in hiding, and my father was helping to conceal him.

My Uncle Tobias the Nazi.

He hadn't stayed behind in Germany because he didn't have the money for the fare. I had wasted many hours wondering how my father

could let mere money stand in the way of helping his brother come with him to the New Land. Now, I know. It wasn't money. It was shame.

***

Nevada could feel Toby's embarrassment over his family's connection to the Nazis seeping from the lines on the page. She had had episodes in her own past when confession and atonement seemed the only way to get past the pain. Now, she could understand Toby's desire to publish this book.

She could also understand the family's desire to keep it quiet. Especially Uncle Tobias, if he was still around. She would have to look into that.

And she would have to speak with Toby's son, Royce.

But first she had to get back to the office and find out what was going on with this delivery that Bernadette texted about. When she walked back into the Fraser Greene lobby, she was shocked to find a pair of uniformed NYPD officers and Detective Travers waiting there.

"Bernadette, what's going on?"

"I called the police because this package addressed to you might have come from the man who was here on Tuesday," she said.

CHAPTER 20

Nevada looked around the circle of people. "The man? Tuesday? You mean the shooter?"

"Yes. Michael Diotte. I believe that's his name."

"It is, Ms. Shanley," Detective Travers stepped in. "Let's go into your office, shall we?"

Bernadette looked around at the group. "We'll use the small conference room on this floor."

Once they were all settled around the table, Travers reached forward with the package and put it in front of Nevada. "Open it, please."

"Wait. What makes us think it came from Michael Diotte? There's no return address."

"I asked the delivery guy, and he said the man who came in to their office and dropped it off was shortish, clean-shaven with gray hair. Just like the shooter on Tuesday," Bernadette said.

"You've just described about four million men in New York." Travers stared at the *Personal and Confidential* handwritten note on the package, then reached out for it. "We won't need a warrant because it's addressed to you, Ms. Leacock, and I presume you're giving us permission."

Nevada watched as the police officer carefully took off the brown wrapping. Inside, a box contained a roll of parchment

paper, tied with a gold ribbon. Travers lifted it out, untied it, and read:

National Book Award. For Fiction. Sable Ogilvie.

A note, folded in half, lay in the bottom of the box.

Nevada: You'll be sorry you didn't believe in me when you had the chance. I may be the runner-up right now but I'll be in the top spot in a matter of weeks. And I'll be in the running for the major awards.

"So." Nevada said. "Not from Mr. Diotte. Not anything to do with Jasper's killing."

"Well, in a way, it does," Bernadette said. "And I'd say, it's a threatening letter."

"I don't feel threatened," Nevada said. "I had threats, back in my journalism days, and this doesn't really compare."

"I agree," Detective Travers said. "This Sable Ogilvie might stand to benefit from Mr. Inniskillen's death. But it's not a tight link. And maybe she was jealous of him. But most people who are jealous or competitive never kill anybody. The tone of this is like something out of high school."

"Still, don't you think it would be good to question her? Find out where she was on Tuesday?" Bernadette asked.

Travers set the package down and backed away from the table. "Maybe. How about you let us do our job, Ms. Shanley?"

Bernadette looked as if she might protest—people who run one situation often think they will be in charge no matter where they are. Nevada felt the need to step in to neutralize the atmosphere. "I'm sure Detective Travers has a procedure he'll follow and lots of his own ideas," she said. "It's only been two days, Bernadette. The investigation is just getting started."

Travers' phone buzzed, and he pulled it from his pocket. "I'll have to take this."

Looking at his back, while he moved the length of the conference table into a far corner of the room, Nevada tried to decide what to say to take the next step. One part of her

wanted to keep her reading of Toby's autobiography completely confidential, for now. She didn't want Bernadette to hear anything about it. But the other part thought she could let the detective in on at least some of it.

She walked over to Travers just as he was ending his call.

"I've seen the pages of Toby Encell's autobiography that Jasper was working on," Nevada muttered, so that only he could hear.

That captured Travers' attention. "I'll want to talk to you about that."

Nevada nodded. "Now? Or are you leaving?"

Travers had his hand on the conference room door knob. "I have to get back to the station now, so we'll talk later. We've picked up Diotte."

CHAPTER 21

After trying to insist that Travers call her to tell her what he found out from Diotte, Nevada had to let that go and just hope he would take her call and answer her questions later. Her next move was to confront Sable Ogilvie about the completely inappropriate letter the witch had sent.

Somehow, despite Bernadette's warning that she take Sable seriously, Nevada couldn't see the woman as a legitimate suspect in Jasper's death. She felt Sable was the type to write about crime, not the type to engage in it.

It was an opinion reinforced when she talked to Ryley Fedor, Jasper's former agent.

Ryley's call came in just as the meeting with the police officers was breaking up. "Nevada? I got your message to call. What's up?"

"Just wanted to connect, Ryley. Are you having a good Book Fair?"

"Well, it's difficult to focus, after Jasper's death," she said.

Oops, that was an insensitive question.

"Of course," Nevada said. "A terrible tragedy."

"Yes." The sounds behind Ryley's voice indicated she was in a crowded, noisy space. "I'm here at the Convention Center now. Other clients besides Jasper … and I have about a dozen meetings between now and five. What can I do for you?""I

Well, that was a question she had no answer for. They weren't anywhere near the serious negotiation point.

"Was there any room to change his royalty percentage?" Fiona persisted. "Because over at Mondarix Press, the percentage was comparable, but the advances were a lot healthier. And there was talk of finding a way to put him on the staff pension plan. Could he have a pension at Fraser Greene?"

How could Nevada answer questions like that?

Daniel seemed to sense her discomfort. Maybe he found the questions quite weird, too. "Fiona, I think you're probably asking about things that are better left for another day. You're upset. We all are. Let's just walk."

Of course, that was it. Fiona was in shock—weren't they all? A sudden cool breeze came up and Nevada crossed her arms, pulling her sweater tighter.

"Nevada, do you need a ride back to town? Or anything else?" Daniel asked.

"No. Thank you." Odd, but she hadn't realized how close she was to losing her grip. Her professionalism was fraying around the edges, no question, and she was inches away from showing too much emotion to these two strangers. *Thank you, Daniel, for pointing out, so quietly, that it was time for us all to leave.*

She turned to Fiona and reached out to hug her. "Fiona, again, I am so sorry. Please let me know if there is anything I can do for you. Do you have family coming? To help you with the arrangements? Help you deal with the police?"

"Jasper's daughter, Daphne, will be here tonight. She's driving down from Boston."

"That's good. Please, do call me if there's anything I can do."

"Thank you, Nevada. I'll keep in touch."

As Nevada drove away, looking back in her rearview mirror at these two people, so important in Jasper's life, she still couldn't shake the feeling that the entire day had been surreal. She knew it had happened; she'd been right there through all of it. Yet she felt as if she were watching a movie or having a dream.

CHAPTER 8

At the Fraser Greene office the next morning, everyone seemed to walk as if the floor were littered with upturned razor blades. The police had finished their investigation of the scene and had allowed them back in. Nevada could almost smell the fear, suspicion, and mistrust that oozed from almost every mind in the place. She wondered how long it would take until they were back to some sort of normal.

Would they ever be? Maybe the execs should be thinking about offering the staff some sort of post-trauma counselling. She'd suggest it to Crawford, if she got the chance.

She stuffed the pages she needed, plus two copies of Cori Lowe's new novel, fresh off the press, into her bag. There would be dozens of them, stacked up at the booth, organized into creative pyramids on the tables, and stored in boxes behind the scenes, to replenish the piles as the booksellers and librarians took away their sample copies. But she needed to have a few near at hand at all times: who knew if she might find herself standing at a mirror in the ladies' room next to the head buyer for Riverrock Books?

As she walked out of her office, she found Hannah hovering by the doorway. "Could I speak to you for a moment,

Nevada?""Just briefly, Hannah. I have to be at the Javits Center in twenty minutes."

Hannah frowned. "Maybe this is bad timing."

"No, it's okay. I remember you wanted to speak to me yesterday on the Book Fair floor. What is it?"

Hannah hesitated, her twentyish face pale and hollow, as if she were recovering from a weekend in Vegas or a twenty-two-hour flight to Sydney. "It's about the panel coming up tomorrow.I heard—"

A deep voice, coming from behind Nevada's right shoulder, interrupted. "Excuse me, Nevada. I need a few minutes of your time."

When Crawford Burr spoke, everyone in the office dropped what they were doing and gave him full attention. In Nevada time at Fraser Greene, she'd seen numerous examples of his complete dominance of the publishing house, and she'd heard from others that throughout his thirty-year tenure he'd never wavered in his image as captain of the ship. With his silver hair, broad shoulders, and graceful posture, he looked like he could star in movies about drama in high political places. Nevada smiled; publishing houses were nothing if not political.

"Yes, of course, Crawford. Excuse me, Hannah. Let's catch up later."

She followed Crawford down the hall to his corner suite. He closed the door behind her—an unusual move in these days of men and women becoming increasingly aware of the dangers of inappropriate office conduct.

"What I have to say is very confidential," he said, as he motioned to her to sit down on one of the two leather couches, facing each other across a marble coffee table. "Would you like coffee or something?"

"No, thanks, Crawford."

"I understand. You're in a hurry to get over to the Book Fair. I won't keep you long. I just want to get something on your radar." He leaned toward her, forearms on knees, and made serious eye contact. "I'm hearing that Jasper's death may not have been an accident."

Nevada felt a need to inhale deeply. She didn't know Crawford to be a gossipy sort of man, passing along hearsay, and his manner was so solemn that she doubted they were launching into a speculative conversation. "Hearing? From whom?""Can't say. But a reliable source."

"He was shot."

"Yes, and at first, they thought it happened while he was cleaning a gun."

"But?"

"But now they think ... there might have been a second person present."

Nevada had a momentary flash of irritation at the ambiguity of his language. In his former life, Crawford had been an attorney, and they were trained to speak that way. And sometimes it was absolutely the best way to communicate, especially if tact and diplomacy were required. But sometimes she much preferred a direct statement.

"He was shot by somebody. Is that what you're saying? Deliberately or by accident?"Crawford shook his head. "Nobody's addressing that aspect yet."

"Who is the 'nobody'? The police? Is it a source in the police department you're getting this from?"

"I can't tell you anything about where I'm getting this information, Nevada. You'll just have to trust me. So far, all we know is that there are questions about Jasper's death."

"Why are you telling me this?""Because I know you were close to him, even though he'd left our roster. I also know you have a very important week coming up, with the Book Fair underway today. At first, I was inclined not to tell you anything because of the Book Fair and because you, and everybody else here, had a horrendous experience yesterday morning. But then I decided it was something you should know. It's something that might have an impact on your reactions to whatever goes on this week."

Nevada nodded. "I would do the same. Alright, what can you tell me? Besides the fact that there are 'questions'?"

"Just what I've told you. That it might not have been an accident—apparently, Jasper wasn't known for ever cleaning a gun."

"I didn't know he even had one," Nevada said.

"And apparently there was some evidence at the house that someone else was there that morning."

"Someone other than Fiona." When Crawford nodded, a thousand questions came bubbling to the surface for Nevada. "What evidence? Found by who?"

"Whom."

"Whom. What person? And what's happening next? Are the police on top of this?""I've heard that they are, and that every possibility is being examined," Crawford said. "I wanted to tell you about it in case you hear anything on the Convention floor today." He stood up. "You'll keep me in the loop."

Nevada knew when she was being dismissed. On her way to the door, she said, "I'll call you tonight."

"Please do."

***

The anticipation in the air at the Javits Center lobby was intense. Nevada had attended many conferences and conventions in her lifetime, most of them in her role as a reporter, and this one was no exception in its power to create a new community out of the simple fact of thousands of people, gathering under one roof. The whole was greater than the sum of its parts, and all that.

Today, the first day of the industry gathering, would be big, but the excitement on Saturday, when the Book Fest for fans and readers began, would be even wilder. Nevada had seen photos of last year in Chicago, when thousands of people lined up before the doors opened, and she knew that in New York the interest level would be just as high.

On this first day of the industry segment of the show, the librarians and booksellers were no less avid, if a little more methodical. Many had come in pulling empty roll-a-board suitcases, ready to be filled with advance reading copies of upcoming titles, bookmarks, brochures, bags, mugs, and all manner of swag. As Nevada walked toward the Fraser Greene booth, she noticed a large area cordoned off with velvet ropes and isolated on three sides with immense hanging curtains. Attendees were encouraged to check their bags in this holding space and Nevada could already see half a dozen people returning to their bags, arms full of hardcover books to fill up their empty suitcases.

Her path to the company booth took her past the autograph area, where long lines of tables and chairs stood ready for the authors whose fans would line up to get their signatures on a new book. Nevada could see that a lot of organization went into the setup, with each table adorned with a small vase and a flower, several gel pens in various colors, and a name card. A large display board showed the schedule for signings, with dozens of bestseller list names lined up under two-hour time blocks. Another showed the authors' names, with the day and time of their appearance in lettering more than a foot high. The author signing was due to start in an hour, right after the opening session.

Nevada joined the crowd surging toward the River Pavilion where tables awaited the hundreds who had signed up for the opening breakfast. She'd heard that the speaker was to be some Hollywood star who planned to release an autobiography next fall. The seats filled up quickly, and she ended up at a table near the back. Only one place was open and she grabbed it, even though it left her with her back toward the stage and the podium.

Her tablemates were senior editors from some of the largest publishing companies in the U.S. Nevada leaned into the opportunity to collect names and pass on her own. Through the croissants, the frittatas, and the fresh fruit, she chatted to her left and to her right. Then the people across the table leaned back into their chairs and tilted their heads toward the front of the room. The buzz in the Pavilion settled down as everyone got ready for the post-breakfast entertainment.

When Nevada first heard the voice, she almost dropped her fork. What was Toby Encell doing onstage at the Book Fair opening breakfast? Promoting his forthcoming autobiography, it turned out. Even though there was no manuscript and virtually no sign of any interest in actually producing a book! Nevada tugged her chair around to face the stage, then sat through Toby's ten-minute story about his beginnings as a sales clerk in a big-box electronics store. She had to hand it to him—he was a skilled storyteller. He had the crowd at his feet like a crowd of dogs waiting for a trainer to hand out treats. They laughed, they watched his face, then they applauded at the end of his speech.

If only she could count on his book delivering as well.

Nevada joined the crowd heading back to the conference floor. She was on her way to the booth, ready to stand for hours to talk to any bookseller or librarian who cared to chat about

Toby Encell's upcoming autobiography or the new historical novel coming from their major fiction author, Cori Lowe.

Jasper had been the star racehorse in the stable when he was at Fraser Greene. When he left, Crawford had moved to replace him with another prominent author. He brought Cori in himself, then turned to Nevada to be her primary contact. Cori had written half a dozen solid historical novels and Nevada felt convinced that, with the right advice, the right editors, and the right marketing, this new one, *I Remember Paris*, she could take a place at the top of the bestseller list.

For the past year, since Jasper had left, Nevada had been working with Cori. The Paris book was to be introduced at this Book Fair, with advance reading copies handed out and a full-on launch coming in July. Cori would be here later today to sign her other books and meet her fans, and Nevada decided to go over to the Author Autograph Zone and double-check on the timing announced for Cori's appearance. Just make sure their understanding of the schedule matched the Book Fair's.

She choked up for a minute when she saw *Jasper Inniskillen* written on the card on the table nearest the main aisle. Of course, the news of his death was so recent that Book Fair hadn't had time to adjust to his absence.

Nevada looked around for someone who might be in charge. Just as she was trying to decide between going over to the management offices behind the scenes to request a change and simply removing the cards and signage herself, a tiny woman in an expensive suit and aggressive shoes swept up to the table and dropped a stack of a dozen hardcovers. She came equipped with her own sign, too. *Sable Ogilvie.*

Jasper's closest competitor on the bestseller list.

CHAPTER 9

Nevada was shocked that Sable would be so brazen about her intention to take over Jasper's seat as king of the thriller writing world. Literally. She'd never liked her much, but even if she thought Sable was the best thing since Miss Congeniality, she wouldn't let this go by.

"Sable, I think you're in the wrong seat," Nevada said with what she hoped was a friendly smile.

Sable looked at her, then without a word went on settling herself at the table, putting her bag at her feet, lining up the pens, and patting her hair into perfect place.

It turned out she wasn't the only one. The organizers of the Book Fair were buzzing about this turn of events and eventually, one of them was confident enough to step up.

A fifty-something woman with gray hair and a clipboard appeared at the front of the table. "Ms Ogilvie, I'm afraid you're lost," she said with a big smile. "We have a chart for every author's spot and everyone is organized by genre. Your mystery readers will be looking for you over there." She waved a hand toward a spot several rows over, where half a dozen authors were setting up to greet their readers.

"No, ma'am, I'm not lost at all," Sable said. "You're organized by genre, but you should have me over here, in the Suspense Thrillers section."

"Well, I realize it's not an exact science. I suppose there's an argument to be made for placing you here."

"You shouldn't have Suspense as a separate category." Sable picked up her bag and began digging through it, looking for something. "Every good story has suspense. It's not a genre at all."

Nevada happened to agree with her but that didn't override the fact that she was offended by Sable's presumption in usurping Jasper's seat. If anything, they should set aside a huge section of this autographing space in his memory, the way sports teams retire players' numbers or stables set aside a stall for a champion who's passed on.

"We're getting off the point," the Book Fair woman said, to her credit. "We can move you to a table in the Suspense Thriller section if you think your readers will be better able to find you there. But you can't sit here."

"I also realize," Sable said, "that you have the best table for each genre set aside for the most prominent author in that category. In Thrillers, that's me."

"No," the woman said stubbornly, "it's Jasper Inniskillen, and this is his spot."

Perhaps the Book Fair woman hadn't yet heard the news that Jasper wouldn't be coming? Sable looked up from her purse and Nevada wondered if she would soften.

"It's mine now," Sable said.

Apparently not.

"I'm afraid it doesn't work that way. Book Fair makes the decisions about assignments of the tables and even though Mr. Inniskillen can't be here to sign autographs, we aren't going to assign this table to anyone else. It will sit empty throughout the Fair."

Sable stared at her for a long moment, and Nevada wondered what she would do next. What could she do, really?

The author stood up, grabbed her purse and name card, and walked to the vacant table next to Jasper's. Nevada didn't have time to see the name on the card before Sable swept it to the floor.

"Happy now?" Sable said.

The crowd around the autograph area was growing. Nevada could see lines of librarians and booksellers forming in the holding area, while dozens of authors were roaming the space, looking for their tables. Would the Book Fair coordinator give in?

"No," she said in a stern parent voice, "that is not your seat. Your seat is over there. I'd be delighted to escort you and show you exactly where it is."

"Sable! Sable Ogilvie!" The voice was excited and the woman owning it arrived in a group of five others. Librarians, Nevada guessed. They had the aura of people used to getting their way and they were traveling in a pack. "Are you ready to start? I have a copy of *Blinding Goodbye* and I would love for you to sign it for me!"

Sable shot one triumphant look at the Book Fair staffer before she sat down, picked up a pen, and reached out for the book.

Nevada and the Book Fair staffer exchange looks. Then the woman shrugged her shoulders and walked away.

Nevada waited until the six buyers had finished their conversations with Sable and moved on to their next author. "That took a lot of nerve," she said.

Sable leaned back in her chair. "Do I know you?"

"I'm Nevada Leacock, from Fraser Greene. Jasper was a friend of mine."

"And you know who I am. Jasper was a friend of mine, too. But I suppose now that he's not here to disagree with anybody, we'll hear about a lot of people claiming to be good friends of his. Anyway, this is business. I can't see that it makes any difference to the Book Fair organizers and it will make a lot of difference to me."

"It's disrespectful."

"It's not." Sable was looking over Nevada's shoulder at the line that had formed to meet her. "This Book Fair is one of my biggest events of the year. Me not taking advantage of the opportunity to put myself in front of his fans will not bring Jasper back." She flipped her hand at Nevada. "Now, if you don't mind, you're in the way."

Nevada stepped away from the table, torn between a state of shock and a desire to laugh out loud. If it weren't so sad, involving Jasper and all, it would be ridiculous.

She was still standing there, at the edge of the signature-seeking crowd, when Daniel Pyne tapped her on the shoulder. The indie author carried a large canvas bag and wore the sneakers you'd choose if you were planning to cover long distances.

"Nevada. Hi. Got a minute?"

More than a minute. She would be glad to shake off the sour feeling of the past few minutes in the company of Sable Ogilvie.

"Hey, Daniel. Of course. How are you?"

"I've had better days. You look as if you're upset about something."

"Oh! Not really. I just had a peek behind the curtain of the Wicked Witch of the West. If that isn't too much messing up a beloved book." She smiled.

"No, I get it. Who was it?"

"Sable Ogilvie."

"Ah."

"Do you know her?"

"She was a new author at Mondarix Press just about the time I was going out the door."

"I didn't know you were there! I thought you were self-published."

"It was my experience there that made me decide to try the independent path," he said. "Hey, do you want to get a coffee?"

"Sure." Nevada followed him over to one of the refreshment tables and watched as he poured coffee into a disposable cup.

"Cream or sugar?""Black. Thank you." She accepted the cup he handed to her, then waited as he poured his own. "Let's sit over there."

The table was littered with discarded brochures and book one-sheets. So much work went into all this selling material and so much was thrown away. No one had ever come up with a way of knowing how many, if any, of the messages registered with the decision-makers.

But you couldn't stop writing the stuff and putting it out there. Something worked, some of the time. The only problem was they didn't know what and when.

"How long ago was it that you were traditionally published?" She asked.

"Until about three years back," Daniel said.

"And what was Sable like when you were at Mondarix Press? Did your paths cross?"

Daniel made a face. "From time to time. We didn't click, let me put it that way. She put on the prima donna character from the beginning."

Nevada sipped her coffee. "There is that saying, 'fake it till you make it' ."

"Yeah, but she took it beyond self-confidence," Daniel said. "She was obnoxious."

"In what way?""Well, for example, she was an advocate for one of the Mondarix Press policies that I thought was just reprehensible."

This was like waiting for the last of the molasses to drip from the spoon. "Which was?"

"Oh, they encouraged authors to post negative reviews of their competitors."

Nevada made a face. "I agree. Reprehensible. You wonder why people waste their time on stuff like that. Why don't they just write better books?"

"And why doesn't their publisher encourage them to write better books?"

"I take it Mondarix Press was just not your cup of tea, in the end."

"I lost interest in the entire scene," Daniel said. "The rivalry and the competition got to me. Plus, as each year went by, the amount of marketing and other sidestreet stuff they expected me to do kept going up, while the royalties went down. It got to where I was making so little money that I was looking at going back to my day job. But I thought I'd give indie publishing a whirl, instead."

This next question was a personal one, but Nevada's curiosity was at a full gallop. "Are you paying the rent, with that?"Daniel smiled. "I have a mortgage, but yes, the indie publishing business has me keeping up."

"What's the main advantage, in your opinion?""The autonomy," Daniel said. "I have control over the way my books look, how they're edited, the timing of the releases, the marketing, and the distribution. Don't get me wrong, it's a lot of work, and I have a lot of days when I'd rather have a team of twenty to do all the stuff I have to do. But I've worked with a big team, and let me tell you, there's a lot of variation in the abilities and the experience of the individual members of the team."

"I've heard some of our authors complaining, usually late at night after a few too many Scotches," Nevada said. "They think their advances should be bigger or their royalty percentages higher."

"Well, advances," Daniel said. "That's a house of mirrors. Everybody thinks that the really big ones only go to the people who can fool the publishing house into taking a gamble on them and that very few are ever earned out."

"There's a lot of truth to that, actually," Nevada said. "But the superstar authors and the mega-selling books carry the rest. The bestsellers support all the mid-list books—not to mention the failures."

"And that explains the massive egos you see sometimes, in people like Sable Ogilvie. But Jasper was never like that." Daniel stared into the depths of his coffee cup. "I know you know that, Nevada. Jasper talked about what a down-to-earth person you are."

Despite herself, Nevada smiled at the compliment. "I worked really hard to live up to his expectations," she said.

"I'll bet it wasn't easy to balance that with those of everybody else at Fraser Greene. Especially with a boss like Crawford," Daniel said.

"Yeah." Nevada looked around; the area was filling up with people taking a break for lunch. "Well, my problem is I try to please everybody. I think it should be achievable, you know? Sometimes it's difficult to figure out what people want, but once you do, you find ways to give it to them, without taking too much away from anyone else."

Daniel was a listener, as many writers are. He cocked his head to one side, then said, "And if you're the one in the middle, managing the giving and the taking, what do you get?"

"The pleasure of pleasing them all, I guess." Nevada laughed. "What is this, therapy 101?"

Daniel Pyne seemed like the sort of man who might take everything in stride: great joy, great sorrow, searing insights. All would be met with the same even balance. Perhaps it was that deep, authoritative voice that reminded her of airline pilots telling you that they could climb a few thousand feet or take a different flight path to solve the problem of the turbulence that had everyone else on board on the edge of a panic attack. Perhaps it was his resemblance to one or two of the brave news photographers she'd seen during the wars she'd covered back in the day. He hadn't seemed like someone who could be easily shaken up.

And yet there he was yesterday, in tears as they walked around Jasper's front driveway or the way he'd reached down every few yards to pat Poe's head as the dog walked along with them. She also couldn't forget his words: "Whatever the truth of this is, Nevada, we have to find it. We were his friends and we have to find it."

"How are you feeling today? About Jasper's death, I mean," Nevada said.

"I miss him. Already, I miss him, because I know how it will be a month, six months, a year from now. Many things will happen and all of them would have been better if Jasper were still here," he said.

They drank their coffee in silence for a moment, then Daniel gazed into her eyes. "I knew him fairly well and I know you knew him well, too. In different contexts. I want to ask you something. Do you think there's more to the story than just an accident?"

Nevada stared at him. "You're the second person today to ask me that. Crawford Burr, my boss, told me this morning that he was hearing rumors that there was a second person present when Jasper died. When that gun went off." She took a deep breath. "Were you that second person, Daniel?"

He shook his head. "No, I wasn't there."

"When you arrived at his house, did you see anyone else who might have been?"

"Only Fiona, like you did, and she arrived late, too," Daniel said. "Nevada, I want to ask you to stay in touch with me about this. Tell me anything you find out about Jasper's death."

What was this all about? Why would she be finding out about anything? She cared about Jasper, sure, and she wanted to know what happened, but that was a long way from 'anything you find out'. What was Daniel asking her? And why?

She ducked her head in an awkward movement that might be a 'yes' and might be just a tic. "I have to go, Daniel. I hope you enjoy Book Fair."

As she roamed around the booths, Nevada was reminded again why she had gravitated to this business after deciding to leave journalism. Every table was laden with new titles: two to three hundred to four hundred to five hundred pages or more in each book, bound and covered by an image that made her want to dive into the author's story. Many of the names on the spines were as recognizable to her as her friends' names. Each of these books represented thousands of hours of thought and work by an author, each one a different story, a different offering.

Some people she'd met in publishing said there were only twelve plots and authors did nothing but recycle them, again and again. Maybe so, but Nevada believed every author had a unique mind and a way of writing a story. The piece of fiction she might write would differ from that of any other person. Her voice, her way of assembling words, her insights—they would all be unique. That was why no one need ever fear another writer stealing their ideas.

But Nevada would never write a piece of fiction. At least, that's what she thought at this stage of her life. Perhaps because she loved books so much that she could not imagine herself ever grabbing the tiger by the tail and holding on long enough to survive the experience of starting, building, and finishing a book. News reports? She had done those by the thousands, if not millions. Academic articles, research reports, even a screenplay. But a novel was beyond her ambition.

The crowd around the author signing area had grown and Nevada was to see a line in

front of the table where Cori Lowe sat. She hoped Cori's author career would take off. If the booksellers and librarians at this conference took to her and adopted her book, it could be her launching pad to a lifetime of full-time writing. They were the people who could make it happen for her, through their channels and the power of word-of-mouth. They were the people who loved books, just as much as any publisher or author.

She watched as two young women stopped in front of the empty table where Jasper's name card sat. They paused long enough for it to be clear that the stop was intended, and Nevada saw one of them put her finger to her lips and press it against Jasper's name card.

Even strangers wanted to pay homage, because of the way his words had moved them.

Nevada's phone buzzed, and she groped eagerly in her purse for it. Was Owen finally resurfacing? When she saw Daniel's name on the call display, she let it go to voice mail.

Five minutes later, when she checked the recording, she felt a little remorse over not responding to him. His voice sounded hoarse and his tone was listless:

> Nevada, thanks for taking the time
> for coffee with me today. It's

really hitting me this afternoon,
that he's gone. I can't begin to
describe for you how much he's
meant to me, over these years,
especially after I went rogue,
out into indie world ... I tried
calling Fiona but she's not picking up. I wanted to know if there
would be a funeral service or a
celebration of life or whatever
they want to call it now. If you
hear anything about that, would
you let me know? If you hear anything about anything, actually.
Anything more about ... about the
gun, or anything. I think we need
to know what happened to him,
right? Anyway, that's all. It's
Daniel. Daniel Pyne.

Oh geez. Her heart ached for him. Hell, it ached for herself. They'd lost a good one, and that just wasn't right.

Nevada felt something start to build inside her. It was what she thought of as anger, but maybe frustration was a better word. Owen said it was her "righteous indignation"; her father used to call it minding other people's business.

It wasn't right that he had died, and if it wasn't an accident, as Crawford had hinted this morning, she wanted to find out what it was.

***

The CEO had suggested she call him at the end of the day, but this felt soon enough.

"Crawford? Hi, thanks for taking my call. I wanted to check in to find out if there was any more news about Jasper," Nevada said.

Crawford's voice was low—maybe he wasn't alone. "Yes, I did invite you to call. I spoke with a contact I have in the police department and he said the coroner will release a report tomorrow, saying it's a homicide."

A homicide. Nevada felt her heart gain forty pounds and sink to her middle. "Is that ... isn't that kind of fast?"

"It can take weeks, but there's some jetstream somewhere that's moving it along. The autopsy itself takes two to four hours, and if there's a result available in twenty-four, you're getting premium service. In this case, it seems the accident explanation just didn't get traction. Now, apparently, the science is going to confirm it."

Homicide. Jasper. Nevada felt numb.

"Nevada? Are you still there?" Crawford sounded distracted. "Look, I have to get back to my meeting, but I wanted you to know. The police are on it, of course, and there is interest in this at the highest levels. But I thought that maybe, with your journalism background, you might be able to ask around and find out something about what happened. At the very least, I want you to keep your ears open. He was a hell of a nice guy and a literary treasure, and I think we owe it to him to uncover the truth."

Nevada couldn't agree more. She owed it to him.

CHAPTER 10

Nevada woke up alone in her bed the next morning. This was not that unusual. Owen often ran into late nights or all-nighters at work. Doctors couldn't demand that their patients stick to a nine-to-five schedule.

What was unusual was how many days they'd gone without talking. He'd returned her voice mail messages with a few short ones of his own and she suspected he was sending them straight to her voice mail without actually trying to reach her. If she weren't right in the middle of Book Fair, she would make a trip over to the hospital and see if she could catch him for a spontaneous lunch.

But it was Day 2 and there was a lot to do. As she walked the convention floor, she noticed that the lineups at each of the publisher booths were even longer. The autograph area wouldn't be opening for another half hour, but dozens of readers were already lined up, books in hand. The private spaces, marked off by heavy curtains concealing tables for meetings or entire rooms set up for lunches thrown by publishing houses for elite clients, were bustling with convention center staff carrying plates and table linen back and forth.

The Mondarix Press people were certainly on their game today. Large posters of Sable Ogilvie, her signature wide-frame glasses on a chain and her designer pant suit coordinated in colors to work with the cover of the hardcover bestseller she held, dominated the exhibit walls and also hung in the open space above.

Any author who preferred to be visually anonymous and to fly under the promotions radar was out of luck these days.

Nevada noticed that the previous day's highlighting of Jasper Inniskillen had been scrubbed. His photos were gone, his banner was gone, his name was gone from the Mondarix Press booth. In the autographing area, they were still holding his table empty, his name card in place. But right next to it, Sable's glossy photo held position on the table until the author herself would show up to hold court.

It left Nevada with a nasty feeling. More than nasty—she could feel the ache of grief in the pit of her stomach. A lot of water had streamed under the bridge since Charles had so graciously brought her in to the Fraser Greene fold and she would never forget Jasper's kindness in welcoming her. And now that his current author-home was showing him such disrespect, would it be acceptable for Fraser Greene to shower attention on his memory? She wondered if that would be something she could bring up with Crawford. He certainly seemed interested in Jasper and didn't seem to be holding onto the anger he felt when Jasper first left.

Her phone buzzed with a video call. Chelan Montgomery. Ordinarily, she would pick up right away; she always enjoyed a catch-up chat with her young friend in California. But out here in the middle of a noisy aisle at Book Fair?

On the other hand, it might be just the sort of thing Chelan would enjoy. She loved words, books, and print just as much as Nevada did, even though they'd first met in a TV station newsroom.

"Hey, Chelan?"

"Nevada! Where are you?"

"You're the digital media reporter. Guess."Chelan smiled. "Fun! Well, obviously, some kind of convention. I see … booths, books … posters … All the Light We Cannot … oh! Are you at Book Fair?"

"I am. I've got a meeting in about twenty minutes and I wasn't going to pick up, but I thought you might get a kick out of seeing this."

"Oh, you know me! Yes, someday I want to get there and soak up all that bookishness."

"How are you?" Nevada asked.

"All good here. I have a few new online assignments and I think I'll be able to fit them in, between all the kids' activities. But I was calling you because I just heard on the news about Jasper Inniskillen."

"Yes. Quite a shock."

"I'm so sorry to hear about it, Nevada. I know you were close," Chelan said. "What happened?"

"What are they saying on the news?""That he died of in an accidental shooting."

Nevada nodded. "That's about right. Except for the 'accidental' part."

Chelan was silent. Nevada knew, from the days when Chelan worked for her in the TV newsroom she managed, that the reporter antennae were up.

"Do you want to tell me more about it?" So were the empathetic friend antennae.

Nevada looked around and spotted a chair by itself in a quiet corner. "Let me just get out of the traffic here, and we'll talk. Here—I'll swoop the phone around once more so you can see all the action."

After she sat down and propped the phone up on her bag, she concentrated on the tiny window she had on Chelan's world. Her friend looked a little weary, but who wouldn't be with three children under the age of four?

"So, it might be that Jasper's death wasn't accidental? What are the authorities saying?"

"Not much, so far. I'm sure they have their hands full—it only happened yesterday. I also don't know where the information came from, about it being suspicious."

"How good is your source?"Nevada thought about Crawford and all his connections. "Very good. And there was enough about his life that was ... I mean, I have questions ... it's plausible that it wasn't accidental."

"Like, what kind of questions?"

Nevada took a moment to think. "He was unhappy. Most of his friends and colleagues knew that. He'd been feeling me out about the possibility of coming back to Fraser Greene as his publisher. I'm sure the people at Mondarix Press wouldn't be too thrilled about that."

"I apologize in advance about this next question, Nevada, but I know you know the police always look at the closest family members when there's a homicide. And that's all we know, so far, isn't it? He died and they think there was another person involved, but nobody is talking about premeditated murder yet, are they?""I don't really know, Chelan. But yes, homicide is all that Crawford has told me so far."

"Might his wife have been there?"

"She didn't say anything about that when I saw her," Nevada said. "She was very upset, but she didn't tell me and Daniel anything."

"Daniel?"

"One of his closest friends. Just as shocked as I am."

"Anybody else you've come across?"

Nevada shook her head.

Chelan's look was sympathetic. "How likely would you say it is that someone killed him deliberately?"

"You mean, did he have enemies? Not that I've ever heard about. But you never know, right?"

"Yeah, well, most of us, in real life, would never think about killing somebody else. And so we have a perception that it's rare. And I suppose, statistically, it is. But people are murdered and for each one of those people, somebody … or a group of people… . wanted them dead."

Nevada watched the people across the way, going to and from the displays and exhibits. Some of them were wandering, and some were almost jogging. It was if the entire floor was a single organism with hundreds of thousands of moving parts.

"You know what you have to do."

Nevada brought her focus back to the phone. "If what?"

"If you want to answer your questions. Go at it the same way you would a major investigative piece in a serious newsroom."

It was a challenge, Nevada got that.

Chelan shrugged. "Or just leave it alone. There are police detectives. You have a lot of your main work to do, and probably, no one will thank you if you get involved."

"I am involved. I'm realizing that. And being thanked is not why I do things."

A shriek emanated from the phone and Chelan looked over her shoulder. "Break time is over, gotta go. Let me know what you decide."

"Oh, I've decided," Nevada said, as Chelan's face and waving hand disappeared from the screen.

First step would be a call to Detective Travers. She didn't know whether he was assigned to this case, but she hoped that her connection with the Fraser Greene shooting incident yesterday would get him to take her call. As soon as she was finished this meeting coming up with Crawford, Bernadette, and the copy editor standing by to meet Toby and receive his manuscript, she would give Travers a try.

Crawford had set up the meeting for one of the side rooms in the Center. It was a bit on the barren side, but at least it wasn't in temporary space on the other side of a curtain. Nevada dropped her purse under her chair and set up her computer. She liked to make her notes only once.

Bernadette was not far behind her, then Crawford, then Aynslee Kinter, the copy editor.

Then they sat and waited. The time inched by.

"Are we waiting for anybody else?" Crawford asked as he looked up from his phone screen.

"Dane from Marketing," Bernadette said. "Oh, here he is."

"Sorry, apologies for being late, so sorry." Dane was often late; Nevada and Bernadette barely looked up.

When Toby was a full fifteen minutes late, Nevada started to apologize.

"You don't have to apologize for him, he's his own man," Crawford said.

"I guess he thinks we need him more than he needs us," Bernadette said.

"From the reception he got at the breakfast keynote, I'd say that's an obvious conclusion. Nevada, could you try calling him?"

"No need to call me, I'm here!" Toby announced as he swept through the door, followed by a young man with an impressive beard and less than impressive clothes.

"This is my son, Royce. I've invited him to sit in."

"Hello, Toby, welcome!" Crawford rose to his feet to shake hands and indicated the chair at the head of the table. "We're eager to see what you have for us."

Toby put an exquisite leather briefcase on the table and spun a combination lock before opening it. "As promised, here is the first draft. Ready for your attentions. Please be kind," he said, pulling out a sheaf of several hundred pages.

Crawford reached for it, but Toby wasn't letting go just yet. "There is one minor glitch that we have to discuss."

You could tell by Crawford's face that he didn't like being blocked in this way. "And that is?"

Toby turned to his son. "Royce, why don't you explain, since it's your issue?"

Issue? Someone named Royce, whom they'd never met before, was being allowed to have an issue with a manuscript they'd paid a four-million dollar advance for?

Royce leaned forward across the table. "Come on, Father, you know it will be a problem for everyone in the family." He turned to address the others. "My father wants to bring out an autobiography that reveals family secrets that will upset many people. Some of them to the point, I think, where it's just dangerous and irresponsible to put these things into print. We don't see why the details can't be left out. The story will be just as good without them, and there is no one who is going to challenge him because no one else knows about these things. Except him. And me."

"And my father," Toby said.

"Yes, well, Rolf doesn't want any of this book coming out. He wants you to cancel the entire publication. I'm not quite that ... crazed ... about it, but I do think you have to remove these chapters."

"No! Absolutely not. I will not be censored by that old man."

The two men glared at each other, and Nevada wished herself out of the room. She'd like to be somewhere on a nice beach, where any tension had a mile of sky and many miles of ocean to blow out over. Surely, Toby should have worked all this out with his family before stepping up to sign a multi-million-dollar contract to produce an autobiography? Never mind seven figures, this one was more like eight. A lot of money was on the line and you wouldn't think a successful, high-flying entrepreneur like Toby Encell would misunderstand that.

But, when it came to people's families and their personal histories, anything could happen.

Bernadette was speechless and Crawford's gaze was darting back and forth along the front of the tabletop, as if he were in a gunnery range, trying to decide which one to unleash on Toby. Nevada decided it was her place to step in.

"This is obviously not something we're going to resolve right now. Of course, you understand, Toby, that Fraser Greene will not want to release anything we don't all want to stand behind one hundred percent. Let me take the manuscript … whatever pages you have so far … and read it. If Crawford agrees, we'll consider it turned in on time, and we'll work together on this other matter. I'm sure if we turn on the rocket fuel, we can resolve the problem and still have it ready to launch next May." She looked around the table. She could see Crawford still fuming over a potential disruption to the release schedule he treasured almost more than he did his club membership. She saw Bernadette flinching at the commitment to speed up any of her processes, but Dane's narrowed eyes telegraphed he could see the marketing potential if there were to be a loud public family feud over this book.

Well, if Nevada had any control over it, there wouldn't be. Whatever it was, she was ready to step in and mediate between Toby and his son, and in the meantime, she would keep this blockbuster on track.

"Royce, if you would share your contact information with me, we'll meet just as soon as I finish my reading of the manuscript and see how we can fix this."

"I'm not sure I even want you to read this," Royce said. "He's written things in there that should be entirely confidential."

"That's not up to you!" Toby's voice was low, but it still sounded like a roar.

"Don't worry." Nevada hurried in to calm things down. "I have kept many things completely confidential over the years and I will do so here. I'll sign a non-disclosure agreement, if that would help. Let's just keep this train on track because time goes by quickly and if we miss a few of the milestones, we'll never make it to print."

As she drove home that evening, Nevada felt as though she'd run a marathon. The day had continued with more meetings and each time she passed the autographing area table with Jasper's name card on it, she felt the loss again. She needed a hug, and she was looking forward to seeing Owen.

His car was in the garage and she could hear the television set as she walked in. "Hey, I'm home!"

A few years back, he would have met her at the door, helping her off with her coat and offering her a glass of wine. Ah well, they'd been married quite a while now, and those romantic gestures disappear, don't they? That's what was normal, she'd heard. Nevada had no template to compare to, since her parents had fought like coyotes over the last chicken in the county.

She hadn't opened herself to the idea of marriage until she was in her mid-forties, and she chose a man quite a bit younger than herself. In fact, she probably would never have married at all, if Owen hadn't come along with his devastating combination of good humor, dependable interest in her, and quiet dedication to his purpose as a pediatric oncologist. He had expressed a few doubts about marriage, but she convinced him that everyone experiences some 'cold feet', as they say. It was a big decision to sign those papers and make those promises, but Nevada had had no regrets.

The past few months, though, she'd had some unease.

She found him in the den, sprawled out on the leather couch with a plate of rice and beans and the baseball game on the TV. "Hey! You made it home."

Nevada allowed herself to collapse into the armchair. "What a day."

"One of those, huh? I saw on the news that Jasper Inniskillen died."

"That was yesterday." She saw his eyes move to focus on the TV screen. "Hey, do you mind if we turn that off?"

"Well, it's the bottom of the ninth and the bases are loaded. Do you want something to eat? Maybe go figure out what you want and by the time you've done that, the game will be over." He turned to smile at her with that amazing smile and she softened. He'd probably had a rough day, too. If a baseball game helped him relieve the stress, who was she to complain?

CHAPTER 11

Nevada was up and out of the house before Owen stirred the next morning. The previous evening had been so uncomfortable that she just needed to give something else her full attention. She didn't want to see him and didn't want to have to make conversation. Perhaps he would want to discuss something heavy and she didn't want to have to face that either. They were just in a phase where they were out of sync with each other, but it would pass.

In the meantime, today she had almost every hour crammed with publisher duties swirling around Book Fair. She had to present Cori Lowe's upcoming historical romance saga at the Editors' Fiction Forward panel this afternoon, and before that she had half a dozen meetings with book buyers and library directors.

But foremost in her mind was Jasper and the questions she had about his death.

Her first call was to Detective Travers.

"Ms. Leacock! You're an early riser," he said.

"I have so much I have to do today, you wouldn't believe," she said.

"Are you calling to find out more about the suspect in your company's shooting incident? The one we now have in custody?"

That stopped Nevada. "No, I wasn't. I didn't realize you had arrested somebody."

"Yeah, it would have been a bit weird if you knew about it already. Just picked him up a few hours ago."

"How did you find him?""Come on now, you know I'm not going to reveal details about our methods. Let me just say that we're fortunate to reap the benefit of the acute observation skills of some of our fellow New Yorkers." He sounded quite pleased with the situation.

"Who is he?"

"Press release going out in an hour."

Nevada sighed. "Alright, Detective Travers.The real reason for my call has to do with Jasper Inniskillen. I heard that you've reclassified it as a homicide and I was wondering if you could tell me more about that."

"We're looking into several theories about that."

"Is it murder?"

"Not at liberty to say … although it probably won't be long."

"Who would want a man like Jasper dead?"

"Could be a lot of reasons," the detective said. "All the motives you ever come across anywhere—jealousy, financial gain, possessiveness, rivalry. Maybe he was just in the way for someone and that person killed him or arranged for him to be killed."

"That's crazy. Isn't it crazy?""I've been in police work long enough to learn never to underestimate any theory."

"What's next?" Nevada asked.

"I talk to people and find out what he was doing and where he was in his last days. And we ask the public for tips. Anybody passing by his place that day, something they might have heard or seen."

"What he was doing in the last few days … is that enough?"

"Let me do my job, Ms. Leacock."

She heard the phone click. The call was over.

Throughout the hours until lunch, she had another track running in her mind. She thought of it as the Jasper track, and by the time she had shaken the last hand for the morning, it was well-worn with ideas and plans. If Detective Travers could talk to people about Jasper's life over the past few months, so could she.

Nevada made a long list of people she planned to email with questions about Jasper's activities in the month of May, starting with Crawford Burr. She had his cell number and for him, it would be text, not email. People jumped faster and answered sooner with text than with email.

> Crawford. Quick question. Did you take any meetings with Jasper this past month?
>
> Yes. He booked a call with me a few weeks ago. First of May, I'd say
>
> To say what?
>
> He wanted to come back. That was no secret
>
> What did you say?
>
> That it was extremely unlikely, but I'd think about it.
>
> Nevada paused, considering her next question.
>
> And have you thought about it?
>
> Moot point now, isn't it?

*She decided to take a run at it
from yet another direction.*

*If things were different, would you
be asking him back?*

No.

So, Jasper was so unhappy at Mondarix Press that he'd actually approached Crawford and risked rejection. And received
it. Nevada wondered how bad it really was for Jasper at the
other publishing house.

She searched her contacts list and came up with a number
for Kristof Dykstra, the marketing head at Mondarix Press.
She didn't know anyone at any higher level than that, in the
company.

Kris, hi. So sorry to hear about
Jasper's death. You all must be
reeling

*It was a shock, yes. What can I do
for you, Nevada?*

*I'm trying to find out something
about his activities this past
month.*

Why?

Helping the cops

Nevada stared at her phone screen, but nothing more
came. Had she offended Kris somehow? Had someone interrupted? She decided to plunge right in.

Do you know anything about anything he was working on?

The long minutes between each of these texts were raising her blood pressure forty points, she was sure of it.

> He was in research mode for a
> thriller about the Mob

Interesting.

> Thanks, Kris

Next on Nevada's list was Fiona. She was reluctant to bother her so soon after everything that had happened, but if anybody knew what was going on with Jasper, you'd think it would be his wife.

> Fiona, have you got a minute?

> *Sure, what's up*
>
> *I'm asking around to try to piece together a picture of things going on with Jasper over the past few weeks*

The pauses were just as long as those she had from Kristof.

> Yes?

> *Would you happen to know about anything unusual he was doing? He was probably working, reading, and so on, but what about meetings?*
>
> *He talked to Crawford. And he did have a meeting with an attorney*
>
> *What about?*

> *He was having a row with our*
> *neighbor over the exact location*
> *of the property line*
>
> *What's your neighbor's name?*
>
> *Brady Roth*
>
> *Anything else?*
>
> *In the past month? He met with a*
> *newbie writer he's been coaching.*
> *Josselyn Madden.*

Why did that name seem familiar? Nevada fumbled in her purse for a pen and came up with one. No pieces of paper, though, so her hand would have to do. Josslyn Madden. Brady Roth. Mob.

Fiona had more.

> He also met with a private secu-
> rity guy. He was worried about a
> stalker fan. She was coming around
> just a bit too much, and it gave
> him the creeps. Wanted to find out
> more about her and what he could
> legally do.

> *Do you know her name?*
>
> *Olivia Theale*
>
> *Thanks, Fiona. This is very*
> *helpful*
>
> *No problem*

Nevada looked at the list in her hand. She had a lot of work to do. She had only about half an hour until the Fiction

Forward panel started, but she wanted to find out what Jasper had been up to on social media recently. Social media postings were a wealth of information. People felt as though they were keeping a diary or just sending notes to a few close friends, but they were creating a lasting, widely broadcast record that anyone could see.

She looked him up on the three major platforms and there he was. Photos of book covers, thank you's from fans, bookstore displays, pics of his book 'in the wild', in someone's hand on a subway or being read on a plane.

She was intrigued to see a few cryptic posts from midmonth about some meeting he attended that seemed to invigorate him with a solid blast of author adrenaline. He wrote about meeting other authors, helping other authors, and getting many new ideas for things he wanted to do.

After contemplating this for a few minutes, Nevada decided to try Daniel on this one. His answer to her text came almost immediately.

> Hey Nevada what's up?

> *Do you know anything about where Jasper might have been last month where he hung out with a lot of authors and talked shop?*

> *Yeah, he was with me. I took him to a self-published author conference*

Self-publishing! Nevada never would have guessed that Jasper had any interest in going in that direction.

> What did Jasper think of that?

He was impressed. By the end, he was talking about going indie. Learning how to publish himself. Said he was doing the best of the marketing anyway, and he was certainly capable of putting together a team of designers and editors

Were you encouraging him in that?

I was encouraging him to do what might make him happy. He was trying to get back home to Fraser Greene but the door seemed to be shut. And Mondarix Press was killing him

Can you send me some stuff about this indie Conference

Will do

Now, please

CHAPTER 12

While she waited for Daniel's material to come through, Nevada made a call to Fiona.

"Hi, I'm sorry if I'm interrupting you. I just have a lot to say and if I try to handle it on text, it will take hours," Nevada said.

"I understand. How can I help you?"

"Do you have Jasper's calendar? Or a way to get it?"

"His computer has a password that I don't know. The police took it away and apparently, their IT people are trying to get into it." Nevada's feeling of disappointment lasted only seconds. "He kept a daily planner on paper, too," Fiona said. One of those small binder-type of things."

Things were looking up. "Did the police take that, too? Or do you have it? Can I see it?"

"Yes, it's still here. But I'll warn you, he wrote everything in there in code. I think he didn't want me to know where he was, a lot of the time. I asked him about it once and he said he had a lot of odd research things he was doing and a lot of them wouldn't work out, or wouldn't ever be useful for a book. He didn't want to discuss them with me, or anybody in advance—said he felt shy about them. Then, he got mad at me for looking into his planner and the conversation went in another direction."

Nevada didn't know what to say to that. It sounded peculiar to her that a person would write in his own day planner in code. Was he worried about someone reading it? His wife? Was there something wrong with the places he was going or the people he was seeing?

"Fiona, I'd like to take a look at it. Would that be okay?""For what purpose?"

"I want to know whether Jasper was killed, in cold blood or by accident, almost as much as you do. The police say there was a second person there. I know many people who knew Jasper and I know how to ask questions. Maybe people who wouldn't talk to the police will talk to me."

Fiona thought over her answer for a few moments. "Alright. Come out to the house tomorrow."

"I can't do tomorrow. It's the last day of Book Fair. But I could drive out on Saturday, before I go in to the Book Fest. The reader fans aren't coming in until noon."

"Saturday is fine."

"Do you think I could meet your neighbor, too? This Brady Roth who had the issue with Jasper over your property line?"

"Sure, we'll walk over. See if they're home."

The drop in Fiona's energy made her feel that she was losing her grip on the conversation. But Nevada wanted to try to work in one more thing.

"Fiona, did Jasper talk to you about this indie authors' convention in L.A. he went to in April?"

"He did," Fiona said. "Lot of nonsense. He had this idea that he could get much more control over his books and make just as much money ... more money! ... than he could with a traditional publishing house. Daniel Pyne was the one stoking him up on this."

Nevada knew the answer to her next question, but she was curious about how much Jasper had shared with his wife. "Did he and Daniel go together?"

"They did. He said it was an outstanding experience, and he wanted to go again next year. Wanted me to go, too."

They both fell silent, thinking about the fact that Jasper would not be going anywhere next year.

"Was it the convention itself he enjoyed?" Nevada asked. "Or was it just the prospect of making more money and having more control over his career?"

"I think he liked the convention itself. Said there was a lot of socializing and he really felt as though he'd found his tribe. Tribe! As if a writer is ever anything other than a lone wolf. He said they went out to lots of restaurants and it was constant talk about writing craft and about selling books. They made quite a fuss about him, apparently. I think that soothed his ego after what happened at Mondarix."

"What happened there?"

"Maybe I shouldn't be telling you this, since you work in publishing, too."

"You can count on my discretion, Fiona."

"They weren't very respectful over there. Even I could see that, and I usually was a lot slower than Jasper to feel that he'd been insulted or disregarded. People didn't return his phone calls, and the editors were making dramatic changes to his work without consulting him. He didn't like the cover they had in mind for the next book. Then they were talking about re-packaging all the old books with new ones. I guess they wanted to rebrand him and wipe out all the evidence of the previous publisher."

"I'm beginning to see why he was so determined to get out of there," Nevada said.

"He was trying to go back to Fraser Greene and he was thinking of going indie," Fiona said. "Meanwhile, the royalties were being paid out very slowly. He was trying to write faster so that he'd have more books to bring out but Mondarix Press said they didn't want to do more than one book a year. He was getting quite desperate about the money ... we both were. That's why he agreed—"

She stopped abruptly.

"Agreed to what, Fiona?"

"Never mind, it's not important."

"Okay, so that was April," Nevada said. "What about March? What do you remember about his activities in March?"

"He visited the doctor a couple of times," Fiona said. "Regular checkup stuff. I used to go with him all the time but as the years go by you stop doing that couple stuff, you know? I usually had errands to do, so I dropped him off at the clinic. He also did quite a few business lunches that month, I remember. But then, he always does. I think he saw the honchos at Mondarix Press a few times, his agent, maybe his financial adviser. If he didn't, he should have."

Nevada didn't know how to take that one. "Well, um, yeah. Anything else?"

"He was doing research for a new novel. Even though Mondarix had told him they didn't want anything until the end of the year, he had already started. It was going to be another thriller, set in Alaska this time I think, or maybe DC. Maybe another one of those political thrillers, the violent ones. He took a few lessons in shooting, said he needed to ramp up his knowledge about various guns. And he did a day trip to Boston one day. Research again. Said it was a contract to write something about biotech."

"Okay, Fiona, thanks for this. I'll see you Saturday morning."

After she hung up, Nevada feverishly tapped all the notes she could remember into her phone. Fiona had certainly added to the picture she had of Jasper. Odd, how you could know somebody for a lot of years and yet find out later that there were so many things you really didn't know about them. She had assumed that Jasper had no money worries at all, given the extravagant advances he'd received for his novels in the past. But, now that she thought of it, she had no idea what his expenses were or how he balanced things out.

And what had Fiona meant when she referenced 'what Jasper had agreed to'?

Nevada had time to check her email before the panel started. The first item to show up as soon as she logged on was the daily news from *Publisher Watch*. Every few days, they listed the latest contracts signed by authors, ranging from fifty grand (a nice deal) to a million dollars (a definitely juicy deal).

Sable Ogilvie's name was there, in bold and at the top of the list. "Bestselling author of HACKED and Book Club Selection of the Year BELTWAY EXILE, Sable Ogilvie's ALASKA CHASE, to Bonnie Lee Vargus at Mondarix Press, from Meaghan Richards of the Richards Agency."

It seemed as though Sable Ogilvie was everywhere.

As Nevada sat and mulled over her conversation with Fiona, she was startled to see the man in the brown clothes again. Way across the hall, near the erotic literature publisher, she saw a man standing with an armful of books, leaning over a table to look at the material piled up there. He certainly resembled the man from the shooting, but was she sure? Her memory was already faltering on the details. She couldn't swear it was the same man ... would it help if she got closer?

Nevada gathered up her files, her briefcase, and her purse and strolled over, as nonchalantly as she could, to a spot about three feet behind the man. He certainly looked familiar. He turned away from the booth and headed across the aisle to a travel guidebook publisher.

"Hey, Mark, how are things?" The salesperson greeted the man in what Nevada took to be a hopeful tone.

"All good," Mark said, as he bent to look over the books and pamphlets on the display.

"And is the Greater Manitou Library District having a good Book Fair this year?" the salesperson asked. "Finding everything you need?"

"We are going to expand the travel collection this year," the man said. "Show me what you got."

Nevada did not know what the connection was between this man, her publishing company, and Book Fair, but now she had something to chase down. She flipped open her laptop, checked that her Wi-Fi connection was good, then started to look up Mark's library.

Her phone buzzed. Fiona Inniskillen.

"Nevada, I just wanted to double check on your promise to keep our conversation confidential."

"Of course, Fiona," Nevada said. If there was one thing she'd had plenty of practice with over the years, it was protecting the identity of a source. "Was there something in particular you were concerned about?"

"When we were talking about money, and I said that's when he agreed ... I shouldn't have mentioned that he agreed to take on the work for Encell."

Say what?

"I don't think anybody is supposed to know just yet ... if ever ... But I thought since you're working on Toby's autobiography, you might already know about this. Maybe you were even the one who put the two of them together."

Not.

"Anyway, I know they were still negotiating the credits on the front cover and both Toby and Jasper changed their minds about a dozen times about whether they wanted to have Jasper's name on there at all," Fiona said. "I don't think it should be you or me who releases that information to the world, you know?"

Oh yes, I do know.

"Of course, Fiona, we'll keep that completely confidential. Thanks for clarifying."

What did she mean, 'take on work for Encell'? What work was Jasper doing for Toby? And should she take Fiona's word for it, or did she need at least one other person to verify that?

One thing was sure, and it made her heart feel like an open wound in her chest. She couldn't ask Jasper anything anymore.

CHAPTER 13

Nevada was in a panic to find her bag and get to the main hall for the Panel. She'd lost track of time—not a smart move. This was one of the pivotal sessions of Book Fair for her. Up to now, she'd played her role as a member of the team but now, she was the leader. It was the Fiction Forward session, the time that a select group of editors had the opportunity to present their top choices for the coming year. The audience would be packed with library decision-makers, major bookstore buyers, media reviewers with millions of readers and followers, and influencers from a dozen different lanes. It was the interstate of book promotion.

Nevada was due to meet Cori outside the hall. They'd decided to go to the session together, to avoid the possibility of either one of them being late or getting lost. Each thought it would be the other one, a notion that amused Nevada. Cori was barely thirty years old and yet she seemed to think she had to be the adult providing the supervision in the room. Meanwhile, Nevada had had enough experience with the frequent childishness of authors to want to do what was necessary to ensure that Cori would be in her seat, smiling and inviting questions, when the time arrived.

Cori wasn't there, so Nevada decided to take a quick moment to try to reach Owen by phone. No answer, straight to voice mail. She didn't know what was going on, but she just didn't have time to find out what it was right now. The New York show came around only once a year, and even though there were the others, London, Frankfurt, Hong Kong, and possibly New Delhi, for the first time for her, none of those lit up her radar the way this one did. She just didn't have time to hunt for him and deal with whatever crack might have opened up in their veneer. She had to be able to rely on him this week.

While she waited, Nevada went back over her recent conversations with her husband, trying to figure what it might be that was in the air between them. The exercise of working back through their dinners and Saturday mornings together kept her from dwelling on the memory of the sight of the silver four-door that she'd seen in her rear-view mirror, pulling into their driveway last week as she'd left for work. Nothing obvious from any of their recent time together emerged.

She searched the crowd but couldn't spot Cori's pink hair or the over-the-knee boots she favored. But she did see Hannah North.

"Hannah!" She could see that the intern was startled when she heard her name called. "Over here!"

Hannah's face lit up, and she plunged into the mass of people streaming toward the open doors. She managed to cross over to where Nevada stood. "Oh, it's awesome that I found you here. I have to talk to you."

"I know there was something you needed earlier, Hannah. I'm sorry that I just didn't have time. But—"

"What are you going to say about my book? Do you want to practice on me for a few minutes before you go on?" These were the first words out of Cori's mouth. It was Interesting how greetings seemed to be going the way of many other endangered species.

Nevada smiled at Cori. "No, thanks. The whole office has had meetings about the presentation of this book and if I deviate from the script, I'll be toast." She turned to Hannah. "I'm sorry, Hannah, but this will have to wait until after the presentation. Come on, Cori, let's get inside."

As she ushered her author into the room, Cori still wanted her questions answered. "What are you going to say?" "I'll be using the key phrases from the blurb on the back cover and some of the advance praise bits from the book description," Nevada said. "The art department has put together some gorgeous slides and a huge poster that will be on an easel beside me at the front of the room. The goal is to make your book title, your name, and the cover as memorable as possible."

Cori was nodding. "And as sales worthy as possible."

"Are the royalties a major concern of yours right now?" Nevada asked.

"Yes. The royalties from the last two books have been disappointing, and this one has to hit big or I might have to go back to a day job," Cori said. "And, as you know, the percentage that goes to royalties has dropped this year."

Nevada wasn't going to respond to that but she could see that Cori was waiting for one. "It's been a tough year for everybody in every corner of the business."

Cori sighed. "It's hard to know what's going on. Some places I look, they're pointing out that the typical American doesn't even read a book a year. Meanwhile, in other places, they say more books are selling than ever before and the average advance has gone up a bejillion percent."

"You can make statistics prove anything," Nevada said. "But I think you have to agree that getting your book on this panel is a sign that your publisher is doing everything possible to get your name out there."

"That's what the marketing department says," Cori said. "Right before they tell me everything else is up to me. I'm doing ten hours a week on social."

"Good for you," Nevada said. "Let's go in."

The Book Fair president latched onto Nevada as soon as she walked in and escorted her to her seat at the front of the room on the panel.

Six women sat in a line, ready to present their 'big book' to an audience of bookstore buyers, library directors, and assorted publishing insiders. Nevada was ready with her phrases: "masterful writing" and "kept me up, reading through the night"; and "when I first read Cori Lowe's *I Remember Paris*, I fell in love with it instantly."

She glanced to her left where Kristof sat, ready to present Sable Ogilvie's big release for this spring, *Hacked*. Mondarix Press insisted on having their Marketing Department take the lead on presenting and representing books. Editors were second fiddle when it came to speaking to booksellers or libraries in their world, apparently. Nevada had heard through the grapevine that Book Fair and a couple of editors on their board had protested but there was no budging Mondarix. And, because they were one of the big players, they couldn't be denied.

She wondered if Kristof knew how much his presence there was resented.

No one sat to her right, which probably meant that she was going first. Not her favorite; she liked to have a little advance information before she spoke, from watching others and gauging the reaction from the audience. But even though her tenure in the book business wasn't that long, she knew she attracted a lot of respect because of her decades of leadership in journalism. Her nerves weren't nearly as jumpy as those percolating farther down the table, in the minds of the thirty-somethings who were just beginning their careers.

The people were taking their time in getting to their seats: there were many old friends from all around the country to be greeted. Nevada took out her phone to pass the time. She had little to say to Kristof Dykstra.

"Good afternoon, Nevada." She looked up to see Charles Delaney standing in front of her. Fraser Greene's editor emeritus seemed to spend more time at book events now that he was retired than he ever had while he was employed full time. "I'm looking forward to hearing about this book from your new discovery." He consulted the program in his hand. "Cori Lowe."

"I think you'll be impressed, Charles. She's an excellent writer and could be one of the best."

Charles looked at her. "That's what you thought about Jasper Inniskillen, and you were wrong."

Nevada was speechless.

"It's true, Nevada. Nobody was particularly upset when Jasper left us for Mondarix Press either, except for you. And maybe Crawford, but I think that was more about his ego being bruised because an author left him."

"Have a good conference, Nevada." And he was gone.

She looked back down at her phone, wondering if she ought to go over her speech notes one more time.

"Nevada?" Hannah stood in front of her, whispering.

Nevada looked down the table, but no one noticed, not even Kristof.

"Could I speak to you just for a minute, please?"

Nevada shook her head. "It's starting any minute."

"I thought you might say that. Here," and Hannah passed a note around the edge of the table.

Nevada glanced at Kristof but he was still completely focused on the phone in his hand.

She unfolded it and peeked at the writing.

Toby is planning to disrupt the meeting.

How on earth did Hannah know that, Nevada wondered. Disrupt, in what way? And why? What was she supposed to do with this information and why had it been sent to her?

"Why are you giving this to me now?" she whispered to Hannah.

"I've been trying to talk to you all morning," Hannah replied.

"Did he give you this note?" Nevada suddenly realized that Kristof had put down his phone and was staring at the two of them. "It's starting. You'd better go."

Hannah hurried away to her seat in a corner of the room. Nevada struggled to get her concentration back, as the panel moderator got things underway, introducing the speakers and describing the scope of the session. She turned to Nevada and invited her to the podium to present the first book.

"Thank you, everyone," Nevada said. Her mind was racing as she stood up to speak. *Why was Toby planning to disrupt the presentation? What was he going to do? How did Hannah know about it? DID she know about anything? Was she a pawn or the queen?*

"Today, I want to introduce you to one of the best books I've read all year. I stayed awake all night finishing it and I couldn't wait to announce Cori Lowe's latest achievement to the world." As she stumbled through her slides and her points, Nevada scanned the room, looking for Toby.

About three minutes in, she saw him. He walked confidently up to the front row and took a seat on the aisle after its occupant, seeing him coming, rose and vacated. Toby looked up at Nevada and nodded to her.

This was nuts.

Nevada concluded her presented, then sat down. She could see that Cori was clapping and smiling, trying to catch her eye, but she was completely distracted. Next, the moderator introduced Kristof, and he got up from his chair to stand behind the podium. But before he could begin, Toby rose and walked up on stage, with an attitude that said *I do this every day.*

Kristof stepped back and surrendered the microphone to the famous entrepreneur without a word. Because he was intimidated or because it was part of the plan?

"Hello, everyone, I am Toby Encell. I'm here today to announce that I have joined the Mondarix Press family. This magnificent, venerable house will publish my autobiography next spring."

Wait, what?

Nevada, along with everyone else in the room, leaned forward in her chair.

"As you may have read, I was talking with Fraser Greene about this project originally, but circumstances have changed and I now intend to have Mondarix Press bring my story to the world."

He spoke as if Mondarix Press were his employee rather than his partner. Nevada felt disrespected, even though she didn't work there.

"I have heard rumors of other manuscripts floating around ... biographies and such ... but rest assured, when this book comes out, it will be the full truth about my life, told by me. No varnishing, no errors, no omissions." He scanned the crowd with a dazzling smile that Nevada was sure had been used to great effect in boardrooms and bedrooms around the globe.

The book world group in the room was stunned. No one on the stage spoke or moved as Toby nodded to the moderator, nodded to Kristof, nodded to Nevada ... *no, really, was that a wink?*

He strode to the stairs, then headed for the door to the hall.

Nevada couldn't leave until the next four editors had had their turn at the podium to present their books. Almost everyone else in the room stayed, out of courtesy, but she'd bet that if you surveyed them, barely five percent would remember hearing anything about the other books discussed—and that five percent probably included staff at the various publishers represented. Toby and his announcement had eclipsed the rest of the show.

She caught up with Hannah at the Fraser Greene booth.

"What was that all about?" Nevada demanded.

"What was what all about?" Hannah looked terrified.

"Did you write that note?"

"No, I didn't write it. He handed it to me this morning and asked me to give it to you."

'Who handed it to you?'"Toby Encell."

"How do you know Toby Encell? Or did he just show up at the office and hand it to the first person he saw?"

Hannah shook her head.

"Here at the booth?" Hannah looked a little unsteady on her feet and Nevada pushed a folding chair at her. "Sit."

"I saw him at a breakfast meeting at Balthazar," Hannah said.

"Why were you at a breakfast meeting with Toby Encell? Come on, Hannah, spill!" Nevada was losing patience.

Hannah took a deep breath. "I am working on a project for him. Most of the communication has been by email and text, and through other people, but he wanted an in-person meeting today."

"What kind of project?"

"A research project."

Nevada said nothing and Hannah seemed to feel the need to rush in to fill the silence. "A lot of interns do this. I'm working in publishing because it's where I want my career to go. But I have to pay my rent and I have a couple of side hustles."

Where Nevada's mind had been dark before, but for a ghost light flickering center stage, now the footlights and spotlights threw the place into full illumination.

"You were working on Toby Encell's autobiography."

Hannah nodded. She looked miserable. "I didn't really want to, but Mr. Inniskillen said it would look good on my resumé."

"Mr. Inniskillen! What did Jasper have to do with Toby Encell's autobiography?"

"He was ghostwriting it."

CHAPTER 14

It did not take Nevada long to track down Toby Encell. Anyone who knew how to use social media could find people.

But finding him, at Sardi's, having a few drinks before going to the theater that evening, didn't mean that it was easy to get him to talk to her. Not easy—full-on impossible. Nevada approached him twice and was waved off.

The third time, the server saw her coming and intercepted her. "If you're not a customer, you'll have to leave. The gentleman has made it clear he doesn't want to talk to you."

As Nevada stood outside on W. 44th trying to decide on her next move, the door opened. Royce Encell beckoned to her, but her hope that he was there to invite her back in to the restaurant was met with disappointment.

"You know, persistence will not get you anywhere with my father. Once he's decided, he's dug in," Royce said.

"All I want is to ask a few questions. Could I ask you?" He pulled out a cigarette and lit up. "Fire away."

"Is this true? That Mondarix Press is publishing his book?""Yes."

"But we have a contract at Fraser Greene."

"He would say, that's what lawyers are for. He changes his mind, then the lawyers have to make the paper that lets him have his way. He can afford it."

Nevada let this settle, staring down the street at the long line of yellow cabs.

"But why?" she asked.

"Part of it is me, I think." Royce inhaled deeply. "I don't want him to include certain things. Certain family secrets that will hurt people if they're in print. He disagrees. After our meeting the other day, he thought he saw evidence that you and Crawford Burr were too open to my opinion, so he made an instant decision to cross the street."

Nevada watched him smoke and almost wished that she still did. She needed stress relief of some kind. "And you're on side with this?"Royce shrugged his shoulders. "He's my father. I work for him, and someday these companies will be mine. We've disagreed before and we'll disagree again. Better I stay involved and try to clean up some of the damage."

"He damages things?"

"Oh, yes, he does."

Nevada tried to get her thoughts in order. "Why does he want these secrets to come out?"

"Because he hates his father. My grandfather, Rolf. Things happened in the old country years ago. Things that just don't matter anymore. Nobody is particularly interested, that's what I say, but he doesn't believe me. Or even if he does, he doesn't care. He just knows that Rolf would be embarrassed and maybe forced into making some restitution if this information comes out. He wants Grandpa in that position. He also thinks that any scandal won't touch the mighty Toby—that there might even be some kind of sympathy support for him. So, he intends to proceed, and fast. Especially now that Jasper is gone."

"I heard hat Jasper was ghostwriting it. Is that true?"

Royce paused, then gazed into her eyes. She'd surprised him. "They hadn't agreed yet on whether it would be actually ghostwritten or whether Jasper Inniskillen's name would appear on the front cover underneath my father's, as co-author. But Jasper had about two hundred pages ready to go."

"But not a full manuscript," Nevada said. "That's why Toby couldn't make his deadline with us."

"I don't think he planned to turn it in, even if he did," Royce said. "He's been talking to Mondarix Press as a backup plan for a while, ever since Grandpa and I made our objections known. In case Fraser Greene wouldn't support his 'damn the torpedoes' approach."

Royce's cigarette was almost down to the filter. He pulled another one out of the pack and lit it from the first. "He talked with the researcher this morning to find out whether she has enough material to cover the parts Jasper will be unable to finish."

"And does she?"

"She doesn't."

"When did Hannah get involved with this project, anyway?" Nevada asked.

"Jasper hired her. He was still releasing his novels at Fraser Greene when Toby approached him. Then, when he went over to Mondarix Press, my dad asked him what their opinion might be about the contents of the autobiography. Jasper convinced him to plan to switch publishers."

"And then, Jasper wanted to switch back to Fraser Greene, but Toby was still convinced he wanted to switch to Mondarix," Nevada said.

Royce shook his head. "I see where you're going. But Toby isn't the sort to kill anybody. Or even to hire somebody to kill anybody. He's more the 'keep 'em alive so you can torture them' type."

Nevada pondered that one for a moment while he smoked in silence. "One more thing, Royce. Did you know your father used Hannah to send me a note before the panel started? Saying that he was going to disrupt the presentation?"

Royce shrugged, then ground out the cigarette butt on the pavement.

"Why did you come out here to tell me all these things?" Nevada asked.

"What? Tell you what things?" He said with a fake naïve smile and raised hands. "I needed a smoke, that's all."

CHAPTER 15

That evening at home, Nevada was aching to tell all of this to Owen and get his read on it. But he didn't show up and he didn't answer his phone, she decided to head out to the Book Fair Awards Dinner on her own. It was the glamor event of the year for the publishing industry and a must-attend. She enjoyed dressing up as much as the next person … occasionally. But generally, this kind of party wasn't her thing, and she regarded it as work, rather than pleasure.

Still, if she ditched it, her absence would be noticed, so she pulled her evening dress out of the closet, cursed the heels she would have to wear, and climbed back into her car for the drive back.

The reception area outside the ballroom was packed, almost shoulder to shoulder. Nevada took a deep breath as she left the elevator and pasted on her business networking face. Once upon a time, when she was beginning her career, she looked forward to events like these. She'd been to many, in the journalism world and as a guest of her father's, in film world. But now, she would rather be at home, wearing something cozy and hanging out with Owen.

Come on, Nevada. Time to go to work. Owen isn't even home, anyway.

"Nevada! Nice to see you!" The Fraser Greene CEO somehow always seemed as if he were the host of whatever party or the owner of whatever room he was in.

Nevada stepped forward to shake Crawford's hand. Her direct boss, Bernadette, stood at his elbow. She said nothing, and didn't reach out for a handshake or a schmoozing hug. Her eyes scanned the room beyond Nevada's shoulder.

"Nice to see you, too, Crawford. Lovely venue, excellent crowd."

"You'll be at my keynote tomorrow, Nevada? We need to have a good showing from the staff."

"Of course, I'll be there. But shouldn't you be at home tonight, working on it?" she teased.

Both Crawford and Bernadette stopped their scanning to stare at her. Oh yeah, she'd forgotten that humor wasn't in abundant supply at Fraser Greene.

"Crawford!" The arrival of two other well-groomed men in tuxedos gave Nevada her opportunity for a graceful exit.

Roaming among the crowd, she smiled and nodded at anyone whose gaze she met. Some of them she knew, most of them she didn't. She didn't have a direct through line to the open bar but she was tacking in the general direction. A few greetings and a lot of knots of groups of people, deep in conversation, delayed her, but eventually she arrived at the bar and ordered a Chablis. It was not a night for anything hard. There were too many people here it would be so wrong to offend by saying the wrong thing with a tongue loosened by liquor.

Along the wall next to the bar, a line of easels had been set up to show off beautifully designed cards for each of the nominees for Awards this year. Author of the Year. Bookseller of the Year. Library of the Year. Publisher of the Year.

Fraser Greene was nominated and so was Mondarix Press. Three other names filled out the slate of five and if the prize didn't go to Fraser Greene, Nevada hoped it would be one of the others. Anyone but Mondarix.

A woman in gold leather and lamé moved beside her to look at the posters. "Hello, Nevada."

"Sable. Hello." She was surprised that Sable would initiate a conversation after their confrontation at the autographing table earlier in the week.

Sable crossed her arms across her chest, her left hand holding a bejeweled clutch purse and her right a rocks glass filled with amber liquid. "I'm looking forward to the awards presentation. Are you?"

Nevada glanced over at the Author of the Year list. Yes, there was Sable's name. And Jasper's.

"Yes, of course, Sable. I—"

"I don't quite understand why they still have Jasper's name up there. It seems inappropriate, doesn't it? I mean, we agreed on that the other day, when we held Jasper's seat empty, didn't we?"

Now, there was a bit of revisionist history.

"We have to acknowledge that he's not here," Sable continued. "Somehow, it seems disrespectful to have him entered in a popularity contest after he's passed."

"Well, I don't think the contest is going on now, Sable. I think the voting was all done weeks ago. If he does win something I think it would be a nice way to honor him and his life."

A man spoke from behind Nevada's shoulder. "I hear there's going to be some part of

the presentation that does that, anyway."

Nevada turned around to see Kristof Dykstra standing behind Sable. Well, great. It was a Mondarix Press reunion. "Hello, Kris. That would be something that Jasper would have appreciated."

"I know. Great marketing mileage, too."

"Even better for you guys if you win the Publisher of the Year," Nevada said.

"I know," the Mondarix Press Marketing Director said. "Between you and me, and I don't mean to be obnoxious about this, but I think we have that sewn up."

You may not mean to be, but you are.

"You two should make a bet," Sable said.

Nevada put on a phony smile. "Pass," she said. "I'm not sure I'm a fan of these kinds of competitions, anyway."

Kristof's smile was just as sincere. "You would be, if you won." He gave Sable a salute, then drifted off toward the bar.

"What was the salute for?" Nevada asked.

"Don't know. Maybe because he works for my publisher and I'm the moneymaker." Sable pulled out her phone and held it up to take a selfie in front of the Author of the Year poster. "When I saw Jasper Monday, he gave me one last piece of advice: don't let the publishers think they can get anywhere without the original idea for your story. Nothing happens until the author creates a story."

"You saw Jasper Monday?"Sable nodded.

"Monday?" Nevada asked. "Monday, not Tuesday?"

Sable took a couple of steps away from the Awards display and Nevada had the distinct impression that she wanted to get back to working the crowd. "Yes, Monday. Tuesday, he died, Nevada. Tuesday morning, he came into town, visited your office, then went home and was shot. Or accidentally discharged his gun. Not accidentally, that doesn't make sense. But if he didn't unload it and then tried to clean it … well …"

Nevada felt as though too many ideas were flying at her, all at once. "Why did you see Jasper on Monday, Sable? And how did you know he tried to visit the Fraser Greene office Tuesday morning? And how do you know anything about cleaning guns?"

"I'm ex-military, Nevada. I know about guns. I still carry one. I have a New York City permit for it. Famous people need self-defense. And as for Jasper … we were friends. Sort of friends. Maybe it's more accurate to say he was my mentor. He told me a lot about the way the publishing industry works and about how to put together a novel that today's reader will buy. I won't tell you about our conversation on Monday. That stays just between him and me. I'm sure you understand, Nevada. You had your own relationship with Jasper. He was an extroverted man, wasn't he? As much as you might have wanted to believe your friendship with him was unique, you had to understand that he connected with a lot of people. And a lot of women."

What was Sable talking about? The author's phone buzzed, and she looked down at the screen. Nevada stared at the top of her head, while she tried to process what she'd just heard. Sable sounded like she had a screw loose, as Nevada's grandpa used to say. Certainly, as if she had a lot of emotions and opinions about Jasper that were news to Nevada. Those last couple of sentences sounded like jealousy … was it possible that Jasper and Sable had something going on? That she wanted that something to be exclusive, or at least more meaningful or with different terms than Jasper had in mind? Was Sable capable of killing someone to prevent him from leaving her side?

Or was she just trying to hint and spread rumors to try to undermine the affection that so many people felt for him?

Nevada had put Sable on her suspects list because she wondered how deep the rivalry went and how ambitious Sable was about occupying the top spot on the bestseller list. Maybe her speculation had been completely misplaced. Maybe love and passion were behind Jasper's death, not competition and the drive for success?

"Gotta go." Sable looked up from her phone screen. "Good luck to Fraser Greene tonight, Nevada. I'll see you around."

The crowd in the reception hall was beginning to move toward the wall of double doors that led to the banquet room. Nevada let herself be carried along, while she tried to think through everything she'd just heard. She had no answers to her many questions, but the one conclusion she was able to come to, by the time she reached her assigned seat at Table 14, was that she should talk to Detective Travers about this. She would try to find time to slip out to make a call during the dinner service and before the awards presentation began.

The meal was extravagant and lengthy, designed and plated by two of the top chefs in New York. Nevada sampled each of the five courses but could barely keep her mind on the food or the conversation from her nine tablemates. Sable! Sable Ogilvie had seen Jasper the day before his death, knew about his movements on the day, had a far closer relationship with him than anyone had realized, and seemed to be jealous of him.

She had the motive and she had the means—the concealed weapon she'd mentioned. But, opportunity? Had she been out to his place on Tuesday afternoon? What were Sable's whereabouts on Tuesday?

Travers could find out about that. Nevada was reluctant to ask Sable any questions, in case she spooked her. But if Travers agreed with her, that this was a lead that deserved pursuing, he would know the best way to approach it.

Nevada was just about to spring from her chair to find a quiet place to make her phone call when the spotlight came up on the stage and the host of one of the late-night television shows took over the podium. Over the next twenty minutes, he entertained the crowd with jokes at their expense, about the dismal future for the book publishing business, the depressing reading rate among the American public, and the threat computers and digital media posed to their industry.

And yet, even with the doom and gloom, people were laughing, and no one seemed particularly dejected. Maybe it was the expensive liquor, the elaborate meal, or the opulence of the surroundings, but it was difficult, during Book Fair, to be negative about their industry. They had wined and dined and been entertained more royally than ninety-nine percent of people anywhere, this evening. They had the privilege of working in this industry, doing jobs that thousands of other people would love to have, all thanks to the ability of a writer to imagine a story and tell it to a reader. Somehow, Nevada didn't believe that essential bond would ever dissolve.

It was timely that the first award on the program was Author of the Year. After a few self-congratulatory speeches from the board of Book Fair and various heads of various industry associations, the TV host returned to announce the list of five nominees and point them out in the crowd, so that they'd have their moment of applause, even if they weren't the award-winner. When he reached Jasper's name, a screen rolled down from the ceiling and a video retrospective on Jasper's author life and successes appeared. Nevada wished she had Sable Ogilvie somewhere in her sightline so that she could see how the other author was reacting.

A young couple in a tuxedo and evening dress walked out from the wings, carrying a golden trophy shaped like a book. At the precise moment the announcement of the winner's name was made on stage it appeared in thousand-point font size on the screen:

JASPER INNISKILLEN, Author of the Year.

The applause was resounding, but somehow, somber at the same time. Jasper's wife, Fiona, appeared from the wings, clad in black and moving slowly. She managed a brief smile as she accepted the trophy and the applause.

Perhaps it might have been Jasper's editor stepping in for this duty but it was difficult to identify who that might be. There was no one person who had guided his career for many years and in the past months, as he had jumped between Fraser Green and Mondarix Press, Nevada supposed Book Fair had a difficult time picturing whom they might ask without offending somebody.

For Nevada, the other awards were an anticlimax. Publisher of the Year was neither Fraser Green nor Mondarix Press. Too bad for Kristof Dykstra. He would have to find another theme for his marketing push next year.

Bookseller of the Year was a thriving store in western Washington which had turned its space into a community hub. Library of the Year was an inner city building that had managed to balance its original purpose with facing the homelessness problem of its neighbors.

When the speeches were done, the crowd, like a giant, living being, rose from its chairs and moved toward the doors.

When Nevada got home, she was eager to talk all this over with Owen, but he was still at work.

She needed to talk to someone.

She tried Chelan, but there was no answer. She wasn't surprised. Any time, in a household with three small children, was a busy time. The other person she thought of calling was another friend from journalism world. It was more recent, but Lillian Howe had been working as a part-time newspaper writer in south Florida for three years now and Nevada knew that asking questions and finding out information was as fundamental to Lillian's personality as Nevada's own. Curiosity is the best tool in the kit, she liked to say.

"Nevada!" Lillian always sounded delighted to hear from her. It was as if she was astonished to be called, every time.

"Lillian, hey. How are things on Alamos Island?"

"As ever. Rainy season is starting."

"What does that mean? A five-minute shower at dinnertime?"Lillian laughed. "Pretty much. Although in a few weeks, we'll see some good lightning storms most evenings. How are things in New York?""Spring time, what can I say? It's the best."

"Anything new?" Lillian could smell a story, the same way that Nevada could. She was always alert to subtext and she was a person who often seemed to have unusual things happening near her—two of the two characteristics an outstanding news person needed. If she were thirty-three instead of seventy-three, Nevada would want to hire her.

If Nevada still managed news, that was, rather than publishing.

"It's Book Fair in New York. I presented Fraser Greene's biggest book of the season today and something very odd happened." She brought Lillian up to speed, then asked the question that nagged at her the most. "Might seem a small point, but I can't figure out why he sent me the note."

The silence that passed told her that Lillian was giving her question serious attention. "Maybe he wanted to distract you from giving a good presentation of your own book. Just mess you up, because he was annoyed about you siding with his son on the disagreement over the contents of his autobiography."

"Yeah, that occurred to me, too. Maybe it's just the beginning of a bunch of ways of messing me up."

"Or ... maybe he was challenging you to change horses in the middle of the stream and present *his* book instead. So that then he could embarrass you even more by announcing he had changed publishers."

"Maybe he just wanted to take over Book Fair, throw his weight around," Nevada said. "You know that type of guy? Who does things just, and I quote, "Because I Can." I think there's a lot of that in Toby Encell. We saw it with the way he showed up at the breakfast, too. And you know, he's such a loose cannon, from what I've read and what I've seen. When I watched him first get up there, I thought he might be planning a spontaneous eulogy to Jasper Inniskillen. Or maybe that he had bought one of the publishing houses and was using Book Fair to announce it."

"Speaking of Jasper Inniskillen, Nevada, I was sorry to hear about his death. I know he was a longtime friend of yours."

"He guided me through my first months at Fraser Greene," Nevada said. "It's not easy to switch careers in your fifties and I don't think I could have done it without Jasper opening doors for me."

"Are you hearing anything about who might have shot him?"

"All that law enforcement is saying so far is that it wasn't 'accidental, while cleaning a gun' and there is evidence of a second person present at the time of death. They're asking that person to come forward, as well as anyone who might have any tips about what went on in that neighborhood that day. Sounds like there's not much information but in another way, I guess based on what I know about Jasper and his life, it feels like there's so much that it's chaos."

"Let's make a list of questions," Lillian said. "You sound like you need to get focused. Do you have paper and a pen?"- Nevada smiled to herself. Lillian had the same teacher instincts that she often felt surface in herself when dealing with younger people who seemed to be floundering.

She grabbed the nearest notebook and flipped it open.

"One. Who might have been with Jasper that afternoon and had a motive to shoot him? Be as open-minded as you can."

"Okay, for starters, how about the entrepreneur's son?"

"Royce? Why? What's the motive?" Nevada asked.

"He wants to prevent his father from divulging family secrets. He can't kill his father but he could kill his father's writer."

"I doubt it, but it's going on the list," Nevada said. "And how about Sable Ogilvie, the number two writer at Mondarix Press who is taking over Jasper's throne?"

"Good one," Lillian said. "How about the shooter, whoever he was, who came into the Fraser Greene office that morning and was shooting up walls?"

"I forgot to mention. I thought I spotted him walking around Book Fair the same day, Tuesday, and I was totally freaked out. Then, I saw him the next day, and I think it might be a double. I overheard him talking about working at Greater Manitou Metro Library. Haven't had a chance yet to check it out."

"Have to nail that down," Lillian said. "Add him ... or them, I guess ... to the list. How about his agent?"

"Doesn't have anything to gain by him dying," Nevada said.

"I wasn't really thinking of her ... or him ... as a killer," Lillian said. "Just a good source of information about his life."

"That's an excellent suggestion. I'll make a point to talk to her. Ryley Fedor. At The Olmsted Agency."

"How about Mr. Inniskillen's wife?" Lillian asked. "I know it seems inappropriate especially when he's just died ... but did she stand to gain more, financially, by his death? Were they happy?"

"I'll add the questions to the list," Nevada said. "Also, there's an avid fan that Fiona told me about. Named Olivia Theale. Hung around the Fraser Greene office and went out to his house uninvited."

"Any long shots? People in his life you've heard about who didn't seem to like him much?"

"It's a long step from that to murder, but I understand what you're saying," Nevada said. "Fiona has mentioned that Jasper was stressed about a conflict with a neighbor over property rights. I'll ask her more about that."

"That's quite a list," Lillian said. You're going to check into all of them?""I'll start, but I'm also trying to learn more about Jasper's activities in his last months and days. If anything turns up, I'll pass it on to the detective. They've got more resources than I have."

"And what you have from the police so far is that they have evidence of more than one person present at the time of death. Any chance that second person could be completely innocent?""Of course," Nevada said. "And just terrified of coming forward. But I'll let you go now, Lillian. It's late."

"Alright. Let me know if there's anything I can do to help."

And you, Detective Travers, Nevada thought as she ended the call. Let's see what you can do to help.

CHAPTER 16

He picked up on the second ring.

"Detective Travers. Nevada Leacock, as you can tell from the call display. Do you always keep such late hours?"

"Do you?"

"Fair point."

"Why are you calling me?"

Enough chit chat, then. "I had a conversation with someone, and I think I have another suggestion for us to consider in the investigation of Jasper's death."

"Us. Huh."

Verbose he was not. Nevada waited a few more seconds, then plunged back in. "Sable Ogilvie is the number two author in the country, behind Jasper."

"Number two in fame, or in actual sales?"

"Sales. Although looking at the results here tonight, they are … were … number one and two in the other category. Jasper won Author of the Year, but Sable was one of the four others nominated."

Travers sounded interested. "And what did Sable tell you?"

"She saw Jasper on Monday. She knew what his activities were on Tuesday. She carries a gun. And she sounded as if she had some kind of relationship with him, something more than just business competitors."

"Sounded as if? What did she say exactly?"

Nevada had to stop to think. "She said he was her mentor. That he was an extroverted man, and that you couldn't expect him to make any relationship exclusive." She waited for a response, but none came. "She sounded jealous, Detective Travers."

"Alright, Ms. Leacock. We'll look into it. At least, have a chat with her, as a former associate of Mr. Inniskillen."

"While I have you on the phone, Detective, could I ask you a question?"

"Ask away, and I'll decide whether to answer," he said.

"What is the evidence of a 'second person' present at Jasper's home Tuesday afternoon?"

Travers said nothing, but Nevada decided just to wait him out. Strong as her urge was to rephrase the question and pepper him with supplementary inquiries, she just waited in silence. After a while, he moved in to fill it.

"I don't know that I'd use as strong a word as 'evidence'. Although we did find some physical clues that we're holding on to, as we go on with our investigation."

What? What did you find?

"I think you know how Mr. Inniskillen died."

Nevada waited, then realized that she had to participate. "Shot," she said.

"Yes. And when we were at his home Tuesday night, we found physical signs of a second gun on the property. Not a gun that Mr. or Mrs. Inniskillen owned."

Nevada inhaled. "I see. That's why you're not just nailing it down right away as simply Jasper's mistake with his own gun."

"Exactly."

"What happens next?"

"Can't tell you that. Look, I know Jasper Inniskillen was important to you." Travers's tone was softening. "And I know you'd like answers about his death. As many of his friends do. Not to mention his wife. Be assured that we're working on it. As soon as there is something concrete to tell you, we'll pass it on. In the meantime, thanks for the heads-up about Sable Ogilvie. We'll look into it. But you know, this one conversation you had with her doesn't mean it adds up to a case against her. Even with a couple of other coincidences. Good night, Ms. Leacock."

"Good night, Detective."

Doesn't mean it doesn't.

CHAPTER 17

The next morning, Nevada had her computer open before her coffee was ready.

She had a long list of questions that had arisen from last evening's events, and most of them couldn't be answered until the next day dawned. But she could attack some of them with an online search. The first one was easy. Mark Diotte was on the online staff list of the Greater Manitou Metro Library. Programming Librarian.

What should she do? Email him to ask about his whereabouts on Tuesday morning at 8 a.m.?

No, plunging in that way would make her seem like a crazy person. She sent a polite, friendly email, introducing herself and asking whether he might have half an hour to meet with her at Book Fair Friday, if he was there.

She had just pressed 'Send', when an email from Daniel Pyne arrived.

"Hi Nevada, I've been thinking over our conversation with Fiona, and the material I sent you about the Indie Authors conference I took Jasper to, and realizing that there may be some misunderstanding about the event. Do you think we could have lunch so that I could tell you more about it?"

She pressed 'reply' and composed her answer. "Hi, Daniel. Ordinarily, I'd say yes, but today is Crawford's keynote, and I have to be there in the audience, waving the flag. Do you want to watch it with me and then go grab a bite?"He sent a thumbs-up emoji, leaving her with one more question: why did he care what she thought about his relationship with Jasper Inniskillen? What she thought, or anybody else?

Should she add him to the list? But what motive could he possibly have?Nevada gave herself a shake. She was becoming overly suspicious, and perhaps of the wrong people. What she need was more information and, even better, some solid clues.

She heard a car pull into the driveway. "Hey, good morning," she said as Owen walked into the kitchen. "Coffee?"

"Yes, thanks," he said with a smile. "How was your night?"

She poured a cup full and thought about how she'd answer that. Was it the right time to grumble to him that she thought he would be home for the evening and able to escort her to the Book Fair dinner?

It turned out that the decision wasn't up to her. It was a rhetorical question, and he wasn't waiting for a reply. "I was in surgery till late, then I fell asleep in the doctors' lounge. I've got a full morning of patient appointments after rounds, so as soon as I shower and change, I'm on my way. See you tonight." He waved toward her as he went out the door.

Well. Nevada was used to the busy pace of his doctor life, but it seemed these past few weeks it was at a new level. Maybe it was just perception, though, not reality. She was on edge about the things going on in her life and maybe her view of Owen's was slanted because of that.

She felt worried for a moment, but just a brief, fleeting moment. She had a massive day in front of her, with Day Three of Book Fair, her boss's keynote speech, preparation for Book Fest tomorrow, investigation of Jasper's death, and probing the Tuesday morning invasion of Fraser Greene's office. She didn't have time to linger over coffee and try to read something into Owen's behavior. They'd had droughts and misunderstandings in the past, and they'd always cleared themselves up. Sometimes, all it took was a little time.

She opened her laptop to check her email. Mark Diotte from Greater Manitou had replied.

"Thanks for reaching out, Nevada. Yes, I'd be pleased to meet with you to talk about my library and Fraser Greene's catalogue, and yes, I'll still be at Book Fair today (Friday). How about the mezzanine café at ten?"

Nevada glanced at her watch. Plenty of time. "See you there!" She hit 'send', then went off to get ready for the day.

***

Day Three of Book Fair reminded Nevada of the last hours spent at a party or a vacation hotel: low energy, a little flat, even a little repetitive. Most of the deals had been made, and most of the excitement had waned. There were still people around who were going to wring every last drop of publishing convention potential from this day, but many others were now so tired they were going through the motions. Some had collected their suitcases full of free books from the holding pen and were in a cab on the way to the airport. Some were still in their hotel rooms, recovering from the bad choices at the dinner the night before. To those who had attended many previous Book Fairs, today's Day Three was just one more day in a blur of days.

To Nevada, it was a day without nearly enough hours. She had a meeting with the librarian from Greater Manitou, a meeting with Daniel Pyne, Crawford's keynote speech, a conversation to pursue with Detective Travers, and a list of people to interview about Jasper's last months of life.

The mezzanine café in the convention center was crowded, even though it was only just past seven. Nevada saw Mark Diotte, sitting in front of his open laptop, a cup of coffee near his elbow. He resembled the man she'd seen from the Fraser Greene elevator as the doors closed three days ago, but she couldn't be sure. He resembled a lot of men.

"Mr. Diotte."

"Ms. Leacock?"

"Thank you for meeting with me," she said, taking the seat opposite him. "I was going to bring you a coffee, but I see you're already equipped."

"Yes, I'm doing fine," he said with a smile. "What can I do for you?"

"I want to ask about your whereabouts on Tuesday."

He looked startled, but that proved nothing. It was the kind of question that would startle anybody. "I don't know why you're asking, but I've been here at Book Fair all week. I flew in on Tuesday morning."

Could that be proven? By a cop or a private investigator, maybe. Maybe that had been done, and it was why Travers had said, so definitely, that this was not the man who shot up the Fraser Greene offices.

Nevada was deep in thought, trying to figure out where to go next with this, when Mark Diotte took the initiative for her. "Why are you asking?"

"I work for Fraser Greene, as you know—"

"Yes, I do know. I thought that was why you wanted to meet with me. To talk about our library's acquisition policy and your upcoming catalogues."

"Not quite." Nevada stopped her scanning of the crowds around them and made full-on eye contact. "Mr. Diotte, I was in my office at Fraser Greene Tuesday morning and I was shot at. By you."

She wasn't sure of that, but maybe the direct approach would yield the best result.

"Not by me," the man said firmly. "I've already been over this with the police, but I'll repeat to you what I said to them. I was on a plane, not walking through your office, shooting at walls."

"How do you know it was shooting at walls?"

"Because that's his style."

"Whose style, Mr. Diotte?"

He drained his coffee cup. "I am not the only Mr. Diotte, Ms. Leacock. My brother, Michael, is my twin. We look the same, but that's about all we have in common. I'm a librarian. He is a former soldier. I read books. He thinks he can write them."

"He's an author?""He wants to be. He talks about writing a book all the time. I'm not sure he's ever actually finished a chapter. He also talks about becoming a bestselling author. He's been trying to get an agent and get published for about twenty years."

"Does he have a beef against Fraser Greene?"

"Against all publishers. He thinks they're all stupid, because they haven't recognized his literary genius. A beef against a lot of authors, too."

"Is that why he went to Fraser Greene on Tuesday morning?"

Mark looked at her sharply. "We don't know it was him. You've told the police you saw someone who looks like me. That could be him, yes."

"Have you talked to him?"

"No, he won't return my calls."

Nevada watched half a dozen expressions sweep across Mark Diotte's face. "Do you think it was your brother?" Her tone was gentle.

"It could have been." The thought left him sad, and, Nevada thought, embarrassed. "He was constantly going to other writers, celebrity authors, and asking for help. Introductions to agents and publishers. He met Jasper Inniskillen a few months ago, and that was his latest 'pipeline to the big publishers', as he would put it."

"Jasper!"

"Yes. They met at a gun range when Michael was there to do some practice and apparently, Jasper was researching for a new thriller he was writing. They got to talking and afterward Michael said he was sure that Jasper had promised to introduce him at Fraser Greene."

"Do you think that's true?"

Mark hesitated. "I think it's fair to say that Michael was the type to read between the lines of something someone said and imagine promises had been made when they really hadn't."

The silence went on for a while. Mark didn't seem inclined to say anything more.

"So, your brother went over to Fraser Greene to confront Jasper?" Nevada prompted.

"Or to use his name to get through the door to meet one of the senior editors."

"Then, when it didn't work, he started shooting at things?"

"He's been known to handle his frustration in unacceptable ways, yeah."

Now, there's an understatement.

"Have you told the police all this?"

"Yes, of course. They've haven't been able to find him so far. Neither have I, although I haven't really been looking. Just calling and leaving him voice mails."

Nevada's next thought hit her like a wave slamming a boat tied up to a pier in a hurricane. "Mr. Diotte. Mark. Did Michael know where Jasper lived?"

"No idea."

***

Two hours later, Nevada was in the disorganized crowd pushing toward the open doors of the main meeting room, searching for a seat. After speaking with Mark, she had stepped outside, just to get a breath of fresh air before the next event. But New York was tight in the clutches of an unseasonably warm June day, and after ten minutes outdoors, she was wilting from the heat.

Crawford Burr's keynote speech was one of the highlights of Book Fair, and after the gunshots at Fraser Greene, the discovery of Jasper's death, and the defection of Toby Encell to a rival publisher, you had to bet money that the CEO's words were eagerly anticipated. By the booksellers, the librarians, the Fraser Greene employees, the other publishers, the authors … and the Fraser Greene shareholders. Not to mention the hedge fund that owned the majority position.

She strode forward to the front of the room and found a seat at a table in the first row. She wanted Crawford to know she was there, and she didn't want to miss a word of his comments.

"Hello, Nevada." Charles was about to claim a chair next to her.

"Hello, Charles. How are you? Do you need any help?" She watched him wrestling with the chair while trying to lean on his cane at the same time.

"I'm fine." He seemed impatient.

"I want to hold that seat for an author I've invited to join me here," Nevada said. "Would you be comfortable in this other one?"

"Fine, yes, okay." Charles shuffled over to the other chair.

Daniel arrived and immediately pitched in to help Charles with the challenge of getting settled. "Here, let me help you, Mr. Delaney." He pulled the chair out and held it steady while Charles sank into it.

"Have we met?" Charles demanded.

Daniel stuck out a hand. "No, I'm just familiar with your name because of your career in publishing. I'm Daniel Pyne."

"Daniel is a formerly traditionally published author who has launched himself into indie publishing world," Nevada said.

Charles snorted. "Good luck," he said. "What is this 'indie publishing' anyway? Isn't it just a fancy way of saying self-publishing? Or vanity publishing?"

"Come on, Charles, you know you're just baiting him," Nevada said with a laugh. "We all know that vanity publishing would be Daniel paying some company to print hundreds of copies of his book and sell them back to him. Or charge him thousands to turn a manuscript into a printed book, while promising him a bestseller and delivering zero sales."

"With indie publishing, the author is in control," Daniel said. "I hire the editors, the designers, the printer."

"So, that's self-publishing," Charles said as he dug into his lunch. "Nobody evaluating your work, nobody putting a professional eye on the cover, the interior, the dozens of choices made in creating this book. No marketing expertise, no publicity expertise."

"Well, these days, most authors would tell you their publishers have turned most of the responsibility for marketing back on their shoulders," Daniel said. "Hey, this chicken isn't bad. What do you think, Nevada?"

"About the chicken or about indie publishing?" Nevada grinned. "I think there's room for both models within publishing. Traditional works for some authors and indie for others. There should be no stigma attached to either."

"Huh." Charles had made quick work of his lunch and was leaning back in his chair, focusing on the stage. "There's never been any stigma about traditional publishing. Goes back for centuries. Thousands of eminent people involved."

"Indie publishing and self-publishing go back centuries, too," Daniel said. "D. H. Lawrence, Gertrude Stein, Edgar Allan Poe, Mark Twain, L. Frank Baum, T. S. Eliot, Beatrix Potter, John Grisham. Charles Dickens, for heaven's sake!"

"*In Search of Excellence* and *What Color is your Parachute?*, if we want to talk nonfiction," Nevada said.

"And as far as no evaluation, the indie published author has the reader doing the evaluation," Daniel said. "Money talks."

"Alright, alright." Charles raised his hands in mock surrender. "Enough, you two. What did you think of the awards last night?"

"Very appropriate and comforting somehow, that they gave Author of the Year to Jasper," Daniel said.

Nevada looked at him sympathetically. "You miss him, too."

"I still can't quite believe it. It's only been three days, but it feels like he's been gone forever."

"Do the police have any leads, Nevada? Do you know? I heard they no longer think it was an accident," Charles said.

"That's true," Nevada replied. "They have suspects, but nobody's been charged."

"Well, whoever it was, I'm sure they had their reasons."

"Charles!"

"What? All I'm saying, perhaps rather clumsily, is that anybody who shoots somebody is motivated by something. We might disapprove of their reasons, but we can't deny they were passionate enough about them that they took this action."

"So they should shoot somebody?""No, I'm not saying we should approve of their methods. Just understand the intensity of their belief in the rightness of their choice."

Nevada shook her head. "I feel like you're mixing everything up, Charles. Are you condoning murder? Jasper's murder, in particular?"

"No, no, that's not what I'm saying. You're the one mixing everything up."

"I know you didn't like Jasper much, the past few months, but does that mean you have to say his death is justifiable?" Nevada put down her fork. Suddenly, she was completely put off her food. "Why were things so prickly between you, anyway?"

"Let's call it a disagreement about gratitude," Charles said.

"What do you mean?"Charles looked toward Daniel, but Daniel remained silent. "Jasper thought he was a self-made man," Charles said. "I mentored him early in his career and he chose to forget all that. He had very little use for passing it forward, and when new people came to him, asking him for help, he blew most of them off. There were a few exceptions, like you, Nevada, but most people couldn't get the time of day from him. It was a one-way street."

This was not a side of Jasper that Nevada had seen, but that was exactly Charles's point.

"And you, Mr. Pyne. I'm guessing that you were helping Jasper and he made you feel that he had become your friend. It was only because you had knowledge and connections he wanted to exploit. The relationship didn't continue long enough for you to find out that if you wanted help after Jasper had everything he needed from you, his door would be closed to you."

"Charles, this is all sounding incredibly bitter…" Nevada began.

She didn't get a chance to finish her sentence because the program was about to begin. The five people at the head table turned their attention to the Book Fair committee chair who rose to introduce Crawford Burr, then the Fraser Greene CEO stepped up to the podium.

Even though she was tremendously distracted by Charles's comments, Nevada was able to concentrate on Crawford's remarks enough to notice that he was not doing well. The speech itself was relatively well written and paced, but it was as if Crawford was seeing it for the first time. He delivered some of it directly from cue cards and read many of the slides. Did he really need to read the slide, or was he just taking an opportunity to turn his back on the audience?

Nevada had seen Crawford speak many times before, and she'd never known him to be shy about facing and interacting with an audience. What was going on?

Shortly after the presentation ended, and the pavilion emptied, she found out.

Charles and Daniel went on their way, along with the hundreds of other luncheon guests. Nevada found herself not to be the only one waiting for Crawford. Bernadette hovered in front of the stage, too. After all the hands were shaken and the committee head table guests dispersed, Crawford gathered his folio from the table and slowly walked down toward Nevada and Bernadette.

"Well, I suppose you're wondering what that was about," Crawford said.

"You didn't seem to be at your best." Nevada said.

Bernadette planted herself in Crawford's path. "What is it, Crawford? What's going on?"

He seemed to sag and shrink about three inches. Nevada pulled a chair out and he let himself sink into it. She and Bernadette pulled up chairs beside him, then waited for him to speak.

"We're being sued," he finally said. "Fraser Greene, you, me, and Jasper's estate."

"Me?" Nevada and Bernadette asked, simultaneously.

"You, Bernadette. Not you, Nevada." Charles looked around as if he were in a fog. "Have they taken everything away? Can I get a coffee or something? I didn't eat a bite of my lunch."

"Just give us the bullet points, Crawford, and then we'll go somewhere and find you something to eat," Bernadette said.

"And drink."

"And drink. Now, come on. Pull yourself together. What's going on? Who's suing us? About what?"

Staff from the convention center and the caterers were passing back and forth, clearing tables and getting the room back to its ready state, but they gave a wide berth to the three of them, sitting huddled at one of the tables just at the foot of the stage. Crawford glanced at them, then began to answer the questions.

"A writer named Josselyn Madden claims Jasper plagiarized her work. Stole her idea and turned it into *Burning Path*."

"The novel I edited," Bernadette said.

"His first big bestseller." Crawford reached up to loosen his tie and shirt collar. "She also claims half a dozen others of his were stolen from her."

"Is she some kind of weirdo?" Nevada asked. "Did Jasper even know her?"

"She has boxes full of notes and letters he's sent her over the years. Says it started out as a mentoring arrangement but that he turned it into a cover for his theft of her intellectual property." Crawford put his hands on the table, then shoved himself to a standing position. "She's suing us for forty million."

CHAPTER 18

In a quiet alcove down one hallway outside the exhibition halls, Nevada sat, checking her messages while trying to absorb the information Crawford had just announced. Sued for forty million! That would mean the end of Fraser Greene. She couldn't imagine what arguments might be made for such a colossal damages award, should this Josselyn Madden win a case—and that had to be a long shot.

Get a grip. You're letting your mind take you off down the road toward disaster, and there are many miles to go before the company would be anywhere near catastrophe.

Josselyn Madden. Why did that name sound familiar? Nevada scrolled through the contact list on her phone but nothing turned up there. Someone she'd met through Owen? Someone from Savannah? Or her journalism days in Canada?

She relaxed and tried to let her memory open itself to a ray of light. And there it was! She'd met Josselyn Madden during set-up day on Tuesday at the convention center. Josselyn had approached her and introduced herself as a thriller writer who was a big fan of Jasper's. She said she was there looking for an agent and tried to get Nevada's card when she realized she had bumped into a publishing exec. Nevada had dodged the conversation, as she had a few others that day, and left Josselyn behind in the crowd.

Could this be true? That Josselyn was much more than a fan of Jasper's and that he'd mentored her? Nevada supposed that was a possibility. She had been a friend and colleague of Jasper's, but she didn't know everything about his life, just as he hadn't known everything about hers.

Fiona would know.

Nevada called Fiona's number, but there was no answer. It was far too touchy a topic to raise in a voice mail or an email, so Nevada decided to leave it sit until she could reach Fiona directly.

She looked up from her phone to see Daniel standing in front of her. "That was a strange keynote," he said.

"I thought so, at first, too. But I saw Crawford afterward, and he admitted he wasn't exactly on his game."

"Is he not well?"

Nevada shook her head. "It's not that, I don't think. Something in his personal life, bothering him and distracting him." Now, that wasn't exactly the front page news, but it was sort of true.

Crawford hadn't directly told her to keep the news of the lawsuit confidential, but it felt as though she should. She was vaguely suspicious of Daniel and besides, what right had he to know about Fraser Greene's troubles?

Daniel nodded. "Definitely seemed as though he had something else on his mind. Maybe Jasper's death? Maybe he's heard something more about the police investigation?"

Nevada looked back down at her phone, fighting against her inclination to stare Daniel in the eyes. What was wrong with him? Why was he so interested? Yes, Jasper had been a friend of his, a close friend. But there was just something too intense about the way Daniel was asking these questions.

On the other hand, what was wrong with her? Was her scrutiny of Jasper's activities and acquaintances infecting her mind with suspicion about everything and everybody? Here was Daniel, who, outside of his connection to Jasper Inniskillen, seemed to be a nice, ordinary, well-balanced man. Yet she was looking at him with the mistrust she'd give a conman who'd scammed her out of thousands and now was proposing a new investment.

But, on yet another hand … should she add Daniel to her list of suspects? Just based on his curiosity? What motive could he possibly have for wanting Jasper dead?

Her phone buzzed, and she saw Fiona's name. "Excuse me, Daniel, but I have to take this," she said, then stood up and walked away down the hall.

"Nevada? You called me?"

"Yes, Fiona. How are you holding up?"

"I can barely move. Thanks for asking. Jasper's sister, Wendy, is here, and she's helping me make arrangements." Her voice was not much more than a whisper. "Is there something I can do for you?"

"I wanted to ask you about a few things that have come up," Nevada said. "Is now a good time?"

"Yes, it is. Yes, ask me anything. We have to find out what happened to Jasper, and if there's anything I can do to help the police or you or anybody who cares, I'll do it."

"Alright. Some of these questions might seem a bit … abrupt. Maybe even brutal. But …have you heard anything recently … very recently … about Jasper being sued for plagiarism?"

The silence went on for several seconds. "No."

"You haven't received any legal papers or requests for a meeting?"

"No, but the mail has been piling up since Tuesday. Why do you ask?"

"Fraser Greene has had an official letter. The plaintiff is somebody named Josselyn Madden. Do you know that name? She claims to have been a close working contact of Jasper's. Says he mentored her for years, and stole her ideas. That *Lockdown* and several other books are actually hers."

If she anticipated an excited, indignant response from Fiona, her expectation was unmet. Jasper's wife's tone continued to be flat and tired. "No, I've never heard of a Josselyn Madden. And I knew about most of Jasper's friends from fiction world. Not all of them, maybe, but he did talk a lot, over the breakfast and dinner table, about the people he was meeting and emailing and so forth." She took a couple of deep breaths. "A plagiarism lawsuit. Oh, God."

"I know. It's terrible. I'm sorry to be the one to tell you about it," Nevada said.

The silence hung between them like a San Francisco fog.

Nevada changed course. "Just a couple of other things, Fiona. What about this stalker that you mentioned to me a while ago? Olivia Theale. You know, I bumped into her at Book Fair, on the setup day, Tuesday, and she was looking for Jasper. Said she was a big fan. I had no idea, at that point, that she'd been stalking him. Has she contacted you since he died?"

"No, nothing. She was spooky, but I never felt her as someone who was dangerous to Jasper. There have been a few other superfans sending me emails, but I'm not answering anything yet. Wendy told me there are a dozen people hanging out near the front gate and there's a lot of flower bouquets. The police have a car there, making sure no one comes in." Fiona's voice had been dwindling. "Anything else, Nevada?"

"Just two more questions, Fiona, then I'll leave you alone. Was Jasper sick, by any chance? Seriously sick? Or was there anything else going on in his life?"

"No, not sick. Not that I knew of, anyway. I mean, people sometimes keep secrets, and I suppose it would be up to him. It's his business whether he wanted to reveal something like that to the world. Or even to me. But no, he never mentioned anything negative about his health to me."

"Alright, Fiona, and thank you. Just one more thing. The man who came into our office Tuesday and took shots at the walls. Detective Travers told me he's a man named Michael Diotte, a writer. He met Jasper at a firing range where Jasper was doing research, and he expected Jasper to help him with his career. Did Jasper ever mention a Michael Diotte to you?"

"No, I don't know that name," Fiona said.

Nevada waited to see whether she had anything to add. No more. "Thank you, Fiona. I know this can't be easy for you. None of this. Are you sure you're okay? Would you like me to come out to see you?"

"If you want." Her mood was so listless Nevada wondered if she was about to fall asleep.

"I'll drive over early Saturday, before Book Fest starts."

Nevada felt she needed to stretch and find a new set of four walls to look at. She walked over to the elevator and rode up to the top floor. The convention center offices were quiet and she didn't see anyone else in the hallway. She sat down and tapped in Detective Travers's number. He picked up on the second ring.

"Ms. Leacock. What's up?"

"Thanks for taking my call, Detective. I wanted to ask you whether you've found out anything more about Michael Diotte and his whereabouts on Tuesday morning? Or even his whereabouts now?"

"Nothing I can share right now."

It was a terse, full-stop answer, but Nevada wasn't giving up. "Because I've heard something more and if there's any kind of link … to Michael Diotte or anybody … it might be worth pursuing."

"What's that?"

She wanted to get the detective's take on the news about the plagiarism lawsuit. She hesitated, wondering whether Crawford would have any issue with her passing on this news to the police. But he hadn't told her not to, and for all she knew, it was all public by now, anyway. "We've just had notice that Fraser Greene is being sued by a writer who says Jasper stole her ideas and words. She believes her name should be on *Lockdown* and several other of his novels."

"What's her name?" Obviously, news to Detective Travers.

"Josselyn Madden. She's suing Jasper, too."

"Definitely, important info. Although … I have to wonder why she'd kill him if she stood to make millions from a lawsuit."

"I suppose if she pursued the case, she could go after the estate," Nevada said. "If she was angry enough to want his money *and* his life."

Detective Travers thought this over. "Alright, we'll talk with her. Anything else?"

"I spoke with Fiona Inniskillen today. Asked her about the lawsuit and this Josselyn Madden. Also about the stalker fan she mentioned, Olivia Theale. And about Michael Diotte and Jasper's meeting him."

"You've been busy," he commented.

"I have. I'm serious, Detective Travers. I hope you can see that. I want to know who killed Jasper, and I'm asking questions."

Several seconds went by. "And giving answers," the detective finally said. "Alright. I have Josselyn Madden's name now, and you have Michael Diotte's."

"Do you know where he is?"

"We're looking for him, and if we pick him up, I'll let you know," Travers said. "Please keep in touch and let's share what we have."

"Guaranteed," Nevada agreed.

"I'll give you one more," he said. "The latest thing we found out. Toby Encell's family includes a branch in Minnesota. Manitou, Minnesota. Where the Diotte's live."

"Michael Diotte is related to Toby? What does that mean, Detective? Do you think Michael was involved in Toby's autobiography in some way?"

"I don't know. We're following up."

When he wouldn't participate in speculating with her, Nevada couldn't get off the phone fast enough. She had to talk to Toby. She was unsuccessful last time, when she'd tried to speak with Toby at Sardi's right after he announced he was moving his autobiography away from her company and over to Mondarix Press, but she was determined to talk with him now. She would camp in his driveway if she had to.

She was looking him up in her contacts list when her phone buzzed. Owen.

"Hey! Long time no see," she said. What an odd thing to say. It was an expression her grandparents used and it had just popped into her mind, uninvited. She must be feeling nervous about talking to him for some reason.

"Hey, Nevada." His voice was somber.

"Hey, babe, how are you?""Not great. It's been a rotten week. We lost a couple of patients. Really young ones. Everybody is feeling miserable."

"Aw, I'm so sorry to hear that," Nevada said. "What can I do?"

"Nothing, thanks. I know you're having a busy week, too. And I appreciate that you have so much important stuff going on in your life that I don't have to worry about taking care of you, too."

Nevada didn't quite know how to take that.

"Listen, I know we haven't had much time together lately," Owen said. "And I know you still have another full day and a half of Book Fair to go. Plus, everything to do with Jasper's death. I really need to get away for a few days, but I'm not going to pressure you to come with me. I'll just go on my own."

"Where are you going?"

"I picked up a ticket for a weekend in Key West," Owen said. "I want some sunshine and blue water. I'll be back Sunday night."

"Well, I think—"

"Sorry, I hear them paging me and I have to go. I'll call you from Florida."

Nevada stared at the phone in her hand. It was not as though he hadn't traveled on his own before, to medical conferences and on one-time consulting appointments, but this was different, somehow. Because it was so abrupt? Because they had been so distant lately? Whatever it was, she felt pressure, even though he said he hadn't wanted to add to her load.

All in all, she'd rather have the pressure of him asking her to go with him. Now, she was left with a stressed-out, spooky feeling that there was a lot more between the lines.

CHAPTER 19

It wasn't hard to locate Toby Encell's main office address. Nevada was surprised she hadn't come across it before, but every previous meeting they'd had was held in a fancy restaurant or the Fraser Greene boardroom. She had to speak with him and she would not be brushed off this time. She would confront him in his own office and get the answers she needed.

The taxi dropped her off in front of an impressive skyscraper on the Upper West Side. While she waited for the elevator, she ran through her questions and tried to plan to direct the conversation. She wanted to find out more about the connection to the shooter in her office Tuesday morning, and if she could, she wanted to find out why Toby was breaking his autobiography contract with FG and going across the street to Mondarix Press.

The lobby of Encell Enterprises was chic and subdued. After Nevada gave her name to the receptionist, she sat on a grass-green velvet couch and examined the art on the walls. Someone had good taste—she thought she recognized a Hockney at the far end of the space, near the cantilevered staircase leading to the second floor. She decided not to look too interested and didn't bother to go across the room to check the signature.

Besides, much as she hated to admit it, she was nervous about this meeting.

"Nevada Leacock. In my office." Toby emerged from the space behind the reception desk. Past his shoulder, Nevada could see a bank of elevators. Apparently, the receptionist did guard duty, in addition to receiving.

"Toby. Thank you so much for meeting with me."

"I haven't met with you yet," he said, his smile reaching his gray eyes and contradicting the unfriendliness of his words. "My curiosity is in fifth gear, though, and I have five minutes until my next meeting, so tell me what you want."

Nevada felt she should probably stand up, but if she stayed seated, maybe he would sit down, too, and give her a little bigger word count.

"I want to talk more about your autobiography, Toby."

"My attorneys"—

"It's not about the contract … although I would still like to know why you took the project over to Mondarix Press and why you announced it at Book Fair."

"Without a heads-up to you."

"Yeah, well…" He had reminded her that she was still ticked off about all that. But it was business and they could sort that out another day. Her priority was getting the story on Michael Diotte's connection to the Encell family and his reason for assaulting the Fraser Greene office.

Toby glanced over his shoulder toward the reception desk. "What is it about, then?"

Nevada had the feeling she was running out of time. "I've found out that your family tree has a branch of cousins in Minnesota. That branch includes Michael Diotte, the man we think shot up the Fraser Greene office on Tuesday. I want to know whether he knew anything about your autobiography and whether there's anything in there that would lead him to take out his anger on the people he thought were going to publish it."

Toby sat down on one of the chairs opposite the couch.

"And I want to know whether he knew Jasper Inniskillen was your ghostwriter."

"I see where you're going with this," Toby said. "I'd like to know, too. Just a minute."

He reached into his jacket pocket for his phone and tapped out a message. Thirty seconds later, an assistant appeared at his side and handed him a box.

"The two hundred pages that we finished before this week," Toby said.

Nevada felt like the room had tilted on an axis. "You're going to let me see them?"

"I am. I want your opinion. And I want you to understand the background."

Nevada reached for the box and Toby handed it to her. "You and Jasper got a good start on it," she said.

Toby nodded. "But these two hundred are only the start. It's probably about a third of it."

"So, once it's all done, it'll be a brick."

"Yeah, well. In more ways than one," he said. "Let me know what you think."

As interested as Nevada was about Toby Encell's autobiography, she didn't want to spend the hours reading it just to satisfy her curiosity. She had a pile of manuscripts she was being paid to work on, and that was where her attention should go. "The connection to Michael Diotte is in here?"

"You'll see," Toby said, then motioned her toward the private area of the office. "I'm sure you'll understand that I don't want to let those pages out of here, or risk having the wrong people seeing them. I have a desk set up for you and you can go through them here. Now. If you want."

She hadn't expected this, but she didn't want to take a pass on the opportunity.

Ten minutes later, Nevada was settled behind a closed door with a coffee in a massive mug on the desk beside the stack of Toby's pages. Jasper's pages, actually. Nevada wondered whether his distinctive voice would come through, even in a ghost-written autobiography of Toby Encell.

Only one way to find out.

***

Preface

I was eleven years old when I realized how paranoid my father was. And how different from everyone else. In 1961, the world was opening up. Strangers talked to strangers, teenagers voiced opinions that were listened to, singers wrote songs that expressed the feelings of a new generation. I was a happy-go-lucky kid, and I made friends easily. I was invited everywhere in my neighborhood on Flatbush in Brooklyn. The kids at school, the guys at the basketball court, the old people around the corner … they all welcomed me into their homes.

I wanted to invite them back. The first time my father came home from his work as a refrigerator repairman, and found my friend Vito watching TV with me, he lost his temper and told Vito to go home. He didn't shout—he gritted his teeth and muttered the words at Tony, "Get out of here."

Later, he shouted at me. "Don't bring people in here! We don't know them and they don't know us. And don't talk about us to anybody, either. Keep our business at home."

This was not the only thing my father said to me, fortunately. He also taught me how to use my hands, and with his help, I mastered several trades. He was never tightfisted with his time and we spent many hours in his workshop, building and fixing things. Over the dinner table, we talked politics and economics, and we even watched the occasional TV show together, after my mother convinced him to get a set.

But he didn't ever introduce me to any of his buddies or invite me to a game when I was a teenager. Mainly, because he had no buddies. He practiced what he preached. I'll give him that. He didn't want me to have friends around or talk about our family to anyone, and he didn't allow himself any outside companionship, either.

It didn't occur to me that I could live my life differently until I went to college. Both of my parents worked two jobs to scrape together the money to send me, and I made good use of every nickel. They had instilled in me many values, including hard work, family loyalty, and discretion, and over the past decades I've often had occasion to question the beliefs they insisted on. But at a very deep level, those views were there throughout my life: play your cards close to your vest, don't trust anyone outside the family.

Whether those attitudes led to some, or all, of my success, I don't know. I hope that the writing of this autobiography will help me answer that question, as well as a few others I have: Why was I able to succeed in a field where I had no training or education when so many others failed? Why was I not satisfied with starting a company in one industry? Why did I leap from challenge to challenge, business to business? Why have I never had any fear of taking a risk?

And why did I let family loyalty triumph over human decency?

Chapter One

My mother introduced me to the magic of technology when she let me watch The Jetsons on TV when I was twelve. She introduced me to the magic of branding when I was nine and she gave in to my relentless pleading for a Gunsmoke lunchbox to take to school.

I knew from an early age that names mattered and that a major part of your identity had to do with the physical objects you surrounded yourself with. I chose my brand of soft drink, of shirts and jeans, of car, my favorite sports team, when I was in my twenties and I almost never wavered.

Technology, branding … and mentoring. Those were the three tent poles for my business career. I sought out mentors early on and as each year passed, I became more convinced of the importance of following in the footsteps of the winners and the stars. At first, I found my mentors just in books. I didn't know Steve Jobs, but I could read his words and follow his career. I tried to model myself after him, and learn from his triumphs and his mistakes. I called him a mentor.

Later, when life introduced me to a few people I admired and gave me the opportunity to ask for help, I sought out real life mentors in technology, in sports, in all the industries where I wanted to make a mark. As I succeeded, I held out a hand as a mentor to newcomers, too.

But even through all the years of networking and team-building, my parents' early training never left me.

I was born in 1950 in Cumberland Hospital and I grew up in a small apartment with a brother, a sister, and my parents. My siblings were like charcoal sketches to me, shaded edges and light gray centers only hinting at the people they might be inside…

***

The prose was gripping, and Nevada would have continued to the last word on the last of the two hundred pages if her phone hadn't buzzed with a text from her boss.

> Get back to Book Fair right away.
> A package delivered for you

She replied to Bernadette instantly.

> Who sent it?

Just get back here

Nevada gathered the pages into their box and stepped out of the office to return them to Toby. Like magic, his assistant appeared at her elbow, holding out her hands to take back the box.

"Please tell Mr. Encell thank you, and I'll be in touch."

All the way back to the Javitz Center in Midtown, even with the ominous message from Bernadette on her mind, Nevada couldn't shake her thoughts free of the story she'd just read. The Encell family—two elderly parents, Toby's father Rolf and mother Sigrun, Rolf's sister Ursula and his brother Willem—carried their few possessions out of Germany in 1940 and made their way to America. Toby was born ten years later and named for an uncle he'd never met: Rolf's other brother, Tobias, who had remained behind in Germany. He could not afford to make the journey, apparently, despite the efforts of the other family members to throw what they could into a pot to buy a ticket for him.

Growing up, Toby was told glowing stories about the uncle for whom he was named. Tobias, the exceptional teenage athlete. Tobias, the winner of all the academic prizes at school. Tobias, the target for all the girls at the dances and parties. About twenty years after World War II ended, Toby's father, Rolf, announced that Tobias had decided to move to America to join them after all these years apart.

For Toby, his uncle was still a glamorous, mysterious figure. The man he'd never met but had been named for. He had built a thriving business as a cattle rancher in Argentina but was tired of the climate, Rolf told them, and wanted to live nearer to his family. Rolf handled the paperwork and helped Tobias emigrate, and after he was installed in an apartment in Brooklyn, he was a regular fixture at Sunday dinner.

was just wondering whether you'd have any idea why Jasper set up a meeting with me Tuesday morning then didn't show up."

"I'm sorry, Nevada, but I don't."

Nevada hesitated, then dove in. "He did tell me he might be interested in returning to us. And Crawford knew something about that."

"Really? He didn't say a word to me." Was Ryley annoyed by this? Surprised? It was impossible to tell.

"Anyway, never mind. Maybe I'll never know what he wanted to talk to me about. I'll ring off now, Ryley. I have to take care of this silly letter Sable Ogilvie has sent me."

"Sable? What did she send you?"

"Oh, she's hot for the seat she thinks Jasper's death has left open. Wants to be Number One."

"That I know about. She came to see me. To talk about us representing her."

"What did you say?"

"That I felt there might be a conflict of interest, since I represented Jasper. Especially, given their history of animosity."

Nevada felt a moment of confusion. "But you don't represent Jasper now."

"It was earlier in the week that I spoke with Sable. Tuesday."

"Morning or afternoon?""Afternoon."

So, at the moment that someone shot Jasper, Sable sat in his Manhattan agent's office, having a meeting.

"What's your position on it now?" Nevada asked. "Would you be open to Sable's pitch?"

Ryley sighed. "I just can't think about it now. I want to get through to the weekend and go home to take a long bath. You know?""I do. Thanks for returning my call, Ryley."

Nevada thought over the conversation, then made a few quick notes. The afternoon was getting on, and she still had a lot of work to do over at Book Fair. But she wanted to make a stop at the detective's office. She doubted he would let her into the interview room with Michael Diotte or let her know what was said, but she had to try.

***

The 10th Precinct building was not as familiar to Nevada as the police stations in other cities during her years as a reporter and a news director, but the atmosphere was. She waited for her turn to approach the officer on duty and asked to be shown to Detective Travers' office.

"Not in", was the reply, which might or might not have been true. Not in for her, anyway. She scribbled a note with her name and phone number, as the desk guy suggested, then found her way back to the street.

She would have to rely on his interest in her information about Toby Encell's autobiography and hope he would call her back. Nevada glanced across the street at a small hotel where café tables and chairs were set up on the sidewalk up front. She needed a break … just a little time to think.

Dropping into a chair, she resisted the urge to take out her phone immediately and look for messages. Five minutes, just five minutes … she needed it and she was going to take it.

The traffic on the street was surprisingly light, but the foot traffic in and out of the police precinct was constant. Nevada watched the people go by and let her mind drift over the events of the past four days. She'd had dramatic times during her reporter years: had been under fire; had pursued killers and kidnappers; had risked personal disaster to expose corruption. But this past week, surrounded by publishers, librarians, and other bookish people had been one of the most disturbing she'd had.

No doubt that was because of her personal connection with Jasper. She still felt like the wind had been knocked out of her every time she made herself come face to face with the fact that he was gone. She would miss his sense of humor and his down-to-earth way of pointing out the weirdness of human behavior. She knew a few other smart, witty commenters on the ridiculous way people fumble their way through their days, but none were so brilliant and kindly as Jasper was.

As Nevada watched the line of people leaving the police station pass the line of people going in, she realized she recognized someone. Sitting up straight in her café chair, she stared as hard as she could, trying to keep him in focus as people passed in front of him. Medium build, gray hair, clean shaven. Could that be Michael Diotte, leaving the precinct?

Nevada timed her move from one sidewalk to the other, crossing the street in between taxis and a garbage truck. She intercepted the man just as he turned a corner.

"Mr. Diotte! Michael!"

He stopped and looked at her. She thought she had never seen such a belligerent pair of eyes. "Yeah?"

"I'd like to speak to you for a minute."

"What about?" What about? She had no plan when she'd run across the street to stop him. What did she really want to know? She already knew he'd been the one shooting in her office. She wouldn't forget him. She thought she knew why … that his anger over having his author ambitions frustrated had boiled over into violence. But what she didn't know was whether that same anger had been directed later that day against Jasper.

"Jasper Inniskillen." She had his attention now. "I worked with Jasper … on his books … and I'm hoping you know something about where he was on Tuesday. Before he went home … and…"

"You worked with Jasper?""I'm Nevada Leacock. I'm an editor at Fraser Greene." She stuck out her hand and he shook it. This had to be one of the strangest interviews she'd ever done but she was just going to go with it. "Jasper told me he worked with you too, and that he mentored you with your writing."

"Jasper talked to you about me?"

She nodded. "What were you doing at the police station? I was just across the street having a coffee outside the hotel and I saw you."

"They let me go. Told me not to leave town. That I might be called to be in a lineup." He looked at her sharply. "Were you at work Tuesday?"

She decided to go for it. "Were you there? Was that you with the gun?"

"If I wouldn't tell them that, why would I tell you?" He turned and began to walk away quickly.

Nevada jogged to keep up with him. "I know you were. I was there. I was the one on the elevator."

That stopped him. Whatever Nevada said would have a big impact on the way the police treated him. Maybe if Nevada and the others said nothing at all, if there was no eyewitness evidence, that would allow him to wriggle out of the mess he was in. He took a step toward her and she was thankful for the hundreds of people walking shoulder to shoulder along this New York sidewalk.

"Your best bet is to talk to me, Michael. We can help each other. Come on, let's sit down in a diner somewhere."

She was quite surprised when he heaved a sigh then moved to follow her toward a corner place. Once they were in a booth, each with a coffee, Nevada leaned forward.

"I know you weren't trying to hit anybody. If you had wanted to, you could have, but all you did was shoot at walls."

Michael nodded and stared into his coffee mug.

"So, why were you there? Why were you shooting?" "I'm not admitting anything."

"I think you just lost your temper," Nevada said. "I think you lost your temper over the bad treatment you think you're getting from the publishers.. Just lost it." She signaled to the server to refill Michael's coffee cup. "How did you happen to have a gun that you could bring into our office like that?"

"I always have a gun," he said.

Nevada couldn't speak for a minute. She would never feel complacent about that aspect of American life.

Alright. What now? "So, you were angry enough at the publishing people that you came into the Fraser Greene office to make a scene."

"I didn't say that."

"Were you also angry enough to go out to Long Island, to Jasper's home, and shoot at him?"

Michael stared at her. "No. I didn't shoot at him. I wouldn't shoot anybody. I was angry at him, yes. He promised to mentor me and to help me get started in this business. My trilogy is the next level when it comes to fantasy. But how am I going to get anybody to know that if nobody will even read it?"

"How long is it?"

"Fifteen hundred pages."

"I guessed as much. Michael, the problem so many first-time writers like yourself have is that you write far more than anybody is willing to commit the time to read," she said.

"I'm not a first-time writer. My book is different from anything coming from anybody else." His tone was becoming belligerent, and she realized that arguing with him would not get her the information she needed.

"Alright. So, you have a good book that Jasper wouldn't take the time to read—"

"And wouldn't introduce to anybody to could get it into print and onto the bookshelves!" Michael grabbed the sugar bottle and poured it into his black coffee.

"Michael, I think you have an inflated view of what a mentor can do for you." Nevada used as calm and controlling voice as she could. This man seemed to be a powder keg two inches away from a burning match. "Jasper tried to help you but not even an influential, well-connected mentor can get your book published if no one wants to buy it."

"He said he would take my trilogy in to Fraser Greene."

"And no doubt he did that," Nevada said. "He was always a good one for following through on his commitments. But just because your name or your work is introduced somewhere doesn't mean anything else is going to happen."

"My writing is publishable! It's just as good as a lot of the garbage I see on the bookstore shelves anywhere. Better!"

"It may be. But you have no idea how many variables go into a decision to publish. Or not to publish. Things going on behind the scenes—"

"Like what?" Diotte demanded.

"Economics. Whether the publishing company is having a good year or about to go under. What other books like yours are already in the pipeline. Office politics. Whether the editor who wants you is staying on or is just about to move to a different house. Or a different career! All those factors have nothing to do with the quality of your submission but they will affect your future as an author," Nevada said. "You can't blame Jasper for any of that."

Diotte seemed to hear her points. His face wasn't quite so red, and he'd stopped gripping the edge of the table. He gave his coffee his attention and Nevada took advantage of the break in the conversation to study him. Like so many others she'd seen in the aftermath of violence, it was difficult to visualize him shooting at walls … even holding a gun. He looked ordinary. Maybe a little anxious, and frustrated by his failure to force his life to take the path he thought ought to reveal itself to him. But also, ordinary.

"Michael, what have the police said about the shooting?" she wondered. "Did they charge you with anything?"

His eyes narrowed. "I'm not saying I was there. Are you saying that?"

"No, I'm not saying anything."

"Good. Cops told me to get a lawyer. Not to leave town." Diotte finished his coffee and stood up. "You don't have to worry anymore, Ms. Leacock. I have a new opportunity opening up for my manuscript. I won't be visiting Fraser Greene anymore."

"There's another thing I wanted to ask you about. Would you sit down?" When he let several seconds pass, ignoring Nevada's request, she plunged in. "It's about your family. You might know that I was working on an autobiography with Toby Encell . . . a book that is going to reveal some very sensitive family secrets. I've just learned that you are related to Mr. Encell—"

"Distant cousins," he said. "I've been estranged from my family for years. We don't see things the same way."

"Including your brother?"

But apparently, the conversation was over. Diotte turned on his heel and left the diner.

Well, Nevada thought. I guess I'm paying for your coffee. My treat.

CHAPTER 22

When Nevada got Detective Travers on the phone ten minutes later, he was keen to hear the details of her conversation with Diotte. As they traded information, though, they realized that neither one had heard anything from him that the other hadn't.

"If you remember anything else, Ms. Leacock, call me," Travers said. "Or if he calls you."

"Or comes by the Fraser Green office, I suppose."

"There's a restraining order against him there."

"Ah. Good. I would bet that Crawford and Bernadette are pleased about that."

"They're in the loop, yeah."

"What's your next move?" she asked.

"We want to know where he got the gun and we're tracking that down."

"Is it the same gun as …"

"As on Jasper Inniskillen? No. But I'm not drawing any conclusions. He might own two. One more thing, Nevada. We've completed our sweep of Jasper's property. The …" he hesitated.

"Murder scene. You don't have to be delicate with me."

"The murder scene."

"Anything turn up?" *Something must have; otherwise, why would he mention it?*

"A woman's scarf. On the ground in the yard. We assumed it was his wife's but then one of the K-9s made a fuss over it. We checked it out with Mrs. Inniskillen. It's not hers."

The foot traffic on the sidewalk outside the diner was heavy and Nevada had to steer a zigzag course toward the curb to raise her arm to get a taxi. All the way back to the Javits Center, she assessed the information he'd given her. What was her next move?

She still had pretty much finished the process of tracking Jasper's activities during his last few months and nothing startling had turned up. It created a picture of a man starting a change of direction in his life: the trip to the indie publishing conference; the contract to ghost-write an autobiography; the feelers out to his former publisher about returning to the fold. You'd start to wonder what the motivation was, for someone so successful and famous. Wouldn't he feel that he'd achieved every goal he'd ever set, and that he had nothing more to prove to anybody?

Nevada also wondered whether his driving force wasn't curiosity or restlessness. Was it despair? Was Jasper depressed? So depressed that he would consider killing himself?

But everything Nevada had ever known about the man, seen him do or heard him express, pulled her away from that theory. Besides, it would be something Travers would raise, wouldn't it? Everyone would be looking for a note, and if suicide were being seriously considered, wouldn't Travers have asked her if she knew anything about that? Wouldn't there be something about the death that would point the police that way?

Nevada wanted to get more of a sense of Jasper's movements and thoughts on that last day. She still didn't know why he wanted a meeting with her at the Fraser Greene office that day. She could guess, but she didn't know.

She couldn't put her finger on the reason but when she visualized Jasper waking up that day, leaving home but not keeping his appointment with her—it all gave her a vibe of a man tussling with fear. What was Jasper afraid of?

As she rode along 11th Avenue, watching the sidewalk through the taxi window, she tried to relax her mind and make it welcoming to any as-yet unreceived thoughts she might have. She often played a 'And what do you do?' game with herself when she watched people, and this afternoon she spotted four accountants, two restaurant servers, and a bank president while sitting at a red light. As the taxi started up again, Nevada saw a clump of what she guessed to be book editors and readers carrying large bags for collecting their free galleys from Book Fair. Those were likely to be accurate guesses; the taxi was just a few blocks from the convention center now.

Her scanning of the crowd stopped at a small woman with long, white hair. She carried a canvas bag with a photo of Anne of Green Gables on the side, and she clutched it with hands covered in white lace gloves. It was the Jasper fan Nevada met on Tuesday ... what was her name? Olivia Somebody. The one Fiona had identified as a stalker. Jasper had never told Nevada anything about any stalker, but there were probably many things Jasper had never told Nevada. And if his primary mood on Tuesday was fearfulness, dodging a stalker was certainly right up there on the list of experiences that would put you there.

Nevada fumbled in her bag for her wallet, then paid the taxi driver. They were rolling along the street at about ten miles an hour in thick traffic and it was easy for Nevada to hop out of the taxi right in front of Olivia.

Olivia ? Theale! That was it.

"Ms. Theale. Do you remember me?" Nevada planted herself right in Olivia's path. "We talked about Jasper Inniskillen and you told me you are a big fan."

The woman gave Nevada a bright smile that was friendly and simultaneously completely withdrawn. "Of course! I remember you. Not your name, I'm sorry, but I remember talking to you."

Olivia stepped sideways, past Nevada, and headed off toward the convention center. As much as she was able, Nevada kept pace with her, walking by her side. It wasn't easy with so many pedestrians to dodge and the brisk pace Olivia set.

"Did you hear about Jasper?" Nevada finally managed to gasp.

"I did," Olivia said. "I stopped by and left flowers at his house."

"You know the police suspect murder and they're interviewing possible suspects."

"I didn't know that." Olivia stopped abruptly and Nevada almost bumped into a linebacker coming down the sidewalk in the opposite direction. They both swerved, then Nevada came to her own stop and turned back to face Olivia.

"Someone like you could be a suspect," Nevada said.

"Why, because I'm an admitted super-fan? There are a lot of us in this world."

"Because you've been stalking him."

Olivia snorted. "Hah! Says who? I'm not a stalker. And I was nowhere near Jasper Inniskillen's home on Tuesday. My neighbor was with me, here at Book Fair, and he'll vouch for me." She waited for Nevada to ask her grandfather's identity, then grew tired of waiting. "My neighbor is Charles Delaney."

***

Nevada let Olivia hustle away from her, toward the convention center doors, and took a moment to write notes about this on her phone. So, Charles Delaney had a neighbor who thought Jasper Inniskillen walked on water! And Charles was her alibi … yet she was female and one of the few female suspects. It was a woman's scarf that had been found, the detective said. That would seem to point toward Olivia or Sable. Or perhaps the one suing Jasper, Josselyn.

Nevada tucked herself into a doorway and found Detective Travers's number in her Contacts. He took her call immediately and thanked her energetically for bringing him the information about Olivia Theale.

"I think that eliminates her as a suspect," Nevada said.

"You sound disappointed about that," Travers commented.

"Not really. I just feel overwhelmed by how many people there are and how far we seem to be from an answer."

"It's only been three days," Travers commented. "But yeah. I think you wanted it to be a simple … and quick … conclusion that a stalker murdered Jasper. By the way, what was the source of your information about Olivia Theale?"

"Fiona."

Nevada barely time to let that one sink in before Travers was adding to the load. "We're investigating Fiona Inniskillen thoroughly. Normal practice in a murder case, look at the spouse. Anyway, turns out they took out a large insurance policy about three months ago. No pre-existing conditions and they were able to get quite a good deal. Beneficiary, Fiona."

Nevada looked around the exhibit hall and took a moment to process this latest information. She'd heard from Jasper and from Toby that Jasper had some short-term money problems. They knew he had taken on ghost-writing work and was looking for new publishing deals that would leave more of the revenue in his hands. Was he also trying to find a solution in an insurance windfall?

Or was that Fiona doing that?

CHAPTER 23

The first person Nevada saw when she put away her phone and began her walk through the hall to the Fraser Green booth was Daniel Pyne.

"Nevada! How are things, is everything okay?"

"All good, Daniel. How about you?"

He shrugged. "I'm kind of just going through the motions, you know? I didn't want to sit around my place all afternoon, but I'm finding it difficult to get interested in new book releases or presentations on marketing when all I can think about is Jasper."

"I know what you mean." Nevada glanced around the room, looking for an easy escape. She liked Daniel, but she didn't like the way he'd asked her, the last few times she'd seen him, to be an information source for him.

This time, though, he was the one with the news. "I spoke with Fiona a while ago. She and Jasper's daughter, Daphne, have arranged a memorial service for him Sunday."

"That soon."

"Yeah, well, I guess family have been arriving all week, and people don't want to leave until after they've had the chance to attend the service."

"He knew many people all over the country … all over the world, really … and a lot of them are here for Book Fair, too," Nevada said. "Sunday will be convenient for them, too."

Nevada was ready to move on but Daniel seemed to have something on his mind.

"Nevada, this might seem weird but I want to ask you something about Charles Delaney."

Several of Daniel's questions and comments over the past few days had seemed odd to her. She braced herself for the next one.

"What about Charles?" she asked.

"Do you have time to grab a coffee with me?"

"I don't, Daniel. I have a few more meetings yet this afternoon and then there's teardown, after five. We have to get everything, including the booth, back to the office."

Daniel nodded. "Alright. I'll try to be brief. But let's just step over here, out of the way where we won't be overheard."

Nevada let him guide her away from the main aisle toward the end of a quiet row where very few people were approaching the booths. The publisher staff were talking to each other, or staring at their phones, and they took no notice of Nevada and Daniel. In a few moments, the browsers had moved on. It felt as though they had this entire section of the exhibit hall to themselves.

"Alright, Daniel. What's up?"

"I think there's some kind of monkey business going on with Charles."

"Charles how? In what?""I think he was interfering in Jasper's author life somehow. Don't you think it's strange, how Charles is trying to smear Jasper's reputation, all of a sudden? Yesterday, at the keynote, he said Jasper wouldn't give most people the time of day. Made fun of them behind their backs, was very judgmental and critical. Was only nice to those he thought could help him in his career. Was a nasty, sour man."

"I don't think Charles said all that."

"A lot of it." Daniel stopped to wait for her confirmation.

"Yes, you're right, he did say some of those things." Nevada thought back on her encounter with Charles on the first day of Book Fair, when he said she was mistaken in thinking Jasper an excellent writer. "But maybe that was just Charles's take on Jasper. Not everyone has the same opinion of everyone. And maybe Jasper wasn't friendly and charming to everyone he met."

"Maybe he *was* unpleasant and mean to some … maybe, or especially, to those who were close to him or knew him well. Lots of people are like that, and it's always a surprise to the ones who liked or loved them to find out that there was more than one side to the person."

Nevada nodded. She'd certainly run across that many times in her journalism days, when the next-door neighbors of a killer or a criminal thought he was the kindliest guy on the block and were completely surprised, even disbelieving.

"But I think it's more than Charles showing a lack of tact about someone who's passed away," Daniel continued. "I think he came out of retirement deliberately to try to take Jasper down."

"Well, he's always been out of retirement. Kind of. He's been active for years."

"Yes, but more so, lately, don't you think? I've heard he's been joining committees, inviting people to lunches, volunteering to judge awards, even hanging out at some of the clubs and bars."

"I've heard that too, but I just thought 'Good for Charles! I hope I'm that active when I'm over eighty'," Nevada said.

"But everywhere he goes, he's talking down Jasper Inniskillen. Why?"

"Did Jasper notice this, too?"

"He never mentioned it, if he did. And he had so many things on his mind this past winter," Daniel said. "He's with Fraser Greene, he's not with Fraser Greene. He's at Mondarix Press, he wants to leave. He's considering indie publishing and going to conferences, he's wondering if it's too much work. He's outlining a new novel. He's ghost-writing for Toby Encell."

And he's worrying about his bank balance.

"But why would Charles Delaney want to undermine Jasper's reputation? Or his success?"

Nevada felt her experienced instinct for speculation slide into action. *Maybe he was mentoring or wanting to champion a challenger to Jasper's status as number one bestseller? Maybe Sable Ogilvie? Maybe he'd been burned or insulted by Jasper and wanted to get payback? Maybe he knew something about the Toby Encell autobiography? Maybe there was some sort of business connection between them and Jasper's financial problems had an impact?* She shook her head. She wasn't about to share all this with Daniel Pyne at this moment. She barely knew him. "I don't know, Daniel. But if I come across anything, I'll get in touch with you."

"So will I," Daniel said. "I'm asking around."

"Now, I really have to get back to the booth. Thanks for letting me know about the funeral" she said, then walked off toward the main aisle as quickly as she could.

"Nevada! You're back!" A line of a dozen industry people stood in front of the last remaining stack of advance copies of Cori Lowe's book, where Bernadette stood behind a table, handing them out. "Good!"

"I'm here now for the duration," Nevada said. "Right through tear down, tonight. What can I do?"

"Cori is doing a presentation in twenty minutes and she's asked that you confirm you'll be there."

"I always intended to, yes. Do you know what room it's in?"Bernadette shook her head, impatiently. Obviously, this was below her pay grade.

"Okay, I'll shoot her an email. Anything else? I have a meeting with the French publisher later, too."

"I'd like to talk to you about this plagiarism suit, if you can spare fifteen minutes. We both edited Jasper books and worked with him intensively and I'd like to compare notes."

Nevada nodded. She was interested in Bernadette's experience with Jasper, too. And she wondered whether Bernadette had heard any of the slurs that Charles had been spreading.

"Let's do that now," Nevada said. "Is there any update on the plagiarism suit?"Bernadette ushered her behind a curtain and to a small table where two folding chairs were set up. "We're finding out more about this Josselyn Madden. She's had a couple of novels published by a tiny press in one of the flyover states. We haven't been able to confirm the nature of her connection with Jasper, of course. We haven't had much luck in getting through to his wife to ask what she knows about Josselyn. Maybe you could help with that?"Nevada nodded. "I'll try calling Fiona about this again. But come on. Her husband just died and the police are investigating a murder. I don't think I'd be that approachable, either."

"Fair enough. But there must be other ways we can find out more about it."

"What about Josselyn herself?"

"We've been advised by the lawyers not to have any direct communication with her. Only through them. They did send over the other side's initial filing and she seems to have emails and texts that establish they knew each other. She isn't just some nutcase who's pulled his name off the front page and is claiming to be his long-lost sister or something."

"Do you think she's telling the truth, that he was mentoring her?"

"Entirely possible. Despite what Charles Delaney is saying, Jasper helped other writers. A lot."

So, Bernadette had heard the word that Charles was trying to put on the street.

"Are Josselyn Madden's published novels anything like Jasper's?" Nevada asked. "Yeah, same genre, same approximate page count. We have a couple of the interns reading them for comparison and analysis." Bernadette gave a heavy sigh. "You knew Jasper a long time. Just like I did. What do you think? Would he have copied somebody else's work and passed it off as his own?" Nevada shrugged. "Who knows? Who ever really knows anybody? I mean, I think I would trust him not to do anything like that deliberately. He was talented and experienced. He didn't need to steal anybody else's work … especially from someone relatively green, like this Josselyn. So no, I don't think he intentionally plagiarized a book. But things do happen accidentally. Writers pick up ideas in many places. Maybe they both saw the same news headline and decided to spin it out into full-length fiction."

"It's certainly true that we see two movies or books come out around the same time with similar plots or characters. It's almost as if there's something in the air and a bunch of people inhaled it. Is Josselyn claiming IP theft because his novel has the same premise as hers?"

"It's more than that. Characters, plot twists, language style. The brief claims it's almost word for word, except for a few places, on minor story points, and they theorize that Jasper put those in, consciously, to try to muddy the waters."

"Whether it was cold-heartedly, calculatedly intentional or not, it still needs to be called out," Nevada said.

"Of course, there's the ethical issue, but there's also the practical question. Some people would say it's the more important question. Who deserves the money?"

The two women sat in silence for a moment, as the power of the question sank in. Hundreds of peoples' jobs, incomes, and their families' wellbeing rested on this conflict over the ownership of a story. "Well, I suppose this first step, of having our readers go through it, will give us a response to that," Nevada said. "But what if the two novels are almost identical? And hers was published first?"

"It's a nightmare. We don't have Jasper around for the other side to question. But our attorneys say they're likely to request pretty much every piece of paper or record in his study. Diaries, planners, appointment books, research notes." Bernadette shuddered. "I don't know whether Fiona is up to the task but someone is going to have to sort all that."

"She might be, since the success or failure of this lawsuit is going to have an impact on her bank account and her life."

Bernadette shook her head. "You have such a way of understating things, do you know that? Yes, Fiona will be motivated big time, but that doesn't mean she can give us what we need to defend this suit."

"Who can?" Nevada asked. "Wait a minute. Are you looking at me?"

Her boss leaned back in the flimsy chair and crossed her arms. Ready to take charge. "Crawford is suggesting that you'd be a good person … the best person … to run point on this, and I agree."

"But I don't want to take on a project like that, Bernadette!"

"You're one of our most senior editors. You worked with Jasper and you know his style. Inside out. Fiona knows you, and won't mind having you in her home, going through Jasper's things."

"We don't know that. But that's not the point, Bernadette!"

"What is the point, Nevada?"

"That I don't want to spend my time defending a lawsuit! I want to work with authors, developing books. I want to read proposals, even go through the slush pile. I want to help make books that will be in readers' hands in the future, not comb through actions from the past."

"Well, Nevada, sometimes there is the greater good to consider, isn't there." Bernadette stood up. "I have a meeting with Crawford coming up and you have Cori Lowe's presentation to get to."

Nevada sat through Cori's talk and she thought it was solid. At the end, once the sporadic applause died out, she walked up to the front of the room to wait to speak with her author. Only one other attendee wanted to talk with Cori, and Nevada waited patiently while Cori answered questions about historical research, then wrapped things up with her host and retrieved her computer from the technician.

"Nice job, Cori," Nevada said, when her turn came to be acknowledged.

"Nevada! Thank you for coming," Cori said. Then, she turned to the other woman waiting to shake her hand. "Do you know Josselyn Madden? She's an author, too."

Nevada felt as though she'd suddenly fallen into a weird, parallel universe. Was Cori kidding? Did she have any idea what was going on, between Fraser Greene and Josselyn Madden? Maybe, Josselyn had told her about it, but it also seemed like the sort of thing an author might keep to herself.

But it was also possible they were close friends, and she'd told Cori everything. If that was the case, though, you'd think

Cori wouldn't be quite so blasé about the way she was introducing them.

Nevada peered into Josselyn's glasses, the black frames guaranteeing that anybody's attention would be drawn to her eyes, although her Russian Red lipstick made her lips a close second.

"Thanks, Cori," she said, "but I already know Josselyn. Or, I should say, I know about her. She's the writer who's claiming Jasper stole her novel and published it as his own."

Cori's head jerked back and her smile froze. "Excuse me? Nevada, are you joking?"

"Please tell her, Josselyn. Why not?" Nevada's smile registered partway between a glare and a grimace of pain.

The only word to describe Josselyn's face was anxious. "That's not really the complete story, Cori."

"What more can there be?" Nevada asked. "You've sued and you're after forty million dollars. It will sink my company. And as you and everybody else here knows, there aren't many of the mid-size publishing houses left."

Josselyn fixed her gaze on Cori. "There's much more to it than that. It started with Jasper looking at my manuscript but a lot of things happened after that."

"And it ends in court?" Cori asked.

"That wasn't my choice!" Josselyn said. "All I did was ask my dad for advice and suddenly, there were lawyers and meetings, and everything was getting away from me. Really, Cori. You have to believe me. I don't want to hurt anybody."

Nevada looked back and forth between them. It seemed this was not a situation of two authors crossing paths at Book Fair.

"Come on, Cori. You've known me since forever. You know this isn't my style."

The two women could not find the next words, so Nevada stepped in. "It may not be your style, but the fact is you've sued Fraser Greene and you've sued Jasper. Or his estate now, I guess." She looked at Josselyn and couldn't even find the polite words to say to end the conversation. 'Nice to meet you?' Hardly. 'Good luck with your writing?'

"Cori, I have to go," she said.

Cori nodded. "Thanks for coming, Nevada. I'm sorry…"

"Nothing for you to be sorry for." She took one more look at Josselyn Madden. What would the next room be where she'd find herself with this woman? A courtroom?

CHAPTER 24

When she saw Toby Encell's name on her list of voice mails from this morning, Nevada listened to that one first.

"Nevada, I want to talk to you about the autobiography. Can you spare me half an hour today?"

Today? Today was almost done; it was just an hour until the end of Book Fair and then the booth would have to be dismantled, with all the gear and any leftover books delivered back to the office. It felt to Nevada as though this day had gone on forever already and it would be many more hours before she could go home.

But yes, she could spare half an hour for Toby. Even though he'd walked out on her and Fraser Greene, and informed her of that decision in a very public, almost humiliating way, she didn't think ignoring him or refusing to take his calls was the best plan.

She dialed his number and took note of the fact that he picked up immediately. Did Toby Encell do that often?

"Hi Nevada. Thanks for getting back to me. When can we meet?"

"I'm at Book Fair until late this evening."

"I'm uptown. I'll be over there by 4:30."

That was optimistic, but who knew what resources tech billionaires had for getting through traffic that the rest of us don't have? Nevada settled the details with him, then went to find Bernadette to tell her about meeting Josselyn Madden.

"So, how would you describe her?" Bernadette asked. "Young? Old? Simple? Glamorous?"

Nevada wrinkled her brow. "I don't know, what do you say nowadays without getting into trouble? I didn't notice her appearance that much, to be honest. I was kind of startled to find out she and Cori Lowe are old friends, and that she didn't seem like the sort of monster who would sue a publishing company for tens of millions of dollars."

"I hope you'll stay in touch with Cori about this," Bernadette said. "And reconsider your reaction to Crawford's request that you run point on our response to the lawsuit."

"Yes, I'll think about it," Nevada tossed over her shoulder as she hurried out of the booth.

Toby had suggested they meet at a small corner bar, walking distance from the convention center. *The Apple Core* was set back about twenty feet from the street and two steps in through the door, Nevada felt as though she'd transitioned from day to night, from an open field to a cave.

The bartender looked up as she walked in, nodded, then looked back down to the glass he was polishing. A few customers had started their Friday night happy hour and were lined up along the bar, enjoying their beers. In one of the back corner booths, Toby sat with a full rocks glass in front of him.

Nevada slid into the booth. "Hello, Toby."

"Nevada. Thank you for coming over." He looked tired and preoccupied—almost a different man from the one who had captivated the Book Fair audience with his announcement of a new publisher for his autobiography. "I won't keep you long, and I'll get right to the point. I know you've been speaking with my son, and I have to tell you, I won't allow Royce to ruin or stop this book."

"I don't know that I'd call it 'speaking with Royce'," Nevada said. "Just one time."

"But enough time for you to hear his objections and his argument that these family secrets belong to everyone, and that we should have some sort of vote or something!" Toby was becoming agitated. "And not just about the publication of my autobiography, but about many of the details in it! I can't have that, Nevada. I'm not having it. This book is the culmination of a lifetime of work for me, and I'm committed to making it as honest and as complete as I can. I won't do it twice … and I have to get it right this time. I was hoping by showing you the pages that have been done so far I would convince you of the importance of getting them published. But I haven't heard a word from you since you read them."

Nevada had no idea why he would care about her opinion, now that he'd changed publishers. But she couldn't help but feel some compassion for him, as she began to understand how upsetting this all was. Some compassion, yes, but that wasn't her only emotion. He had embarrassed her, by pulling out of his contract with Fraser Greene, and not only that, but by going over to their primary rival. She wasn't sure how she felt about him taking advantage of Jasper's financial need by hiring him as his ghostwriter, and then ordering him to keep the project secret. Someone as talented as Jasper was a national treasure, she believed, and Toby should have been helping him get back on his feet, financially, while leaving him alone to write the novels he was meant to write.

And even though, on the surface, it would seem that Toby would have no motive for hurting Jasper, since he needed him to write more pages, was it possible that something had happened between them that pushed Toby to violence?

"I've had a very busy week, Toby," Nevada said. "So have you. We haven't had a chance before now to sit down to talk about your autobiography. About the contents, about Royce's … and your other family members' opinions about it."

"Now that you've read it, and know the secret, don't you understand why I thought the truth needs to come out?" It wouldn't be too long a stretch to describe Toby as anguished. "I'd been hating myself for years because I knew about this and I did nothing about it. How could I? It's my family and he's my uncle. Even if he's such a tough old bird, he could withstand the consequences, whatever they might be, I don't think my mother could."

"And your father?"

"My father would be furious. It's hard to predict what he would do. Royce thinks his grandfather would come after me in some way, and he says that's why he was trying to prevent publication of my book. Maybe. But that's not really what I was worried about. I have security and I can stay out of my father's way … or anybody else's, for that matter."

"What was it you worried about, Toby?"

The businessman stared into the bottom of his drink. "I guess 'worried' is the wrong word. It just tortured me that I've known about his Nazi past for decades now and I've never done anything. Never done anything to bring him to justice or to reveal him for the scum that he is."

"Did you ever think of blowing the whistle on him before this?"

"Yes … and no. I think I've always known it would be the right thing to do, but then I'd put it out of my mind … or promise myself to do something once I had time for it. Once the current project or fiscal year was over, or whatever. I wanted to do something about it, but at the same time, I didn't, you know? So many obstacles … and probably the biggest was wanting to avoid my family's disapproval."

"What changed your mind?"

"I think working on these pages with Jasper was almost like therapy," Toby said. "I didn't tell him the entire story at the beginning. He asked me where my name came from, and I made something up. Then, after a few weeks, I revisited that question, in my mind, and the answer just felt really stupid to me. Stupid, and false. I started to think more about a few other things I'd told him, about my past. My personal past and my business past. What if someone came along, someone who had a few facts to add, or even proof about what really happened, during some event or other?

"And one day, he asked me a few questions that made me realize he knew I was fudging the facts. Then he asked me did I think I could control all the information, all the time, for all the people, forever?

"What should I do now? Keep on adding to the details and trying to build the story into something no one could penetrate? When I thought about that, it just felt exhausting. I wasn't sure I could remember every point, every … "

"Every lie?"

Toby looked up and stared at Nevada. "Yeah, I suppose that's what it was. You have to understand, Nevada, all my life I've been a direct kind of guy. Blunt, you might call it. I answer questions, I say what's on my mind, and I get to the point fast. I wanted to have a career and build a mega-business in a hurry. On steroids, you know? And I did that. Took as much advice as I could get, copied every leader, studied every word I could find.

"So, when I sat down to work on this autobiography with Jasper, it was just agony to have to pick my way through minefields like this. Thinking twice, three times … even more!

About how I was going to phrase something. What would be clear enough to defer any further questions but not so clear that the whole truth was out there."

"Were there a lot of 'events', as you call them, in your past, like the story of your Uncle Tobias?"

"Not really. That was the main one. But it was huge. It was an enormous secret, with so many consequences for unsealing it. But the thing was ... who owns it? Whose secret was it? Who owned it? Uncle Tobias? Did he need to face up to it and do the right thing, by coming forward and facing the penalties? The rest of the family, because every one of us would be affected by this news going public?"He stared at Nevada for such a long time that she felt that they weren't rhetorical questions, and she was supposed to answer them. But she had no answers. This was Toby's life and Toby's family, not hers.

"I decided, at the time, that it was Uncle Tobias's secret, not mine. It was about twenty years ago. I met with him ... he knows I know, and that Royce, and some of the cousins in the next generation, know. But I told him then, that it was up to him to do the right thing, and then I shut the door on it, in my mind. I got even busier, buying companies, investing in inventions, doing what I do.

"But it caught up with me eventually. I've felt for years that I need to redeem myself for agreeing to keep this horrendous secret and for agreeing to protect Tobias from judgement."

Nevada finally succeeded in attracting the server's attention and getting a drink ordered. She really needed it. "So, you saw writing the autobiography, and revealing your family's secret there, as a way of compensating for the way you hid it for so many years?"

Toby nodded. "I thought it would be liberating ... and Jasper thought so, too."

"Was Jasper in favor of you switching from Fraser Greene to Mondarix Press as your publisher?" Nevada had so many questions, and since Toby's desire to confess about his role in hiding his uncle's secret seemed to have made him ready to communicate, she wanted to take advantage.

"Yeah, we were both Mondarix Press fans there for a while," Toby said. "Although, that was mostly about being non-Fraser Greene fans."

"But why?"

"You'll have to ask Crawford Burr about that."

Nevada had to let several moments pass while she let that sink it. "But why?" Repeating the question might work.

Toby bent, a little. "Let's just say he displayed some opinions that neither of us had time for."

"Another question, Toby. If I may. Why would an author of Jasper's stature take on a ghost-writing assignment?"

"Money," Toby said. "Every task has a top price, for everybody. A fee that can't be rejected, no matter how much you don't want to take on the task. I found Jasper's, offered it to him, and he took it. Held his nose and tried to pretend he wasn't doing it, but he took it. Actually, though, I think once we got into the work, and he forgot from time to time that he was a hired flack, he was committed to the story. I think that's partly why he was pushing me to go one hundred percent into revealing the Encell family history. It made a terrific climax for the story."

Nevada nodded slowly. "That sounds like Jasper. He was a magician with a story. So, Toby, do you think there's a connection between this last project of his, your autobiography, and his death?"

Toby screwed his face up into an unmistakable expression of dismissal. "Not at all. I think it's completely a coincidence. I think it's a great tragedy that Jasper died and I hope the police find whoever did it, and why. I've offered to do whatever I can to assist them, if they ask it. But I don't think his work on my book had anything to do with it.

I hope nobody interprets the pause on the book as me being intimidated by Jasper's killing, because it wasn't."

Nevada couldn't hide her surprise. "Excuse me? The pause on the book?"

"That's a big part of the reason I wanted to speak with you today," Toby said. "I've decided not to finish the book. At least, not now. Maybe not ever."

"May I ask why? Were you disappointed with the support you were getting at Mondarix Press?"

He shook his head. "Nothing to do with that. Royce came to see me last night. Asked me to stop working on the book. Again. And I looked into his face, that face I've known since he was five minutes old, and I just couldn't keep on saying no. Even though I think Tobias is an old crook. A man who deserves to be exposed and to pay for his crimes. Even if they were committed seventy-five years ago. And even though it would soothe my soul to have some of these truths finally out into the world."

He waved his glass toward the bar and they sat in silence for a few minutes until the server arrived with a fresh Scotch. "I couldn't continue hurting Royce, Nevada. He's my son, what can I say? When you love somebody and they ask you for something, you give it, don't you?"

"Maybe not when it has to do with crime," Nevada said. "War crimes."

"The old man is over ninety." Toby seemed to withdraw into his own thoughts and his voice became softer. "Who knows what torture, what guilt he's lived with all this time?"

"Nowhere near the torture he inflicted on others, and their families, during the War," Nevada said. "I don't buy it, Toby."

His voice dropped even lower. "Whether or not you have sympathy for Tobias, Nevada, I'm telling you that this secret is going to rest. I won't be publishing my autobiography."

"Not at all? You're not thinking of doing it, but leaving out the part about Tobias?"

Toby shook his head. "I'll either write and publish the whole truth or I won't publish," he said. "The secret remains. And for that reason, I want you to confirm that you will not pass it along to anyone either." His voice was now so low, she almost felt a shiver. "I require your agreement on that. You must promise to keep all this confidential."

Or what?

CHAPTER 25

Nevada noticed almost nothing that was going on around her as she walked back from the diner to the convention center. Crowds of people filled the sidewalk, as they did all day every day, but at this hour on a Friday afternoon there was a different buzz: done work for the week, feeling the sunshine on a beautiful June day, heading into a weekend of freedom.

Her phone pinged with an incoming email, and she pulled it out to check it. So much had been going on this week and she felt she had to be on call every minute. Owen often talked about how little control he had of his time, especially when he was on call at the hospital, and about how Nevada's job didn't have that pressure. This week, it did.

Lillian's email was brief.

> *How are things going?*
>
> *Good. You?*
>
> *It's very quiet here on Alamos. Season is over and the rainy, humid season is here. I've been thinking about you in New York and your friend dying. Chelan and I have been talking, and we thought*

we'd get together for a group brainstorm. Is this a good time? I thought you might have more freedom to email than talk.

This is perfect. Too many people are around to talk freely. Yes, bring Chelan in, too.

Ok, here we go. Hi Chelan, we've got Nevada copied in.

Hey everyone. How's Book Fair going, Nevada?

It's been challenging, staying focused … especially with all the side stuff going on.

And losing Jasper, I imagine. Any developments?

The police are on it, of course. The detective is keeping me informed … I think. I don't know how much more there is to know that he's not telling me, but the latest thing he dropped was the fact that they've found a woman's scarf at the scene that doesn't belong to Jasper's wife.

Lillian:Okay, that narrows the field.

Chelan:It blows Sable Ogilvie's alibi out of the water—and makes me suspicious about her agent, Ryley Fedor. It moves Josselyn

Madden into the spotlight, with her anger about Jasper the alleged story thief.

Lillian: And we have Nina Theale, the avid fan that Fiona the wife thinks is a stalker.

Nevada smiled. She could always count on these two.

Nevada:Wow. Have you two been keeping notes all week?

Chelan's email reply was almost instant.

Spreadsheet. You've got a lot of people over there.

Nevada:I don't think we should be quite so quick to shift gears just because the police say the woman's scarf is the only physical evidence.

Chelan:No fingerprints at the scene? No conclusions from the blood spatters? No fabric fibers or hairs?

Nevada:No, and no footprints or tire tracks. 3D laser scanning hasn't helped either, as far as I've heard from Detective Travers.

Lillian:I agree with Nevada about the scarf. Any man might wear a woman's scarf. What is a 'woman's scarf', anyway?

Nevada: I think this one is one of those silk square numbers that Grandma's in the eastern European countries wear. I haven't seen it though, so I don't know for sure.

Chelan:Let's put all the men back on this unofficial suspect list. Jasper Inniskillen had quite a few people in his life with the motivation to want him gone.

Lillian:But not everyone with motivation and opportunity has the personality to be a killer. There are better ways to achieve whatever goal it is you think you have.

Nevada:True.

Lillian:So, Nevada, which of the people on this list are potential killers?

Nevada:I really have no idea. Maybe none of them. Or maybe any of them. I don't know any of them well enough to know.

Chelan:Then, I think to be safe, you need to go forward as if any one of them might be.

Nevada:If I had to pick one to be most careful of, it would be Michael Diotte, Jasper's disappointed protégé. The wall shooter in our office on Tuesday.

Lillian:Good choice.

Chelan:But just generally, Nevada, watch your back.

As she signed off, Nevada took a moment to appreciate their concern. Neither one jumped at the sight of their own shadow, but each had a sensible level of caution and she took their advice seriously. Toby's threatening tone earlier this afternoon had startled her. Michael Diotte wasn't someone she'd trust, and she couldn't decide whether she thought Sable was dangerous or just mean.

She was about to close her laptop when she saw an email from Detective Travers.

Update. Surveillance team on Michael D. followed him to lunch with Encell's son.

Michael Diotte and Royce? But she'd been told the Diotte branch of the family was estranged from the Encell side. Out of touch, anyway. Had they just connected because of all the police attention and the news about Jasper and Toby's relationship?

Or had the information about the cousins being distant and disconnected been false all along?

CHAPTER 26

Nevada arrived back at the Fraser Greene booth just in time to see Dane Saunders and a few of his marketing staff appear with trolleys and boxes.

"Just half an hour till we pack up," he said.

"I'll be here to be an extra pair of hands," Nevada said. Owen was out of town, in Key West, and she didn't relish the thought of going back to her car to drive home to an empty house. "What's the summary page on how we did?"

"At the entire Book Fair?" Dane asked. "No way to tell, at this point. There seemed to be a lot of traffic here at the booth. All the advance copies went."

"For everybody?"

"Yeah, the librarians and the booksellers seemed very interested in the new ones we offered. And for Jasper's older books, if you can believe it. Some people seemed to think we'd have stacks from his backlist after the news on Wednesday. I told them to contact the distributor, make an order in the usual way."

"That's nice, that there was a lot of interest in mine." Nevada turned to see Cori standing next to Dane at the booth table. "Nevada, do you have a minute to talk?"

"Of course, Cori. Excuse me, Dane. Let's just go over here, okay?" Nevada guided Cori over to a spot out of the sightlines of both the last-minute browsers and the Fraser Greene staff. "What's up?"

"It's about Josselyn. First, let me say, though, thank you for coming to my presentation. You've been just great all week, supporting me and my book. I can only imagine what it must be like, in the midst of the news about Jasper's death and what you went through at your office at the beginning of the week."

"Well, thank you, Cori. It's nice to be appreciated."

"I wondered if you'd seen this." She opened her laptop. The screen showed a website anchored by images of stacks of books and an author photograph of a young woman with large black-framed glasses. Josselyn Madden.

"No, I haven't," Nevada said. "What of it?"

"It's Josselyn's blog I want you to look at," Cori said. "it's about Jasper. She posted it today. And it's linked to another she did a couple of years ago, praising him."

Nevada was disinclined to look at anything Josselyn had written, but she had no quarrel with Cori. "Alright, let me see it."

The blog was a eulogy for Jasper. The language was some of the most complimentary and heartfelt that Nevada had ever read. Josselyn described their meeting, the help Jasper had given her, and the admiration she had for his work. After about a thousand words, in the final two paragraphs, Josselyn dealt with the plagiarism suit, telling her readers and fans that they probably would hear that she was suing Jasper in a dispute over intellectual property. She wrote that it was 'just business' and hinted that she didn't think the courts were the best place to handle their disagreement.

Cori was scrutinizing Nevada's face as she read. "Well?"

"Well, what?"

"What do you think?"

"Of this blog post?" Nevada shrugged. "I'm happy to see any warm, admiring comments about Jasper … and I have a feeling we'll hear a lot in the next few days."

"I read in the news that there's a celebration of life for him on Sunday."

Nevada looked down at the computer screen and reread some of Josselyn's words. "I'm sure it will be packed. But Cori, I don't think Josselyn's blog post changes anything. As she said herself, there's a dividing line between her feelings and 'business'.

Cori put down the laptop and closed the screen. "What will it take for you to change your opinion of her?""You're a good friend, Cori, I have to say. If Josselyn sent you here to ask that, tell her she has to drop the suit. Leave Fraser Greene … and Fiona Inniskillen … alone. Call off the lawyers, or get her father or her business partners or whoever it is that she says is pressuring her into this to drop the suit."

"But what if it's the truth? What if Jasper did copy her novel and present it as his own?"

Nevada shook her head. "I just don't believe that, Cori, and I'd have to see proof before I did. To a lot of people in the world, all it takes is an allegation. What's that old saying? Where there's smoke, there's fire. That's not enough for me. An allegation is nothing more than that. Where there's smoke, there's smoke. That's all. And sometimes the smoke is artificially pumped around, on purpose, to blot out the truth."

Cori stared at her thoughtfully. "Alright. I believe you. And I know enough about Josselyn's situation to be wary about the advice she's getting."

"What do you mean?"

"I can't say more. But I think you get the picture—it's not cut-and-dried. Lots of moving parts, behind the scenes."

"Do you have a lot of influence with Josselyn, too?" Nevada asked.

"I do," Cori said. "She's a lovely woman, but she is easily swayed. At school, we used to tease her about believing whatever she'd heard most recently and we'd play games with her to prove it.""Do you think you can get her to drop the lawsuit? And to stop smearing Jasper's reputation?"

"I think she's already on track with that last bit," Cori said. "You saw her blog post. I'm having dinner with her tonight and we'll see what happens after that."

***

The Book Fair doors closed at five, and by six, in between counting books and tossing bookmarks and other swag into boxes, Nevada picked up her phone twelve times to look for a text or voice mail from Owen. It was Friday night, after all, and they'd barely spoken all week. He was a long way away, in Key West, but he could call or text from there, couldn't he?

But there was nothing.

That wasn't completely true. Nothing from Owen, but Daniel Pyne had texted to ask whether she was going to attend Jasper's service on Sunday.

Of course.

Nevada sank into one of the folding metal chairs. Time to take a break. She didn't understand it, but a strong feeling of fatigue suddenly overtook her. She was not a person who often felt overwhelmed, but this week seemed to have tested her to the limit of her perseverance.

She had no suspects, and she had too many. If the woman's scarf even *was* a woman's scarf, she had Josselyn Madden and Sable Ogilvie, with their plagiarism and rivalry reasons. And there was Olivia Theale, the so-called stalker. For that matter, she didn't want to discount Fiona Inniskillen and the financial worries.

If the woman's scarf wasn't relevant, she had Michael Diotte, who'd shown himself capable of violence; Royce Encell, who wanted the Encell family secret kept; and Toby Encell, who had switched horses.

Dozens of publishing company staffers hurried past the booth, carrying posters, book boxes, and various bits and pieces from their exhibits. To Nevada, they blurred into one shapeless mass, surging back and forth like an ocean in a hurricane. Her gaze went out of focus as she tried to organize her thoughts about Jasper's murder: Josselyn. Sable. Olivia. Michael. Toby. Royce. The Encell family secret.

And what about me? Now that I know about uncle Tobias, what is my responsibility? Is it right or is it wrong to pretend I don't know?

Then there was Brady Roth, the neighbor who had clashed with Jasper over a property line? She hadn't met him yet or had an opportunity to size him up. She also had a few others to consider who had voiced their animosity just in the past few days toward Jasper: Krystof Dykstra, the marketing VP at Mondarix Press who complained so venomously about Jasper's lack of cooperation in pushing his books; Charles Delaney, the publisher emeritus who described Jasper as unreliable, stingy, and undeserving of respect or reward. What about someone completely unlikely, someone who seemed to care about Jasper but would turn out to have a resentment running deep enough that it could lead to death?

Someone like Daniel Pyne?

Nevada looked up to see a man standing in front of her, and her vision cleared. It *was* Daniel.

"Nevada. Hey." He looked exhausted. About ten years older than the last time she'd seen him. "Just about done with Book Fair for this year?"

"We are. How about you? Did you get everything you needed this week?"

"Met some new authors, heard some interesting presentations, yeah. Mostly reinforced my decision to leave traditional and get into indie," he said. "I've only had half my mind on it though, because of Jasper."

"Me, too," Nevada said. *Could it be Daniel? But what motive could he possibly have?*

"When I was at his place Monday, he talked about his plans for the rest of the year. He was really enthusiastic about finishing a novel that he could produce and market himself," Daniel said.

"Did he talk about his ghost-writing side-gig at all?"

"Not to me." Daniel squeezed out half a smile, and Nevada noticed, again, the weariness in his eyes. Weariness and wariness. Was he suppressing some secret, too?

"Are you okay, Daniel? You seem ... I don't know. Tired? Concerned about something?"

Daniel's chuckle sounded hollow. "No, not particularly. I might be coming down with something. Flu bug or something. I have been feeling a little off ... maybe a virus, addition to all the commotion around Book Fair. And ... I just can't get over Jasper being gone."

Doth protest too much?

But almost the instant she had the thought, Nevada felt ashamed of herself. Was she going to suspect every single person who had ever been one of Jasper's friends? Was she turning into some kind of perennially suspicious, mistrustful, cynical bystander?

Have I always been that?

The question was so disturbing that she had to put it into the back of her mind, behind the suspects list.

Daniel had gone off into his own thoughts, too, and after a few seconds, each realized they had no conversational energy left. He nodded to her and wandered off toward the exit, while Nevada stood up to look around the booth and see what else needed doing.

She caught sight of the Fraser Greene intern standing near the back of the booth. Hannah bent over a chair, then reached a hand out to a table to steady herself. She stared at the floor as if she'd never seen one before.

Nevada was over to her in three long strides. "Hannah! What's wrong?"Hannah said nothing, just pointed in the direction of the floor, where a gun lay just beside a stack of unbound galleys.

An uneasy gurgle of fear and nausea followed the first icy wave that hit Nevada. She breathed deeply twice, then pitched herself into action. "Don't touch it! Call 9-11 and tell them we need the police immediately. And Detective Travers from Midtown Precinct South, if possible."

"I can't call anybody!" Hannah whispered. "Not right now."

Geez! Come on, Hannah. Get a grip! But Nevada's frustration passed almost instantly. If Hannah just couldn't handle this, that's just the way it was.

"Alright. I'll call. Don't touch anything and don't let anybody else touch anything."

"There's a note." Hannah whispered.

"A note! Where?"

"Here. On the seat of the chair."

Nevada saw a cardboard folder covered in words. All caps. Black marker.

THE SECRET BELONGS TO ME. BACK OFF

The call to 9-11 was answered instantly. Nevada tried to be clear about how urgent speed was, although she had little hope that they'd catch whoever had left the note and the gun. The convention center was full of people scurrying back and forth, and it would have been so easy for the person to blend in. They also did not know how long the gun and the note had been there. It could have been hours, Detective Travers said later.

"I think it's unlikely a gun would have gone unnoticed for hours, even if people in the booth were concentrating on their work," Nevada said.

Travers shrugged. "We'll talk to everyone who was here today. But please keep your antennae up and ask anyone you can whether they saw any strangers hanging around."

"Will do. Anything else?" Travers hesitated, then shook his head. As he walked off to speak with Crawford, Nevada wondered about the hesitation. What wasn't he telling her?

Or had her paranoia grown into full-fledged incoherence?

Bernadette sat in one of the corner chairs, staring off into space.

"What is it, Bernadette?" Nevada asked.

Bernadette wrapped her arms around herself, and almost imperceptibly, rocked back and forth. "She's telling me to shut up."

"Who's telling you? What are you talking about?"

"The note. Did you see the note?"

"Yes, I saw the note. Bernadette, I don't think it had anything to do with you. Why do you think it does?" Bernadette stopped her rocking and looked Nevada in the eyes. "Never mind. Forget I said that."

"Gladly." *Does Bernadette go through life believe that absolutely everything that ever happened had to do with her, directly? What secrets was she talking about?* But almost the instant she let her impatience with Bernadette surface, Nevada pushed it down and tried to replace it with compassion. Clearly, Bernadette had some sort of secret and someone she feared was insisting she protect it.

Across the aisle, she saw Cori Lowe hurrying toward the convention center exit. Josselyn Madden was beside her, and the two seemed intent on passing by without stopping to speak to anyone. Nevada saw Cori nod at a few people, but she didn't stop.

"I have nothing more to say! Not to the police and not to anyone!" Crawford Burr's voice cut through the buzz around the booth and perhaps through the action of this entire section of the convention center. What was this now? Did Crawford have some sort of secret he had to insist on preserving, too? Was he shouting at Detective Travers to make sure that his intention was heard by anyone lurking nearby who might be a threat?

How many people in and around the Fraser Greene booth had a secret? How many of those secrets had more than one participant, and how many of those thought they had the sole right to decide whether to suppress it or uncover it?

Nevada permitted herself a small smile at her next thought: if the note-writer was truly a threat, and anyone needed to feel fear about the order to "back off", why had he or she left the gun on the floor? Shouldn't they be more fearful if the gun was still in the note-writer's possession?

But … maybe there was more than one gun.

She'd read many thousands of news reports of shootings. There was often more than one gun.

CHAPTER 27

The aisles of the exhibit halls at the convention center were even more crowded than they'd been all week. Nevada wouldn't have thought that was possible, but Book Fest this year had caught the NYC imagination and people had been lining up for an hour before opening time.

It was one day just for the readers. Nevada stopped just inside the entry doors to admire the giant posters screaming *Book Fest!* It was a child of the Comic Con phenomenon, where fans, readers, movie-watchers, and collectors gathered to enjoy their communal love for the products of many imaginations. It seemed to her like a giant shopping mall given over only to books. She had loved bookstores throughout her years as a journalist and her travels as the child of a movie star. This Book Fest was like a bookstore that went on for miles.

"It's inspiring, isn't it?" Daniel Pyne stood beside a booth that appeared to be half the size of a Macy's floor. The name of one of the largest chain bookstores in the country was emblazoned on a banner that ran the length of the booth. Posters promoting some of the top books and authors of the year added to the visual explosion.

"Inspiring? In what way?"

"Indie authors and publishers are always hearing how hard it is to find readers. That nobody reads books anymore. But look at them all!" Daniel waved an arm enthusiastically across the fan landscape. He'd come dressed in shorts and a Hawaiian shirt. Maybe going to a New York convention felt to him like being on vacation.

"Not just indie publishers. Traditional, too," Nevada said. "It is thrilling to see so many avid readers all in one place."

"Are you here for a while? Do you want to grab a coffee?" Daniel asked.

"I'm just here to take a quick look, then I'm heading off for an appointment. Sorry."

Nevada's other destination that morning required her car. Jasper and Fiona's home was an hour's drive from Manhattan, and she had no appetite for a train ride. She decided to do one loop around the exhibit hall, hope to cross paths with Crawford or Bernadette or anybody senior from Fraser Greene, and then take off for Oyster Bay Cove.

A pack of teenage girls, in skater skirts, ripped jeans, and green hair, jostled past her as she strolled near a booth set up by one of the publishers that had decided to have a presence at the reader show in addition to Book Fair. Each one carried a canvas bag, ready to collect all the swag and free books they could find. Nevada grinned at them as they swept past. She'd been young herself, once upon a time.

Nevada headed for a quiet spot behind one of the aisles in a far corner of the floor. She tapped in Detective Travers's number.

"Nevada. I suppose you're calling to check about the gun found on the floor of your booth. No prints. No bullets."

"Thanks, Detective. Any other guns?"

"No, just the one. No leads on it so far, but we're not done checking."

"What about the woman's scarf found at the scene? Anything else turn up?"

"Nothing. And nothing more about the scarf."

"You know, we really can't decide it was a woman who shot him just because that seemed to be a woman's scarf. Anyone could wear it, and it might have been left intentionally, anyway."

"Yeah, that occurred to everybody here, too. No conclusions drawn. And you know it's only been a few days. We're just getting started on the investigation. These things can take weeks. Months."

"Or years sometimes, although that's when they make the headlines," Nevada said.

"Will you be at Jasper Inniskillen's funeral tomorrow?" Travers asked.

"Yes, of course. Will the police be there?"

"We'll be very discreet. But yes. Keep your eyes open, yeah? Let me know if there's anything I should notice. Anybody there who shouldn't be, anybody missing. That kind of thing."

After agreeing to make contact following the service, Nevada checked her watch. She had just under an hour to get to Oyster Bay Cove to meet with Fiona, and if there was the least bit of traffic, she'd be late.

The June sunshine bathed even the dirty sidewalks in a sort of golden shimmer. Late spring and Christmas were the two seasons when New York City was at its finest, in Nevada's opinion. She joined the traffic flow out of the city and headed east toward Nassau County.

Jasper's home was located in one of the priciest neighborhoods in the state. Nevada had been there many times. Her father's friendship with Charles Delaney had generated many invitations to Charles's home when she was young, and during those visits, she'd come to know Oyster Bay, Cove Neck, and Farmingdale very well. The houses were mansions and the backyards were better described as grounds; the average income was one of the highest in the country.

Rolling along the driveway toward Jasper's front door, she took a moment to appreciate the line of sugar maples pointing the way to the house. Fiona's front door now, she supposed. A knife of grief sliced through her heart when she realized, once again, that Jasper was gone.

Jasper's house was not the grand, colonial-style historic manor that Charles had chosen. His was a relatively new, stridently modern one-story construction that extended many thousands of feet to the east and the west—the sort of building you couldn't begin to comprehend until you saw it from above. Nevada's phone buzzed and she let the car slow to a stop while she glanced at the call display. Owen! She put it into park, then picked up the phone.

Just a text, not the call she was hoping for. Ten words. *Key West is great. Hope all is well with you.*

She thought of phoning him right back. She needed more than ten words. But obviously, he didn't, since he was the one who'd chosen to send a text. And there was still something in the vibe, something that was off. She knew she wanted to deal with it. Sometime. But not now. Fiona was waiting, and she was already ten minutes late.

Fiona's housekeeper let her in and led her to the library to wait. After another ten minutes went by, Nevada was wishing she had stopped to make a phone call to Owen. Where was he in Key West and what was he doing? Why had he gone away this weekend? And why hadn't he asked her to go?

Nevada wandered along Jasper's bookshelves, looking at his immense collection. This really was an amazing room. His awards held places of honor on some of the shelves; his magazine covers were framed and filled any wall space not overlaid with the book collection. Jasper's desk commanded the center of the room, with an expansive view through the bay window that led to a fenced meadow to the east. On previous occasions, Nevada had seen the desk piled high with pages, file folders, and open books. Jasper used a computer, but he also liked to see the tangible evidence of his work.

Today, the desk's surface was completely bare, except for a set of bookends that held nothing between them. Obviously, someone had been in to clean since the tragedy. No doubt, the police had examined, labeled, and filed many items. Perhaps Fiona had had her own hours in this room with Jasper's things and her memories. Today, it looked more like a museum exhibit than a working space for an active, eager mind.

The door opened behind Nevada. "Nevada, hello. Thank you for coming out to see me." Fiona still looked exhausted and stricken. Despite the information from the police about the insurance payout that would solve Fiona's financial problems, and despite the many times she'd covered stories where it was the spouse who most wanted the dead person's departure, Nevada had great difficulty in imagining Fiona as Jasper's killer. As *anybody's* killer.

But how many times had she heard a reporter say, "Well, I didn't expect that!" How many times had she said it herself, for that matter?

"I'm sorry I wasn't here when you arrived, but Brady Roth came by and I wanted to ask him to stay to meet you," Fiona said. "And to thank him for the flowers and sympathy note he and his wife sent yesterday."

Where the library was a place of thought, the living room was one of sight and sound. A baby grand piano graced the far corner, near the floor-to-ceiling windows. A television screen dominated one entire wall, while soft, instrumental music flowed from speakers concealed somewhere in the room.

Where the library said "England", with its dark green and walnut color scheme, the living room was all Sweden.

A short man in cargo shorts and a Giants T-shirt stood by the windows, looking out at a pair of white-tailed deer grazing in the field.

"Nevada, this is Brady Roth," Fiona said.

Nevada stepped forward, hand outstretched. "Hello, Mr. Roth. Thank you for agreeing to meet me."

"No problem," he said. "Fiona told me you know about my differences with Jasper over the past year."

Fiona stepped forward. "Brady and I have talked that all out, and the problem is solved. It was just a misunderstanding."

"Is that why you wanted to come over, Mr. Roth?" Nevada asked.

"Please. Call me Brady. Yes, that was the main reason. But there is one other." The man looked uncomfortable. "There's something I want to tell you. I don't have any idea how to handle it, Fiona, or how you want it handled, and I don't want to make anything more difficult for you than it is already. You mentioned you trust Nevada, and that she has a lot of experience with news, and crime things—"

"News, yes, but I'm not a police officer or former detective or anything like that," Nevada interjected.

"I understand. But I thought I could start here and give you this, and you can guide Fiona on what to do next. We've just resolved our differences over the property line, and I want to be a good neighbor now."

"What is it, Brady?" Fiona asked.

"The police came and talked to me on Wednesday. I told them I'd seen someone near your gate on Tuesday afternoon. You knew that?"

Both Fiona and Nevada nodded.

Brady looked around as though he'd like to be invited to sit down. "I was in and out a lot on Tuesday. Doing some pruning on the bushes near the front door. I like to do some gardening, even though we have the regular guys coming every second week." He looked at Nevada. "I have a sightline that goes right from my front yard to Jasper's. It was something that always bugged him and he wanted me to plant a hedge or a row of trees for privacy. There wasn't room on his side of the line … and he didn't want to spend the money to do it, anyway. But there was room on my side, and he thought I should do it. But I didn't want to spend the money, either. And it didn't bug me the way it did him."

He looked upset, and Nevada realized he was hurting from the unfinished business between him and Jasper. "It's okay, Brady. Neighbors often have differences of opinion … even those who have a lot of space and land between them. Jasper wanted one thing, you wanted another. You probably never would have changed your mind, either of you, no matter how long he lived or how many more conversations you had."

Brady looked at her gratefully. "I hope you're right. I keep thinking, 'why did I get so dug in on such a minor issue?' And now, it's too late to fix it."

"It doesn't matter now," Nevada said. "And Jasper, wherever he is, he understands."

"You think?""I do."

"I do, too, Brady," Fiona said.

"Now what was it you want to tell the police about that day?" Nevada asked. "You said you were around your front door, you could see Jasper's drive, and you saw somebody. Was it a woman?""It was," Brady said.

"The police have what they think is a woman's scarf that they picked up at the scene," Nevada said. "It's not one of yours, I assume, Fiona."

"They asked me about it almost right away," Fiona said. "It's not."

"The thing is," Brady continued," there was more than one person. Two people. A man and a woman."

"But you told the police only one person. And you didn't say it was a woman."

"I was flustered when they first talked to me. Upset, hearing about Jasper. And that detective, he asked the questions so fast, and he seemed to know what he thought, so I just confirmed what he said. But I've been thinking about it for nearly four days and I think I have to talk to him again and spell out exactly what I saw."

"I agree, Brady," Fiona said. "Anything that might help identify who did this to Jasper."

"That's what I thought, too, but I wanted to talk with you before I called the police. I didn't want you to hear it from them."

"Thank you. And yes, call them."

Nevada and Fiona escorted Brady to the front door, and as Fiona opened it, Daniel Pyne stepped forward with a smile.

"Good morning!"

Fiona did not seem the least bit surprised. "Daniel, hi. Welcome. The coffee is on. I'll get you a cup and we can have it on the terrace." She turned to her neighbor. "Brady, thank you again for your thoughtfulness. I hope the police will do something with the information you're providing."

Daniel nodded toward Brady and reached out a hand. "Daniel Pyne."

Brady looked slightly confused but took and shook it. "Brady Roth. Thanks again, Fiona."

Nevada watched him go as he headed down the impressive stone steps leading to the circular driveway. She had to admit she was a bit confused, too. What was Daniel doing here and why did he and Fiona seem so comfortable with one another? The last Nevada heard, Fiona was kept in the dark about the trip Jasper and Daniel had made together to the independent authors' conference. Now she was smiling warmly at him. And was that his hand placed in the small of her back as they turned back toward the foyer?

"Nevada, I'm sure you're eager to get back into town for the rest of Book Fest," Fiona said. "Thank you for coming out to see me and for meeting Brady Roth."

"I'll be at the service tomorrow," Nevada said.

"We'll see you then," Daniel said as he turned to follow Fiona toward the kitchen.

We?

CHAPTER 28

iona wasn't quite right about Nevada's eagerness to get back to Manhattan for Book Fest. Since she was already out here, she decided to spend half an hour driving around Oyster Bay Cove, trying to pick up something in the air … a vibe, a feeling … that might help. Jasper had moved far out into the countryside to find peace and quiet: a village, tiny roads, wealthy neighbors who wanted the same protection and privacy he did. How could a murderer find his way in here?

Nevada's phone, lying on the passenger seat, buzzed. *Owen?* She grabbed for it. Not supposed to take calls or texts while driving but she hadn't seen another vehicle in ten minutes. It felt safe.

Toby Encell.

She pulled over to the roadside and started the call.

"Hi Toby. Nice to hear from you."

"I just have a couple of minutes, but I wanted to follow up on our last meeting."

Businesslike, as always, even about something as emotional and personal as a book about his family connection to the Nazis.

"The timing wasn't what I would have wanted," Toby said. "I didn't realize, when I let you see the pages Jasper and I wrote so far, that we would go in a different direction and that there would be no autobiography published."

"Yes, I've been curious about that," she said. "How did Mondarix Press take that news?"

"Don't know, don't care," Toby said. "It's with the lawyers. I'm just calling to make sure that you understand that we are done with that book and I expect you to maintain confidentiality about the information you were given."

"Why did you decide to back away from publication, really, Toby? Was it only because of Royce's request?"

"It's an intricate situation. Some other family difficulties you know nothing about, but trust me, there is good reason to put this all behind us," he said. "I don't really need an autobiography, anyway. People know me. The world knows me. It was just an ego thing and it's best I leave it behind."

Nevada said nothing, as she tried to absorb this. His words or someone else's?"

"Nevada? Are we cool? Can I rely on you to close the door on this, too? What shall we say … it's all off the record?"

"Usually, off the record is a deal you make with a journalist before you start talking or writing," Nevada said. "But, yes. I understand what you're asking, Toby, and yes, I will continue to keep it to myself. It's your secret to tell, if you want to tell it."

"Good."

Toby ended the call quickly. As Nevada pulled back onto the road, she wondered how the conversation might have gone if she'd refused to cooperate. She also wondered what Toby would do now, to deal with his guilt over concealing his uncle's past.

The main street of the village looked like something from another era. Small shops and wide sidewalks invited passersby to move slowly and let the day unfold. Nevada spotted a coffee shop and decided to stop. She needed a little time to herself, to collect her thoughts.

A tiny bell above the door rang when she walked in and a friendly server waved to her from behind the counter. "Sit anywhere you like," she called.

The shop had a bench with bar stool chairs in the front window, facing the street. Nevada usually didn't like the high chairs much but today she wanted to watch some of the pedestrian traffic go by. She also liked the fact that no one else was sitting anywhere near the window counter.

As she sat taking a few deep breaths and tried to get her mind to settle down and focus on all the information she'd encountered this morning, Nevada saw an elderly man walking past with a cane, assisted by a woman with long, white hair.

Nevada slid down from the chair and rushed to the café door. "Charles!"

He looked puzzled at first, then smiled when he recognized her. "Nevada Leacock. Well. Of all the gin joints in all the world..."

She smiled back. A reference you had to be older to get. "I'm out here in your part of the world to see Fiona Inniskillen. Just taking a break before I head back into town. You used to live near here, I remember."

"Still do. Same place. I come into the village most days to pick up a few things and get a coffee." Charles noticed Nevada glancing at the woman with him. "This is my friend, Olivia Theale. She has a house down the lane from mine."

"We've met," Nevada said. "At Book Fair, twice this week. Olivia told me she's quite a fan of Jasper's books."

Charles took a deep breath, then lifted his chin toward Nevada. The message was defiance. "Well, then, perhaps she also told you how badly he treated her."

"Badly?" This was so unexpected that Nevada could think of nothing more to do than repeat his word.

"Yes, badly. That's why I washed my hands of him over the past few months. After all these years, after everything I did for him while I was at Fraser Greene, he wouldn't agree to let me introduce her."

"It's alright, Charles." Nevada thought Olivia seemed uncomfortable with the conversation. "Jasper was a busy man and he just didn't have time for me or my organization."

"Very important cause," Charles said. "I'm not surprised you would devote so many years and so much effort to it. Not surprised, and very impressed. Jasper would have been, too, if he'd given you so much as five minutes of a hearing."

"I'm not so sure about that, Charles. Not everybody cares about animals the way you and I do." It sounded to Nevada as if it were a debate they'd had many times before.

"All I asked him for was five minutes. Even if he didn't want to support an animal rights' group and even if he was tired of meeting with his fans, he could have spared five minutes for me." Charles's face was flushed and Nevada thought the red color was looking a little dangerous.

"Stand down, Charles Delaney," Olivia said affectionately. "I haven't seen you this worked up since ... well, since yesterday, actually when Sofia told you about her friends at the social club."

"Well, it's outrageous that people like that can obtain a weapon so easily." It seemed Olivia knew just how to distract Charles.

"Sofia?" Nevada asked. "Who is that?"

"My housekeeper," Charles said. "She has this club she goes to and a lot of the others there are ... recent arrivals from central America."

"A lot of sad stories," Olivia said. "Many of them have escaped terrible conditions in their home countries. A lot of fear … with good reason. Maybe that's why they're interested in arming themselves."

"I don't really care about the reason," Charles said. "It's far too easy to get a gun in this country … and I just don't buy the self-defense argument."

"So, Sofia has a gun and you don't want her to have it?" Nevada asked.

"No, not Sofia. These friends of hers. The Rubios. Lina and Alejandro. I've met them both, once or twice. She brought the husband around when I needed some extra help for the gardening, and the wife when we had our annual Fourth of July party last year. She helped with the food and the clean-up. Saved me some money on the catering bill. Anyway, they've been here a long time, I think. Over a year. Why would they still think they needed a gun for protection? They're a long way away from whoever it was who attacked them in their home country. They're here now, and they don't need a gun here."

"Many people think you need a gun here," Nevada said. She tried to keep her tone mild; she didn't want Charles to get any more worked up.

He glared at her. "That's not the point."

Nevada was no longer sure what the point was.

"Anyway, I've told her I don't want her to bring them around anymore," Charles said. "She wanted to bring them in to say hello a few days ago. 'Say hello!' I don't need to *say hello* to those people."

"I'm sure she won't," Olivia said, soothingly. "Nevada, it was very nice to see you again. Charles, I'm going to have to get on my way. My daughter is coming over for lunch today. I cancelled her Tuesday when you took me into town to go to the Book Fair and I want to be on time for her today."

"I'll walk with you," Charles said.

Nevada watched as the two old people slowly made their way down the sidewalk. They might have some sort of beef with Jasper about his lack of support for their animal rights cause. Or perhaps Olivia was obsessed with Jasper, as simple as that. But somehow Nevada doubted that either of these two people had the energy to move from whatever complaint they had about Jasper Inniskillen to doing anything about it.

CHAPTER 29

Nevada got behind the wheel of her car and put it into gear. She had a lot to think about, during this drive back to the city. Instead of being dispirited, she was energized. She felt that the encounter with Charles and Olivia eliminated two more possibilities from the list of suspects. They were each other's alibi for Tuesday. Besides, she just couldn't see that either one had the strength or the capability to kill, no matter how emotional they might feel or how much they might hate.

She'd eliminated Brady Roth from her list, too. He didn't seem like the type who would explode into enough anger or nurture enough resentment over a property line dispute to kill a neighbor. And, he was showing an impressive amount of willingness to cooperate—coming forward with his information about seeing a man and a woman lurking around Jasper's home. He hadn't said anything about his activities Tuesday that might suggest an alibi, but he'd mentioned a video camera on his front door and if he was coming and going, a date and time stamp might prove he was at home.

Fiona? For insurance money? Again, she didn't seem like the type. Nevada briefly wondered about her and Daniel, then concluded she would find out soon enough whether they really did have an attraction and whether it would blossom into anything.

Josselyn? She … or someone in her crew … seemed to be after Jasper's money, not his life. But Nevada didn't discount the power of envy and ambition.

Sable? She was the mean girl, not the killer type. In addition, she had an alibi.

Michael Diotte? She didn't have a feeling about him, one way or the other.

Nevada wondered whether Detective Travers spent much time pondering how people 'seemed'. Her instinct was based on years of covering news and reading people; no doubt, he had met even more than she had and assessed even more personalities. Who, in the publishing crowd surrounding Jasper, did he think had the potential, or 'seemed' to be, the killer type?

The streets around the Convention Center were jammed with Saturday shopping and sightseeing traffic. Nevada found a lot for her car, then headed inside. Another couple of hours here, then she would escape for a Saturday evening. No Owen to enjoy it with, but she was sure she'd be able to get him on the phone. She was eager to hear what he'd been doing in Key West and when he was coming home.

The aisles of Book Fest were packed with eager readers, collecting bookmarks, T-shirts, posters, and autographs. You'd think, from the physical evidence at a convention like this, that reading was a booming sport and that all authors were taking truckloads to the bank. But Nevada knew that most of these excited readers were there to see their favorite author, not to meet a new one, and that two or three names accounted for ninety percent of the traffic.

Her phone buzzed. "Nevada? This is Detective Travers. You got a minute?"

"Yes, of course. Let me just look for a quiet spot."

"You're at work?"

"At Book Fest. You're obviously at work, "she said, as she dropped into a chair near a coffee kiosk.

"I want to ask you about your friend, Charles Delaney."

"Yes?"

"He rang me up today and started by introducing himself as connected to you. Then, he told me he was an old friend of Jasper Inniskillen, and a long-time New York City publisher."

"All true. Charles Delaney is one of the pillars of the book industry."

"So, we can believe anything he says?"

Nevada managed a bit of a laugh. "As much as we believe anybody. But I think we can say, he has a lot to lose by being untruthful."

"He told me he believes you suspect a friend of his of having something to do with Inniskillen's death. A woman named Olivia Theale."

Nevada considered her next words. "I wouldn't say I suspect her. I did, for a moment, when Fiona, Jasper's wife, mentioned she was an exceptionally avid fan. But now that I've met her, and heard Charles's endorsement, I'm not inclined to think she had anything to do with it."

"Alright. Well, we might get around to talking to her, but in the meantime, we have a few other avenues in the investigation to pursue. Mr. Delaney also mentioned his housekeeper, Sofia."

"Charles thinks his housekeeper killed Jasper?" Nevada felt as though a baseball had suddenly whizzed at her from left field.

"No, that's not it. He told me his housekeeper mentioned to him that she's met a couple at her social club, a Mr. and Mrs.

Rubio, who seemed unusually interested in Jasper. Asked a lot of questions about her employer's acquaintance with him."

"I've heard about them, too. But I haven't met them."

"I think we might initiate a conversation there," Travers said. "Different topic. Are you going to be at the memorial service tomorrow?"

"Yes," Nevada said. "Fiona has asked me to say a few words."

"Just you?"

"I doubt it. I think it will probably turn out to be quite an event." A thought struck Nevada. "Will you be there? Or any police?"

"I'm working with a detective in Nassau County and they'll have a presence there. I'll probably go along, too." They sat in silence for a few seconds, then Travers continued. "Please keep your eyes open. Killers often show up at the funerals of their victims. And somebody knows you've been nosing around."

"I think I'm just background sound in this whole piece," Nevada said.

"Nonetheless," Travers said. "Be careful."

"I will. But listen, Detective Travers, I have an idea. Since all these people are going to be there…"

CHAPTER 30

The crowd at Jasper's funeral would have been too much for almost any of the churches or cathedrals in town. But his property was more than equal to the challenge.

Attendance at the memorial service was by invitation only. Driving in, Nevada had been asked to show her identification and her name was checked off a list by a security guard at the gate. She'd passed lines of cars parked along the sides of the country lane, some of them with saucer-sized lenses propped against half-open windows. Apparently, there was a market somewhere for photos of people arriving for Jasper Inniskillen's funeral.

Men and women in black vests guided the traffic inside the gate. Nevada followed their directions toward a temporary parking lot that had been set up in a field not far from the house.

Next to it, folding chairs had been set up in rows that stretched almost all the way to the horizon. *Good thing we aren't trying to say goodbye to Jasper in February,* Nevada thought, as she took a program and followed the usher's direction to her seat.

She wished Owen was in town and available to come along with her to this service. Over the years, they'd attended funerals and weddings together, and it was always easier to walk in to these events in his company.

This time, it seemed particularly difficult—partly because of her distance from Owen and partly because of her grief over Jasper.

The program was about ten pages long, filled with photographs, details about Jasper's life, and references to his books, his homes, and his friends and colleagues. Nevada gazed at the photo that graced the front page. Someone had chosen to go with a current picture, rather than one of him in his youth. He was a handsome man, even in his older years. She thought she recognized the shot as one taken during the Brooklyn Book Festival last year and later adopted by Jasper as his favorite to use for any of his public appearances.

Nevada really wasn't that interested in the contents of the program, but staring at it gave her the few minutes she needed to collect her composure and find the strength she'd need to sit through the service. She was happy that Fiona hadn't followed up on her hint that she was going to ask Nevada to speak. She would have done it, if asked, of course, but it would have been tough. She would have felt a bit like an imposter, too. There were many others, much more central to Jasper's life, who would have been the better choice.

The first pair of eyes she saw when she looked up belonged to her boss, Crawford. He was seated in the second row and was turned halfway round in his chair to scan the crowd. He nodded at her and she responded by lifting one hand in a sort of wave.

Next to him was a woman she assumed was his wife. Then, Bernadette, Dane Saunders, and several other Fraser Greene staffers took up seats in the row. Throughout the gathering, Nevada saw many well-known faces from book, newspaper, magazine, and entertainment worlds.

Among those not well-known but certainly of interest to her, Nevada spotted Sable Ogilvie, Josselyn Madden, and Olivia Theale. She had made up her mind not to be surprised by anything or anyone she saw there today, so when she saw Toby Encell, sitting with his son, Royce, in the back row, she simply took note. Neither one of them acknowledged her.

She wasn't surprised or unsurprised, but she couldn't resist a few moments of speculation about Toby's motivation in being present. Simply to pay his respects? To try to ensure that he was still keeping a lid on the manuscript and his family's secrets? To speak to Fiona to try to find out something he felt he needed to know? To watch the other guests and determine whether any of them might pose a threat to his privacy in some way?

Nevada saw Toby's attention drawn toward a group standing at the end of a row midway up toward the front. Somehow, none looked like mourners and as Nevada inspected them more closely, she recognized Detective Travers. He saw her looking at him and raised a hand to beckon her.

Dropping her program on her chair to save her seat, Nevada made her way over to the police officers.

"Nevada, this is Detective Langford. He's with the Nassau County police."

She reached out to shake hands with a very tall man who was chewing gum. "Also investigating Jasper's death?"

He nodded, but didn't make eye contact as he continuously scanned the crowd.

She turned her attention back to Travers. "Are you going ahead with my idea?""It was already under discussion before you mentioned it," Travers said. "And yes, the K9 unit is here."

Nevada looked around the field but didn't see anything.

"The van is parked out of sight," Travers said. "We don't want to disrupt anything. We'll wait until the service is finished and then let the handler do his thing as calmly and inconspicuously as possible."

"You think the killer might be here?"

Travers shrugged. "We'll see. The dog will look for whoever's scent matches that scarf and if she's here, he'll find it."

"She or he," Nevada said.

"She or he."

"Then, what? If I may ask."

"Then, we'll ask some questions," Travers said.

A cellist began playing a somber piece and Nevada felt her head and shoulders droop. She nodded to Travers and the others then went back to her chair. The music continued for about five minutes and then Fiona and the rest of Jasper's family emerged from the house. They walked slowly, holding one another up as they proceeded to the empty row of chairs at the front of the assembly. A table holding an urn with Jasper's ashes and a large version of the photograph on the program faced them.

The ceremony was a brief ten minutes. Exactly what Nevada guessed Jasper would have wanted. The last words had just been spoken, the last hymn sung by the small choir, and a processional of Fiona, Jasper's family, and a young man carrying the urn begun on its way down the center aisle, when a rugged man wearing heavy clothing unusual for a June afternoon led a German Shepherd up the middle aisle between the chairs.

The dog sniffed the grass once or twice but most of its attention was focused on the people. Nose probing the air, it walked slowly past six of the rows. It stopped at the seventh, the one in front of Nevada, then turned toward the chairs.

The couple sitting on the aisle didn't wait for the dog to make its final selection. The man, a short dark-haired young man wearing a badly fitting black suit, jumped to his feet while pulling at the hand of the woman sitting next to him.

"Alejandro!" she hissed, yanking at his hand to try to bring him back down to the seat. She was twice his size and might have won out, in their tug-of-war if the fear of the dog hadn't given him extra strength … not to mention, motivation.

"Lina, get UP!" He jerked her to a standing position, and in a second, the canine investigator was at her skirt, inhaling her unique scent, then turning to its handler.

Nevada watched as Detective Travers stepped forward, a silky piece of cloth with a bright blue, red, and purple design. "Is this yours, ma'am?" he asked quietly.

Dark eyes snapping at him, she shook her head vehemently.

"Then you won't mind coming with us to answer a few questions," Travers said.

Her partner was mesmerized by the dog and didn't take his eyes off it as he stepped into the aisle. "We don't mind," he said. "Ask us anything."

The four of them walked out, leaving everyone else at a complete loss for words. Nevada caught sight of Daniel Pyne, even his usual cool, at-ease-in-any-situation demeanor ruffled, for once. Fiona leaned against Jasper's daughter, then they both turned back toward the front of the rows and headed toward the house. Nevada didn't blame them; she doubted she would have the strength to greet any visitors under these circumstances herself.

CHAPTER 31

Nevada got herself as far as the coffee shop in the village before she stopped the car and tried to get Travers on the phone. She felt he owed her, since the dog idea had been hers. Or, so she thought; maybe the police really had had the idea already in mind. Maybe it was standard, in cases like these. Regardless, she had mentioned it to Travers, and she wanted to know what the result had been.

She listened to the phone ring four times, then go to voicemail.

"Detective Travers? Nevada Leacock. Any news? Please call me back."

Her heart was pounding, and she felt she had to get out of the car or explode. She looked toward the seashore—a long walk on the beach was exactly what she needed to bring her stress level down.

When she reached the sand, Nevada saw that many other people had chosen this beautiful spring day to get outdoors. Hundreds of blankets and beach chairs dotted the shore. This made the fact that she heard someone call her name even more surprising.

"Nevada! Wait up!"

She turned to see Charles Delaney, still in his dark suit from Jasper's funeral, and Olivia Theale, clinging to his arm, coming toward her.

"Hello, Charles. Olivia. I hadn't expected to see you out here. Or anyone that I knew," Nevada said.

"We often come to the seashore on a Sunday afternoon," Charles said. "Although, not usually after a funeral."

"But sometimes we do," Olivia said. "Remember Darren Wales last March? And Samantha Corey in the fall? And—"

"What did you think of the service?" Nevada asked, to interrupt the recounting of all of their recent visits to the beach.

"I thought it was well-done," Charles said. "Dignified."

"Very sad," Olivia said. "His daughter and his wife were just barely holding it together, I think."

"Were you there until the end?" Charles asked.

Nevada nodded.

"Then you saw the police move in."

Did Charles know something about this? "I did. With the dog and all. Charles, you knew a lot of Jasper's circle. I didn't recognize that couple from anyone I've ever met in publishing. Do you know them from the village?"

Charles and Olivia exchanged glances. "Yes. Do you remember I mentioned Sofia, my housekeeper, and the couple she brought around to do some casual work at my place?"

The Rubios. Lina and Alejandro. "Yes, I do. You were outraged when she told you they'd registered a gun."

"We don't know they ever applied for or registered it. Just that Mrs. Rubio said they had one," Charles said.

"That's the couple the police arrested at the funeral?"

"We don't know that they arrested them. Nevada, were you this careful with the facts when you were a journalist?" Charles was leaning heavily on Olivia's arm and his face was beginning to sweat. It was a warm day, and he looked very uncomfortable.

"Charles, it's awfully bright out here and I think we should get out of the sun," Nevada said. "But before we go, tell me, what do you think is going on?"

"You're right, Nevada. Charles, let's go get something cool to drink," Olivia said.

"I think the Rubios were involved in Jasper's shooting." Charles moved toward the sidewalk.

Nevada fell into step beside them. "I assumed that's why the police escorted them out of Jasper's yard," she said. "And the dog seemed to point them out."

"Hired killers," Charles said.

"I beg your pardon?"

"That's what they were hinting at. To Sofia. That's what she implied, to me. That they got the gun because they'd been hired to kill someone. Not for protection. Or to brag about. To kill someone. For a boatload of money."

"Who would hire strangers to kill Jasper?"

Nevada asked the question out loud but neither Charles nor Olivia suggested a name.

***

The minute Nevada was back in her car she was on her phone.

And once again, on voicemail.

"Detective Travers, this is Nevada Leacock again. I have some new information ... well, not exactly new information, but a new way to connect the dots, I think. Please call me back."

She waited twenty minutes, but the phone was as silent and unmoving as a brick.

She needed to talk to someone.

Owen.

Again, to voicemail. Was her phone broken? Why wasn't she getting through?

Nevada went into her contacts and tapped on Lillian's and Chelan's numbers. Both picked up instantly.

"Hi, Nevada. What's happening, on a Sunday afternoon?" Lillian asked.

"Just left Jasper Inniskillen's memorial service."

"Aah. How was that?" Chelan's voice sounded quite low-energy. Like a person who chased three young children around all day.

"Sad. Even when it's someone who's lived a long life and had much happiness, it's always sad. And shocking."

"And of course, in a case like this, with a violent death…" Lillian said.

"That's why I'm calling," Nevada said. "I need to talk about the latest developments and get your take on it."

"Ready to go," Lillian said. "What's happened?"

"The police brought a dog into the memorial service and it identified a woman and a man who've been in Jasper's neighborhood, doing garden and housework. Lina and Alejandro Rubio."

"Work for Jasper?"

"No, for Charles Delaney, one of his friends. Well, once, one of his friends."

"So, the scarf helped," Lillian said.

"Yes. But there's more. I've heard from Charles that someone he knows heard the Rubio's talk about having a gun."

"Any clue about what motive they could possibly have?" Chelan asked. "Assuming the rumor is true, and they do have a gun. And that it isn't just for protection. Do they know him?"

"No obvious motive," Nevada said. "We don't know whether they worked for Jasper, at some point. I wondered the same thing. Why would we assume a connection just because there's talk of a gun?"

"Do we have any information about what kind of gun it might be? Or whether it's the same as the one used to kill Jasper?"

"None. The police would know, I suppose, but I haven't been told or asked about that," Nevada said. "I can't get Detective Travers on the phone."

"Is it possible it was a robbery that escalated?" Chelan asked.

"Could be. Charles Delaney thinks financial gain has something to do with it. But he wasn't speculating about a robbery or a burglary. He thinks they might have been hired to kill Jasper."

"Hired by whom?" Lillian asked.

"That's the next question, obviously," Chelan said.

"Somebody with money, first of all. Or access to it."

"And somebody with a reason to want Jasper dead."

The three women let the silence lengthen. Then Lillian said, "So, we're back where we started. A long list of suspects and many motives."

"An even longer list," Chelan said. "Now, we should add back all the people with alibis."

Nevada heard an incoming call notification. Detective Travers? Owen? "Listen, I have to go, ladies, but thank you for the input."

She caught the call just in time.

"I was just about to leave a voicemail," Travers said. "You phoned me?"

"Yes! Thanks for calling back," Nevada said. "I was there, at Jasper's memorial service, and I saw you take the two people out. Have they been arrested?"

"They have."

"Who are they?"

Travers hesitated. "I assume we're completely off any kind of record here? This has to stay completely between us. I need your help with one more thing, and I can answer a few questions. Maybe."

"Understood."

"Their names are Lina and Alejandro—"

"Rubio."

"You know that?"

"Those are the names Charles Delaney gave me. The couple who worked for him and bragged to his housekeeper about having a gun."

"That's what I needed to know."

"Are they talking?"

"Not yet. We have enough reason to hold them because the scarf is hers and she has no explanation for it being there, near the body."

"Somebody could have planted it."

"Always a possibility. There's more to find out, obviously."

"Mr. Delaney has a theory that they are killers-for-hire."

"Possible."

"Any idea who might have hired them?""Not yet. They've asked for a lawyer, and once he gets here and we all sit down, that'll be a priority question."

***

It took only two hours before Travers was back with the information. Nevada had just settled down to a simple Sunday dinner for one, when her phone lit up with his name on the call display.

"Nevada, I'm calling to ask you to take precautions. When we talked to the Rubios, your name came up."

"What! What did they say?""Nothing very specific, but enough that I just wanted to warn you to be alert and take care of yourself. I'm guessing you probably already do, with your background and experience in news." Travers paused to speak to someone, then said, "I don't have much time. But I can tell you, the Rubios confessed. They were paid $670,000 to shoot Jasper Inniskillen outside his own house."

"Paid by whom? Did they say?"

"By a Mr. Encell, they said."

CHAPTER 32

Back in her news-chasing days, Nevada would not have hesitated before jumping into a car or onto an airplane to get to the scene. Now, in her fifties, sitting at home on a Sunday night in cozy robe and slippers, she had second thoughts about driving ten miles to confront Toby Encell at his Manhattan office. She didn't even know whether he'd be there, although she had no doubt he was working, as always. Always working, men like him. But he might be working at home, he might be on an airplane going somewhere, or he might be at one of his factories or offices anywhere in the world.

She paced around the house twice, then realized she was too restless to wait until she heard the news, along with everyone else, about the outcome of Jasper's story. Were the police on their way to apprehend Toby? Did they know where to find him, right now? Did they feel they had enough to go on, with just Lina and Alejandro Rubio's say-so?

Detective Travers had ended their phone call abruptly when someone called him into a meeting. If he'd stayed on the phone five minutes longer, she'd have been able to ask him about their next move, perhaps even let him know she was going to go in to Manhattan to see whether her reporter luck would send her path crossing Toby's.

Pulling on a pair of jeans, a top, and running shoes, Nevada checked her phone one more time for a text or a call from Owen, then went out to the car. Traffic into the city was light and the drive didn't take long. When she rolled up in front of the skyscraper that housed Toby's office, she had no trouble finding a spot right by the curb.

What now?

She knew the address of Toby's office, but each time she'd been there previously, her name was on some sort of guest list and the security guard was expecting her. Would the front desk even be staffed? Would the door even be unlocked, on a Sunday evening?

Nevada stared at the double doors, about twenty feet away. Then, two men appeared in the brightly lit lobby and came running out to the sidewalk. Both wore jeans and T-shirts. One carried an old-style briefcase: the other ran ahead about half a block and stood at the curb, waving his arms to flag down a taxi.

No cab drivers stopped for a few seconds, and Nevada could see from the body language of the gray-haired man with the briefcase that the frustration was building. She stared harder … he looked familiar. Ah … there it was! It was Michael Diotte, the man with the gun in her office from Tuesday.

While Michael jumped from foot to foot and waved his arms at every passing cab, the other man managed to flag down a cab. She recognized that one too … it was Royce Encell.

Royce yanked the back door open, grabbed the briefcase from Diotte, and threw it in. He scrambled after it, into the street side seat, and Michael followed him, slamming the door shut. The taxi took off, pulling into the fast lane within yards.

Nevada turned on the ignition. Something was going on, and if she'd ever seen two men look as if they were running away, it was those two. But why? The killers had identified

Toby Encell as their employer, Travers said. What did Royce and Michael have to do with it?

Wait a minute! Travers said they named "Mr. Encell". Was it Toby or was it Royce who had orchestrated Jasper's death?

The lights at the intersection ahead changed to amber, and Nevada watched the taxi cruise through it. She couldn't let herself sit for a minute or more at a red light while that taxi went who-knows-where. Pounding her right foot down on the accelerator, she gripped the steering wheel, leaned toward the windshield, and willed herself and her car through whatever gap there was going to be in the traffic.

If the light had turned red, and if someone came through from the other direction, barely missing her rear bumper, she didn't know about it. She was focused on what lay ahead, not behind. She thought she heard a horn sounding to the rear, but that might have had nothing to do with her; there were always horns sounding in New York.

Nevada could see the yellow cab with the two men's heads over the back seat. She thought each of them turned around to look back a couple of times, but she couldn't be sure. So many cars all around them … it wasn't as easy as in the movies, to notice when someone was following you in Manhattan.

She didn't have to run every red light or make a decision about every yellow one. Most of the way, she hit the greens at about the same time as Encell and Diotte. Twice, as they approached a yellow light and slowed down, she was able to tuck her car in behind another vehicle, and so far, she didn't think she'd been noticed.

They headed down Park Avenue, then turned toward the bridge. She wondered for a moment whether they were heading for Long Island and Jasper's neighborhood, but as the taxi ahead made turn after turn, she realized he was heading for the airport. Was he trying to dodge someone he thought was following him or just hunting for the quickest way through the traffic? No way to know, but as the miles went by, she became more convinced they were going to JFK.

But why? And what was in the briefcase?

Traffic was lighter, temporarily, as they cruised through Queens, but then everyone sped up and it took every brain cell in Nevada's concentration arsenal to cling to the taxi's bumper. The vehicle count increased again as they got closer to the terminal—where did they all come from?

Nevada followed the cab to the departures zone, but she knew she wouldn't last long in the taxi lineup. All she could think of to do was abandon her car and hope she'd be able to pick it up later.

She pulled over the curb, put on her four-way flashers, and jumped out. That seemed to work sometimes uptown, when people double-parked and set their lights going, as if to say 'I'm really important and I'll only be a minute here. You, go around me.' Whatever. She was going to try it herself, and if she returned to find her car towed away, she'd deal with that then.

She could see the column of taxis ahead of her and she fixed her gaze on the curbside doors. Family groups, solo travelers, couples hopped or clambered out of the back seats and walked around to the trunk to get their luggage. She leaned left and right, trying to keep each cab in sight as people walking along the curb blocked her view. What she needed was a pair of binoculars! But ... no sense spending precious thought that way. She'd make do with what she had, which was fierce determination and a reasonable amount of speed.

Just after she went toe to toe with a burly man wearing a Giants jersey with the sleeves cut off, she leaned left, went around him, and spotted the cab that had carried Royce and Michael to the airport. The two men were on the curb, Royce clutching his briefcase and Michael reaching into his back pocket. He pulled out a wallet, then handed something through the passenger window to the driver. Must have been a card because the driver passed a credit card machine out through the window. Why hadn't they taken care of that from the back seat when they pulled up to the curb? Nevada speculated that the two of them argued about who was going to pay. Or maybe no one had enough cash.

Whatever the reason, it slowed them down for a few moments. Nevada thought of confronting them … but to say what? She didn't know what they were doing there. It looked as though they might be going somewhere but maybe they were meeting someone. Or picking up something that had been shipped? Or maybe there was a restaurant at the airport that they liked and they were just going there to hang out?

Nevada smirked at herself. That was unlikely, and silly. Besides, she didn't have enough information to justify challenging them … especially, in public like this. Did they even know that the killers had confessed and had invoked the Encell name? What if she said or did something that messed up the evidence or enabled them to wriggle out of whatever corner Travers wanted them in?

How did she even know that it was Royce, and not Toby Encell, with his billions, who was behind the killing? It was also possible that the killers had lied, and neither Encell was guilty.

Nevada knew when she was out of her depth. It was Travers, with his knowledge and experience, who was needed at this point. Keeping the two men in sight, she pulled out her phone and called the detective.

Voicemail. Of course. "Detective, it's Nevada Leacock. I'm at JFK and Royce Encell is here, with Michael Diotte. The shooter. Royce's cousin, let's not forget that… Anyway, they're on the departures level, just got out of a cab and I'm going to follow them into the airport."

Her phone buzzed with another call coming in. She didn't recognize the number but something in her gut told her to answer. She put the detective's voicemail on hold and accepted the other call.

It was Travers, on a speakerphone. "I heard you, you're at the airport. Don't approach them! But keep them in sight, if you can. We're on the way."

"Ms. Leacock? This is Captain Diaz. We also have people coming over from Brooklyn who might get there faster."

"You believe the Rubios actually killed Jasper? And were hired by Encell?"

"We've got some more physical evidence, in addition to their confession."

"Are they telling the truth about Royce? And do we know it was Royce, not Toby?"

"We've had another conversation since I talked to you. Yes, it was Royce."

"He took a cab from his father's office building to JFK. And he's got Michael Diotte with him."

"It's not Michael. It's his brother, Mark."

"The librarian?"

"Mark and Royce were working together to shut down this autobiography. The other cousin, Michael, was going to be the fall guy."

"Where is Michael?"

"With us," Travers said.

Well, that implies a lot.

"How far away are you?" Nevada was puffing as she worked to keep up with Royce and Mark. Their progress through the terminal was swift and direct. They moved like two people concerned about missing a flight. At one point, she had to break into a jog to keep them in view.

"Any clues about where they're going?"

"They're heading for a row of airline ticket counters," Nevada said. "No luggage, and from the way he's clutching that briefcase, it's going to be carry-on. What's your guess on what's in it?"

"Since this seems to be all about covering up those family secrets, I'm figuring it's the manuscript."

"In today's day and age? Wouldn't there be copies? Digital copies?"

"Who knows what precautions Toby Encell took? Maybe they've got laptops or all the copies on USB drives in that case, too."

"Wouldn't they just burn the paper copies?"

"Maybe they planned to once they get to where they're going. They probably don't want to take any chance that a page or two or the whole thing turns up somewhere in the future," Travers said.

"Does Toby know about any of this?"

"We picked him up shortly after the funeral. He's cooperating with us. Didn't know much of anything, except the family secrets they're trying to cover up." Travers said. "How are you doing, Ms. Leacock? Still sticking with them?""Yes. They're in line at the Delta counter."

"Long line?"

"Not too. They're in the Sky Premium line." Nevada sidled up behind a group of about fifteen teenagers traveling together and kept her face turned away from Encell and Diotte. "Are you anywhere close?""We're about five minutes out from the airport. Hang tight. Stay on the phone."

Nevada watched the ticket line like a dog watching a squirrel cross its territory. Her camouflage teenagers moved in a clump toward the airline counters and rolled into the same line as Royce and Mark. She kept her back turned but edged toward the pair, inch by inch.

Then, she sidled within earshot.

"Two tickets to Vietnam."

Nevada switched to her email account and tapped out a message to Travers. "They're buying tickets to Vietnam."

"No extradition treaty," came the reply. "Two minutes out."

Nevada watched, feeling helpless, while cards changed hands and paper boarding passes were offered to the two men. Her phone buzzed with a new notification. "Terminal 4. Gate B41."

She followed as the two men dashed through the airport. But when they reached the hub that led to the B gates, they made an abrupt turn.

She heard a buzz on her phone and lifted it to her ear. "We're at the gate. Where are you?" Travers demanded.

"I think they've made a change of plan," she said. "They've walked right past ... oh! They're heading for the First Class Lounge."

Nevada watched Royce and Mark Diotte go through the smoked glass, sliding doors that led to the private lounge. "I can't get in there."

"Wait for us, we're almost there. You can come in with us."

A minute later, Travers and five other police officers were at her side. Nevada hung back as they spoke with the attendants at the front desk, then followed as they moved in.

She was the first one to spot Royce Encell and Mark Diotte, sitting in a pair of chairs right beside the floor-to-ceiling windows looking out on the runways. She raised her eyes to Travers and pointed as inconspicuously as she could.

"Mr. Royce Encell? Mr. Mark Diotte? We require you to come with us," Travers said.

Royce's face, as far as it was possible to read an expression behind the heavy beard, was shocked. Mark's looked unsurprised, even resigned. She could imagine him thinking, 'okay, ya got me. What took you so long?'

"What's this about? I'm not required to go anywhere." Royce was going to brazen it out. "Let me see some kind of identification."

Travers flipped his badge in Royce's direction. "We can do this quietly, or it can be embarrassing, Mr. Encell. At this point, we just have a few questions for you."

"But no authority!" Royce blustered. "I'm going to call my lawyer."

"Of course, that's your right," Travers said. "Please ask him to meet us at the Nassau County Sixth Precinct."

"I'm not going anywhere until he gets here!"

"Come on, fool," Mark Diotte muttered. "Let's just do what they say. It's done now."

"I need to know who knew," Royce said. "It was fail-safe. Somebody talked. And somebody listened. We'll find out who."

Neither one noticed her. It wasn't November, but she took a moment for thanks giving.

CHAPTER 33

iona wore a flowing, multicolored hippie-style dress that Nevada knew had been one of Jasper's favorites. Daphne had flowers in her hair and a low basket filled with lilies. The two stood beside Daniel Pyne, Charles Delaney, Olivia Theale, and Nevada. Jasper's golden retriever was the seventh mourner.

All the commotion of the previous week had subsided and Fiona was at last left in peace to say goodbye to her husband. She held the bronze urn in her arms, looking out over the green meadows that rested between her house and the village on the shore.

Emotion flowed in waves in the air between them, and Fiona couldn't control her tears. Nevada had a lump the size of a boulder in her throat. It was still hard to believe that Jasper was gone, and she knew, from her experience of other losses, that it would be a long time before his absence became something she felt as real.

They stood for half an hour, almost as if frozen. No one seemed to know what to do, and Nevada didn't feel it was her place to step up to guide them all. That was one of the boons of a funeral, a memorial service, or a farewell of any kind, in any religion: the process was structured, someone ... a minister, a priest, an imam, a rabbi ... steered the proceedings, and a sense of resolution and honor was given to the person's death. The distraction of the police at Jasper's service hadn't erased all that, but coming together to spread his ashes, quietly and without all the drama, added the dignified epilogue that Nevada felt she needed. And if she felt it, certainly Fiona must, as well.

In the end, Daniel helped them all. "Would anyone like to say anything?" he asked.

Fiona shook her head, and Nevada did the same. So much had been said yesterday, and she still felt as if she were in a state of denial and pain.

Daniel reached toward Fiona and she passed him the urn. Gently, he put the ashes down in the meadow under the tree canopy that Fiona had chosen, then spread some of the soft sand they'd brought from Jasper's beloved beach over top. Handing the urn back to Fiona, he stepped away from the site. Nevada and the others followed him, leaving Fiona a few moments on her own there. It would be comforting to her, to have a physical location so close that she could visit when she wanted to contemplate him.

As Nevada stood at the door, saying her goodbye, she reached out a hand to Daniel. "It's none of my business, I know," she said quietly, "but my curiosity is in overdrive. You and Fiona?"

Daniel shrugged. "Maybe, maybe not. It's early days. But she loved Jasper and so did I, so we must have something in common."

Nevada nodded, then turned to walk back to her car. She didn't head back toward the city, though. She turned toward the village and the water's edge. She felt herself drawn, more and more, to this little place. As she pulled into the beach parking lot, her phone rang.

"Nevada? Can you talk?" Lillian's voice was cautious. "We saw you called early this morning."

"Yes, just before I headed out to Jasper's place to support Fiona and Daphne while they spread his ashes."

"What happened after the memorial service?" Chelan asked.

Nevada brought them up to speed on the chase after Royce and Mark.

"Have they been charged with Jasper's murder?"

"Not yet, I don't think. I haven't talked to Detective Travers since he helped me get my car out of the lockup at the airport. But they certainly took them into custody. Lots of bluster about lawyers on the way."

"Was Michael Diotte mixed up in it, too?"

"Don't know. From Travers' brief comment, it sounded as though he had turned informant for them, but I don't know. I know they charged him because of the shooting at Fraser Greene last week, and he's out on bail. But I don't know whether he was part of the attack on Jasper and whether they're pursing that."

"It's a tragedy," Chelan said. "What people will do if they want to keep a secret."

"And how the pain is exponential when it's not clear whose secret it is," Lillian added.

The three women sat in silence for several moments, then Nevada said, "There is one bit of good news. Crawford texted me to let me know Josselyn Madden has dropped her plagiarism suit against the company and against Jasper."

"That's a relief!" Lillian said.

"It is," Nevada agreed. "Crawford says she said it was because of Cori's intervention."

"And yours," Chelan put in.

Lillian asked, "What are you doing for the rest of the day, Nevada?"

"Not sure."

"You sound a little low. Maybe it would be best not to be alone."

"Not much choice, unfortunately," Nevada said.

"Owen is still away?"

"I haven't heard from him, except for a few brief texts, saying he's extending his stay in Key West."

"Now that they've got Jasper's killers and this chapter is done, why don't you go down south and meet him for a little recuperation in the sun?"Nevada winced, then stared out at the water. "Somehow, I don't have the feeling I'd be welcome."

"Why don't you just ask him and find out?" Chelan was having trouble getting her head around this marital communications style.

"There's a lot going unsaid, I think, and maybe Nevada feels the silence shouldn't be broken right now," Lillian said. "Nevada, would you think of taking a break on your own, anyway? You could come visit me in Alamos Island."

"Or me in California," Chelan prompted.

"I'll think about it," Nevada said. "Thank you both so much, though."

"Anytime," Lillian said with a smile.

Nevada's phone lit up with Detective Travers' name on the call display. "I have to go. I'll check back in later."

Travers, as always, didn't waste any time. "We've got confessions all around."

"Really," Nevada said. "You make that all sound very easy."

"It actually was. We already had the Rubio's. Once we got the Encells and the Diottes in a room, they were stumbling over each other, competing to see who would get to tell his side of the story the loudest."

"Encells, you said. Toby was there, too?"

"He was."

"Was he part of it?"

"We haven't untangled all the details yet. Royce and Mark claim he was the instigator of the whole thing. That it was writing his autobiography and planning to tell the world about Uncle Tobias, hiring Jasper and revealing the family secret to an outsider that started everything. Do you lay charges for something like that? Does Toby agree with their description of events? Didn't sound like he would, during the interview we were able to have. But there's more digging to do."

"What happened?""Lawyers shut it down. But the work carries on."

"So, Royce and the Diotte brothers were cousins, I know that part," Nevada said. "But did they just get together recently on this scheme?"

"No. They had a lot of contact as kids, growing up. They'd even formed a little group. Not quite a gang, but getting into a bit of trouble. Nuisance stuff. They called themselves "The Phases". Of the moon, get it? Michael was quarter, Mark was half, and Royce was the full moon."

"Ah! I thought I heard Mark call him 'fool' at the airport," Nevada said.

"It was 'full'. His family nickname."

"Explains the note, too. 'It's not my fault, it's the full moon.' " Nevada said. "So, did Michael hope to get caught? Or to implicate Royce?"

"That's what our psychologist suggested, before we knew the identity of the shooter. When we got Michael Diotte in, and talked with him, it didn't take long to figure out that he wouldn't mind helping us out a little."

"So, then, who left the unloaded gun and the second note at the Fraser Greene booth at Book Fair?"

"The Rubios. To try to plant the murder weapon on some-one at Book Fair."

Nevada felt overwhelmed. "It's not my fault, it was the full moon," she said slowly.

"I think Michael was also hoping the word would get back to Toby, his uncle, or to the police, and he could send the message about who was behind everything without having to come out of the shadows." Travers cleared his throat. "That's all we've got for now, Ms. Leacock, but I wanted to let you know we're confident we got the bones of the story right. We'll be investigating further—the higher-ups are taking a di-rect interest in this, because of Toby Encell's profile. You can feel safe about going about your business again."

She thanked him and they disconnected the call. But it left her wondering … what was her business now?

Nevada turned toward the beach. It stretched out before her, and to her right, the open water seemed to roll out to a horizon a limitless distance away. What a change from where she was a week ago, hunkered down behind a desk, hearing gunshots, fearing the worst. When she thought of going back, up that elevator and through those doors into the Fraser Greene office, she felt sick to her stomach. Yes, she had her job and her new career in publishing, but was it really what she wanted?

And where was Owen?

Nevada walked for what felt like miles. The questions pushed at her from a dozen directions: What did she really want? Eventually, she stopped thinking, and just walked.

When she sat down in the sand and stared out at the water, one more thought floated in.

I want another change.

AUTHOR'S NOTE

Thank you for reading *Monkey Me Monkey You.* I hope you enjoyed it as much as I enjoyed writing it. It's the fifth book in my Media Mysteries series and I'd like to invite you to check out the others, which are set in TV, movie, community newspaper, and social media worlds.

I'd also like to thank everyone who read portions of the book while it was in the story and early draft stages, and the numerous writers and podcasters whose advice, experience, and insight I absorbed while on my own journey through publishing.

ABOUT THE AUTHOR

Gail Hulnick is a former journalist who lives in the Pacific Northwest. In addition to writing novels, she takes photographs, produces travel books, and hosts a podcast about creativity called *The Brainwave*. She enjoys books, movies, dogs, and walks in the forest with her husband, David.

Gail writes a regular, free newsletter and would love to send it to you. Please visit www.gailhulnick.com or www.windwordgroup.com to sign up to receive it.

www.ingramcontent.com/pod-product-compliance
Lightning Source LLC
Chambersburg PA
CBHW060913210726
48293CB00006B/2081